Corie's mind drifted back to Granger Deene.

She wondered if her new "handyman" was busy at work on the walls. She could just picture him, muscles rippling as he swept the paintbrush carefully up and down the woodwork, his hard mouth tight with concentration.

Oh, how she wanted to feel the pressure of that mouth, hard and demanding, on her own. The sudden longing took her by surprise, heating her from her thighs to her breasts. What was it that made her weak every time Granger looked at her, made her long for his hands to touch her, caress her, drive her wild?

And what the hell was she doing fantasizing about a man who could very well be a hunted criminal?

The fact was, the only thing she knew about Granger Deene was that he could be a very dangerous man. In every sense of the word.

Dear Reader,

Welcome to another month of wonderful reading here at Silhouette Intimate Moments. We start right off with a bang with our Heartbreakers title, penned by popular Linda Turner. *Who's The Boss?* will immediately catch you up in the battle raging between Riley Whitaker and Becca Prescott. They're both running for sheriff, but there's a lot more than just a job at stake for these two!

Next up is Sharon Sala's *The Miracle Man,* our Romantic Traditions title. This one features the classic "stranded" hero—and the heroine who rescues him, body and soul. *The Return of Eden McCall,* by Judith Duncan, wraps up the tales of the McCall family, featured in her Wide Open Spaces miniseries. But you'll be pleased to know that Judith has more stories in mind about the people of Bolton, Alberta, so expect to be returning there with her in the future. Another trilogy ends this month, too: Beverly Bird's Wounded Warriors. *A Man Without a Wife* is an emotional tale featuring a mother's search for the child she'd given up. You won't want to miss it. Then get Spellbound by Doreen Roberts' *So Little Time,* an enthralling tale about two lovers who never should have met—but who are absolutely right for each other. Finally, in *Tears of the Shaman,* let Rebecca Daniels introduce you to the first of the twin sisters featured in her new duo, It Takes Two. You'll love Mallory's story, and Marissa's will be coming your way before long.

Enjoy them all—six great books, only from Silhouette Intimate Moments.

Yours,

Leslie Wainger
Senior Editor and Editorial Coordinator

Please address questions and book requests to:
Silhouette Reader Service
U.S.: 3010 Walden Ave., P.O. Box 1325, Buffalo, NY 14269
Canadian: P.O. Box 609, Fort Erie, Ont. L2A 5X3

SO LITTLE TIME

DOREEN ROBERTS

Silhouette

INTIMATE MOMENTS

Published by Silhouette Books

America's Publisher of Contemporary Romance

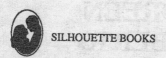

SILHOUETTE BOOKS

ISBN 0-373-07653-3

SO LITTLE TIME

Copyright © 1995 by Doreen Roberts

Printed in U.S.A.

Books by Doreen Roberts

Silhouette Intimate Moments

Gambler's Gold #215
Willing Accomplice #239
Forbidden Jade #266
Threat of Exposure #295
Desert Heat #319
In the Line of Duty #379
Broken Wings #422
Road to Freedom #442
In a Stranger's Eyes #475
Only a Dream Away #513
Where There's Smoke #567
So Little Time #653

Silhouette Romance

Home for the Holidays #765

DOREEN ROBERTS

has an ambition to visit every one of the United States. She recently added several to her list when she drove across the country to spend a year on the East Coast. She's thinking about setting her future books in each of the states she has visited. She has now returned to settle down in Oregon with her new husband, and to get back to doing what she loves most—writing books about adventurous people who just happen to fall in love.

To Bill, who makes me smile when I'm down, cracks the whip when I feel lazy and knows more about American history than anyone I know. Thank you for your expertise on the research, your unwavering support and encouragement, the hundred and one jobs you do for me and for fulfilling my every dream.
I love you.

Chapter 1

He awoke with a start, bathed in sweat. The lights above his head had been turned off, and only the sunlight filtered through the blinds. How long had he been asleep this time? A few hours? All day? It was hard to remember. So many days had passed. Four, maybe five. He wasn't sure.

He waited until his mind had cleared enough for him to sit up. He still couldn't remember anything, though now and again he'd had brief flashes of smoky green fields, and hot sun on tall grass. He didn't know what to call the pictures that formed unbidden in his mind.

He only knew that when they happened, he blocked out everything else around him, to the point where he couldn't function at all. It was just as well he was lying down when the visions attacked him, he told himself, because he would have certainly fallen down on the ground, maybe never to get up.

He climbed carefully out of the bed and moved to the window. From there he could see a corner of a paved yard, where several odd-looking conveyances stood side by side. Every now and again, one would move, making a dreadful noise as it did so.

In fact, he couldn't get used to the noises he heard, both inside and outside the building. He had no idea what caused them, and no one would take the time to explain it to him. All the doctors would tell him was that he would understand everything once he had his memory back.

There was one thing he knew for certain. He could not trust anyone. For some reason, they didn't want him to leave that room. He had overheard them talking outside his door.

Imperative to keep him under lock and key. He cannot be allowed to escape.

Well, he had news for them. He was going to damn well escape. He would do whatever it took, but he was not going to spend one more day locked up in that damn room.

He hadn't thought about the medication they'd given him, until he'd realized that every time they'd used that needle on him, he had become sleepy and disoriented.

Damn it, his name was the only thing he could remember. To lose it again was to lose his identity, and he fought like crazy to hold on to the elusive syllables. Granger Deene.

He had no idea why these doctors were keeping him prisoner. When he asked them, they shook their heads and pretended he was imagining things. It was his mind, they said, playing tricks on him.

Granger was already weak from lying in bed for so long. In order to get his strength back he had to escape from this damn prison. Maybe then, he could remember more about who he was, and what had happened to him.

He awoke the next evening to find that his meal had already been brought to him while he lay sleeping. Soon someone would come and stick the needle in his arm, then leave him alone until morning.

While he was doing his best to stay awake, he heard a key turn in the lock, and his door cautiously opened.

A man's face he didn't recognize peered at him from the doorway. "Sorry to disturb you," the doctor said, looking nervously about him as if he expected someone to spring at him from the shadows, "I have your medication. It won't take a moment."

The man fidgeted with his coat lapel, where a badge had been pinned to it. His neck looked too thin for his collar, and his glasses wouldn't stay on his nose. He kept pushing them up again with his fingers.

Granger studied him from under lowered lashes. The frail-looking doctor presented his best opportunity to escape so far. His own strength would barely hold him up, let alone overpower some of the bruisers who had held him down so effortlessly.

This weak, indecisive little man looked as if he would scare easily, giving Granger the advantage.

He waited until the doctor leaned over him to take his arm. Then, with a swift movement, Granger lifted both his hands and fastened them around the scrawny neck.

Staring into the man's frightened eyes, he said fiercely, "I don't want to break your neck, but I will do it if you don't keep quiet and stay out of my way. Understand?"

The man's eyes were round balls of glass in his red face. He nodded and made a gurgling sound deep in his throat.

Carefully, Granger maneuvered into a sitting position, still gripping the terrified man's throat. From there it was easy to slide off the bed and stand on his feet.

Granger waited for the dizziness to pass, praying it wasn't an onset of the fantasies. After a moment his vision cleared, and he concentrated once more on his victim.

"I'll have to cover up your mouth," he said, beginning to feel sorry for the squirming doctor. "I can't chance you yelling for someone the minute I'm out of here."

The doctor just stared at him with the same glassy expression. Granger let go of the man's throat and shoved him onto the bed. Taking the linen napkin that had been left with his dinner, he folded it cornerwise, placed it across the doctor's mouth and tied it securely at the back of his head.

After trading his nightshirt for the doctor's clothes, Granger tied the man's hands and feet with the sheets to the bars on the bed.

It took Granger a matter of moments to change into the black trousers, white shirt and long, white coat. The sleeves barely reached his wrists, and the pants cut him around the belly, with the hems ending above his ankles. The shoes, happily, fitted him. The doctor had surprisingly large feet for such a small frame.

Taking the key from the coat pocket, Granger faced the little man once more. "Tell them not to come looking for me. I'll kill before I come back to this place."

The doctor frantically nodded his head, obviously relieved that he wasn't the one being killed.

Granger touched his forehead with his fingertips, then closed and locked the door behind him.

Spring was the time Corie Trenton enjoyed her Cape May home the most, when the days were warm enough to appreciate the Jersey shore and all it had to offer, without the hustle and bustle of the crowds that would soon stream there from New York and Philadelphia.

Now she was glad she'd taken the chance on the transfer that no one else had wanted. Not only had the position offered her the escape she'd been seeking, it had provided her with a whole new outlook on life.

Letting out a sigh of satisfaction, she set out on the brisk walk along the shore to the tumbledown, sprawling Victorian house into which she'd invested her life savings.

She had not only bought a home, she'd told herself, she had bought something far more precious—peace and a wonderful sense of independence. And that was worth far more than any palace.

The light had begun to fade, and the beach was practically deserted. The steady swish of the ocean washing the sand relaxed her, and she felt her tension easing as she marched past the hotels that lined the boardwalk.

A fresh sea breeze ruffled her smooth, blond hair, and she lifted her face to it, enjoying the cool, salty air on her skin. She was really looking forward to the weekend, even though it meant more hard work on the countless chores that awaited her.

As she turned into the quiet tree-lined street, the fragrance of woodsmoke from the chimneys of the elegant, century-old houses greeted her.

The sight always gave her a wonderful sense of coming home, something she had never felt in all the years of her marriage. Now she had two whole days to herself. No one was going to interrupt her well-earned break from the office. No one at all.

Once inside the house with the door securely closed, Corie felt completely at peace. She decided to pour herself a glass of wine and listen to her favorite John Denver album before she tackled the chicken stir-fry she'd planned for dinner.

By now the sun had deserted the sky and left it glittering with a thousand stars. Fascinated as always with the spectacle, Corie took the remains of her wine out onto the porch to view the endless wonder of space that never failed to stir her soul.

It was then that she saw him.

She stared at the figure crumpled at the bottom of the steps for several seconds, trying to find the nerve to take a closer look at the man. She didn't want to get close to him.

Darn drunks should stay at home if they couldn't handle their liquor.

Of course, if he was dead she would have to call the cops. That's all she needed ... lights flashing, car doors slamming. That would really please the neighbors. They were so darned fussy about keeping the street quiet for their paying guests. Still, she couldn't just leave him there. She had to at least find out if he was still alive.

Creeping down the steps one by one, she held her breath, ready to spring back to safety should the guy make a sudden move. She reached his side without seeing the faintest flicker of life from the hunched body.

He lay on his side in a pool of light from the porch lamps, his face hidden from her. One wide shoulder hunched under his ear, pushing the collar of his white shirt over his cheek.

His legs were drawn up almost to his chin, and one arm seemed to reach out in mute appeal. He looked vulnerable, and Corie felt a brief stab of sympathy. However, she hardened her feelings immediately. She knew better than to feel sorry for a drunk. Tentatively she reached out and touched the shoulder nearest to her. "Hey, mister! You breathing?"

The feel of his solid frame unnerved her, and she snatched her hand back. Maybe she should call the cops after all. Even if the guy was just sleeping, she didn't need a drunk lying in her driveway all night. Besides, if she left him there he could very well be dead by the morning and that would lie on her conscience. She wouldn't leave a dog alone to die.

Frowning, Corie sat back on her heels and gave the man a hard look-over. He didn't have a jacket on this cool, spring evening, and his clothes were definitely too small. The only piece of clothing that appeared to fit him was his shoes.

Either he'd put on weight recently, or the poor guy was homeless, she thought, then hardened her heart. That was no excuse to spend what money he had on booze. Besides, he looked strong enough to get some kind of job.

The sudden urge to see his face took her by surprise. Cautiously she took hold of his shoulder and dragged him onto his back, assuring herself that she should know for certain if he was dead or not before she called the cops.

The light fell across his features, highlighting a slightly hooked nose. He looked to be in his mid-forties, a few years older than her. His square jaw was clean shaven, and thick dark lashes fluttered above his strong cheekbones. He wore his dark hair a little long, and it curled slightly at the edges, she noticed.

His mouth held her attention for longer than it should have. It was a hard mouth, as if it were used to delivering harsh statements, or even commands. A mouth that belonged to a strong-willed man used to being obeyed. Somehow his face didn't fit his appearance at all.

Startled by her illogical assessment of a complete stranger, Corie forgot her apprehension. Taking hold of his shoulder again, she shook it hard. "Mister, either you wake up and get out of here, or I'm calling the cops."

His eyelids remained closed, his face as still as if it were carved from stone. She couldn't tell if he was breathing. She hesitated for a moment longer, then leaned closer to his face hoping to hear a whisper of breath.

Instead, his eyes opened without warning and stared directly at her. For a long moment he seemed to look right through her, then slowly he focused.

The moment his gaze locked with hers shock waves shivered down her spine. She felt as if invisible arms had enclosed her in a paralyzing grip, squeezing the air out of her lungs. Her hands and feet tingled as if they'd been frostbitten.

He stared at her for what seemed an eternity, then said clearly, "There is a God, after all."

She didn't understand the words. Mainly because she'd listened to the voice rather than what was said. He had a deep voice, rich and husky. She'd felt a strange quiver when she'd heard him, almost an erotic response. Which was ridiculous. This man could be dangerous.

It might have been a trick of the light, she couldn't be sure, but his eyes seemed to be a strange silver color. Not gray, not pale blue, but silver, and glittering like the Lurex threads on her best black sweater. She'd never seen eyes like that in her life.

For several seconds Corie seemed imprisoned by that strange gaze, then she made a determined effort to shake free. "All right, now get out of here. I don't want any drunks cluttering up my driveway."

"I need some help," he said, in a tone he might have used when ordering a meal.

For some reason, Corie lost her fear of him. Scrambling to her feet, she said firmly, "The only help I'm going to give you is to get you back on the street. Then you're on your own." She grabbed hold of his arm and tugged. "Come on, dig your heels in the dirt and shove. You're too darn heavy for me to lift on my own."

"I'm not drunk."

Risking another glance at those strange eyes, Corie was inclined to believe him. Besides the fact that he'd spoken without a hint of a slur, she didn't smell liquor on him. And the stink of booze was one of the things she knew well and despised the most.

"Are you sick?" Letting go of his arm, she squinted down at him. He didn't look sick. But then it was hard to tell in the pale yellow light from the porch.

"I don't know." He patted his chest as if looking for something. "I don't seem to have any pain. I think I'm all right."

He seemed to be concentrating on his words, pronouncing each syllable carefully, as if he were learning the language. She wondered if he was a foreigner. Perhaps he had a hard time understanding her. Besides, she always talked fast when she was nervous.

Corie watched him climb slowly to his feet. He was at least eight inches taller than her, which would put him at about six foot. Now that he stood towering over her, he again seemed intimidating.

It occurred to her that she might have done better to call the police before she checked on him. There was something odd about this man, maybe he was dangerous after all.

Determined not to let the stranger see her apprehension, Corie said in her firmest voice, "If you would like me to call an ambulance—"

"I don't need an ambulance." He brushed his slacks with his large square hands.

Long fingers, Corie thought, feeling the same little tremors that his voice had generated. She had no idea why the sight of his fingers should excite her. Or even interest her. True, he was an attractive man. Impressive, if she wanted to be precise.

He had a certain air about him, a suggestion of hidden strength. She could almost feel the power radiating from him. Which was odd, considering the way she'd found him...

Irritated by her straying thoughts, she reminded herself that he was a man. And men were definitely and absolutely off her agenda forever.

"I should thank you for your concern," the man said, giving her one of those electric looks again. "Mrs...?"

"It's Ms.," she said shortly. "Trenton. I lost the Mrs. some time ago."

Once more she felt the paralyzing effect of his gaze. It was beginning to aggravate her. She was thirty-eight years old for pity's sake. Old enough and certainly experienced enough to know better.

"You are widowed?" he asked, just when the pause was becoming uncomfortable.

She sent him a look warning him it was none of his business.

He ignored it. "My sincere sympathy, if that is so."

She couldn't let that go by, even if it was none of his business. "That is so, as a matter of fact. But don't waste your sympathy."

"I see," he said quietly.

She had the distinct impression he saw more than she wanted him to. "Will you be all right, then?" she asked, hoping he would leave.

To her dismay he held out his hand. "My name is Granger Deene. I do appreciate your concern."

Deciding it would be rude to ignore his gesture, she placed her palm against his. His fingers closed around hers, locking them in a firm grasp that caused chills up and down her spine. Darn the man. He really did have the most peculiar effect on her.

Sliding her hand out of his was like brushing her palm against a live wire. Her voice cracked slightly as she said, "Forget it. I didn't do anything."

He studied her for several nerve-racking moments. "You are a very unusual woman," he said at last.

Taken by surprise, she squinted up at him. "Thank you . . . I think. You're quite a bit different yourself."

Corie watched an odd expression cross the man's face, and couldn't decide if it was confusion or fear. It had to be confusion, she told herself. She couldn't imagine this man ever being afraid of anything.

"I need to sit down," Granger Deene said, taking an unsteady step forward.

Afraid he was going to fall, she grabbed his arm. She realized something was really wrong with this man. Perhaps he'd had a heart attack. She was no doctor, but whatever it was, it had to be serious to put a rugged man like this on the ground.

"You should come inside and sit down for a while," she said, then wondered what on earth had possessed her to say that.

He gave her an odd look, as if he were going to refuse.

Still unsure why she was being so insistent, Corie said, "I don't want to be responsible for sending you out on the street if you're not fit to walk. I'll call a cab and have the driver take you home." She peered closer at him. "Or perhaps you should go to the hospital. They might want to do a thorough exam on you."

"No hospitals," he said, his voice suddenly harsh. "I've had enough of hospitals to last me a lifetime."

So he was sick. "I'm sorry," she said quickly. "Come inside while I call a cab. It shouldn't take long."

She waved a hand at the steps, indicating he should go first. If he looked as if he might fall, she wanted to be there to catch him. Though she wasn't sure how much luck she'd have holding him up. More likely they would both crash to the ground.

The shiver that attacked her spine at the thought of rolling on the ground with this man rattled her teeth. Or maybe it was the cool wind off the sea that sent the shudder throughout her body.

To her immense relief Granger Deene made it up the steps and into the living room. She self-consciously shoved newspapers off her well-worn recliner and plumped up the cushion. "Sit down," she said, "I'll get you some coffee."

"Thank you. That would be very nice." He stood in the middle of the room and took a slow survey of her few pieces of furniture as if committing it to memory.

Once more she was aware of an aura of power. Disturbed by the force of it she added, "Cream and sugar?"

"Black. Thank you." He turned to face her, and she was surprised to see that his eyes weren't silver but light gray. "You have a nice home here," he said. "Lots of charm."

"Thank you." She'd almost laughed out loud. Looking around at the faded chintz curtains and discolored walls, she added, "It's mortgaged to the hilt and falling apart at the seams. I sank every penny I had into this piece of real estate. But it's mine, and that's what matters."

She crossed the threadbare carpet to the door that opened into the long hallway. "I can't afford to have it fixed up, so I'm trying to do the repairs myself. I'm hoping to rent out rooms in the summer, and eventually make enough money so I'll be able to give up my job."

She let the door close behind her as she went into the kitchen, wondering why she'd told him all that. She had to be crazy to take pity on a strange man that way. He might be suffering from some kind of illness, but that didn't explain his clothes, or the odd way he talked.

By the time she'd made the coffee and carried it back to the living room she wished heartily that she had simply called a cab and made him wait for it outside. She was taking one heck of a risk inviting him into her home when she was all alone in that big old house.

Granger Deene had seated himself on the armchair. Again she was struck by the aura of strength surrounding the man. If he was sick, he did a very good job of hiding it.

He took the coffee from her with a slight smile that softened his harsh features. Corie caught herself wondering what he would look like if he really smiled.

"Thank you," he said, balancing the mug on the arm of the chair. "It smells good."

"It's only instant. When you live alone you tend to get lazy about things like percolating coffee."

He again studied her with an intent look, making her uncomfortable. After a long pause, he asked, "How long have you lived in this house?"

"Almost a year. I work full-time, so it's hard to find the time to spend on renovations. So far, all I've managed to finish is three of the bathrooms. But if I don't work, I don't earn the money to fix it up."

He took a sip of the coffee. "This tastes very good."

"Thank you." She wasn't sure what to say after that. A little voice warned her that she should be calling a cab, not making small talk with a strange man who disturbed her senses just a little too much to be safe.

"Do you live around here?" she asked nervously.

He waited a moment before answering. "Here?"

"In Cape May, I mean."

"No, I don't."

Somehow she'd expected that. He was probably sleeping on the beach. She wondered if he was hungry. Trying to ignore her protective instincts, she said carefully, "So where is your home?"

His glance skimmed around the room, then returned to her. "I don't have one at present."

Dismayed to have her suspicions confirmed, she said tightly, "I'm sorry."

He put down his coffee cup in a resolute way that made her nervous. Apparently he had come to some kind of decision.

She eyed the phone, which sat right by his elbow. If he made a move on her, she would never have time to reach it and dial Emergency before he overpowered her. Her best bet would be to make a mad dash for the door. As unsteady as he was on his feet, she should easily outrun him.

"As a matter of fact, that's why I'm here," Granger Deene said. "I'm looking to buy a house."

Again she studied his clothes. Although they were too small for him, they were of good quality. Perhaps she had misjudged him. "So you are staying in one of the hotels?"

"Not exactly."

The tingling feeling down her spine intensified. When he looked at her like that she forgot all her doubts. All she wanted to do was help him, which was out of the question, of course. She'd had all the trouble she could handle in her life. For the first time in years she was content, and she intended to stay that way.

"A motel?" she persisted. "Shall I call you a cab, or is it close enough to walk?"

She could see by his face that he had understood the hint.

He gave her yet another of his long, intent stares, then said carefully, "I was wondering if you would consider a proposition."

Her heart skipped uncomfortably. "What kind of proposition?"

"Would you perhaps consider offering me room and board in exchange for some of those repairs you find so difficult to take care of?"

So that was it. He was looking for a handout. She'd been right about him in the first place.

"I'm sorry, Mr. Deene, but I couldn't possibly—"

"Mrs. Trenton, I understand your hesitancy. But the truth is, I have recently left the hospital after a bout of illness. My clothes and belongings were stolen from me. I had to... borrow these clothes from a doctor. This is all I have to my name at present. I have no money to pay for board and lodging."

Corie frowned at him. "You don't have a credit card?"

His eyes narrowed, and he gave a slight shake of his head. "Credit card? I'm sorry..."

"You're not bankrupt, are you? If you are, you'll have a tough time buying a house."

His chin came up at that. "I am certainly not bankrupt. I'm simply unable to lay my hands on my money at present. As soon as I do, I shall be on my way."

"What about your job?"

Granger Deene shrugged. "I lost that when I became ill."

"You don't have family, friends who could help you?"

"I have no one."

"I'm sorry."

His gray eyes regarded her for a long moment. "So am I," he said quietly.

She hesitated for several seconds, before asking tentatively, "How good a handyman are you?"

He took his time thinking about it. "I am quite good with my hands," he said at last.

Something about the way he said it made her shiver. The man positively oozed sexuality.

"What about your illness? Fixing up a house like this one can be very hard work."

He squared his shoulders, reminding her once more of an indomitable power that seemed to hum just below his surface. "Please don't concern yourself on my account, Mrs. Trenton. My unfortunate weakness earlier was due solely to exhaustion. A good night's sleep will take care of that, I assure you."

Corie stared at him, while the seconds ticked by in ominous silence. She had no idea why she was even considering the proposal. The man was obviously a smooth-talking, no-good bum.

Yet, somehow, part of her couldn't believe that. For one thing, he spoke with a precise, educated accent that seemed to indicate a good background, and that direct gaze of his radiated honesty.

Then there was that sense of authority that almost over-whelmed her. No man with that aura of formidable strength could possibly be a bum. Besides, lots of people didn't have credit cards, for one reason or another.

If he was really down on his luck, she decided, she could hardly turn him out on the street. Anyway, it seemed like a good idea. She had plenty of empty rooms in the house, and she could certainly use the help in fixing up the place.

"All right," she said, ignoring a little flutter of appre-hension, "I'll give you a room and meals. But only until you get your finances sorted out, okay? I'm not officially in business yet, and I won't be, until I get these repairs done."

"Then perhaps we can both benefit greatly from the ar-rangement."

She stared at him a moment longer, wishing she could lose the uneasy twinges in her stomach. "I'll show you to your room, though I'll have to make up the bed first. I'll leave you to finish your coffee, and I'll be back in a few min-utes."

He nodded, watching her with that intent gaze that made her feel as if he could read her mind. She hoped he couldn't. She was beginning to wish she'd insisted on him leaving. Although she was more than inclined to believe him, she couldn't shake that feeling that Granger Deene was more than a little weird.

After she'd left the room, Granger sat with the cup be-tween his hands and stared down at the coffee. There was still so much he didn't understand. Somehow he couldn't seem to think straight, and when he tried, he felt a terrible pain in the back of his head, as if someone held a branding iron against it.

He needed time. Time to discover exactly where he was and what had happened to him. Time to find out why he had been held prisoner by men who insisted he was imagining things.

So far the woman had been cooperative, though he couldn't trust her, of course. He couldn't trust anyone.

He'd first seen her quite by chance, moments after leaving his room. She was talking to a man in a guard's uniform at the main door. She didn't look like a nurse. She wore no uniform, yet from the conversation he'd overheard, it appeared she worked at the hospital.

He wasn't sure what he'd had in mind when he'd decided to follow her. He only knew that he needed answers, and he needed somewhere to hide. He'd heard her mention to the guard that she lived alone, and he'd concluded that she would give him little trouble if he'd had to use force.

Then he'd had that damn attack again, the same visions that danced in his head and tormented his mind. He'd blacked out as he'd reached the steps to her porch. When he'd opened his eyes, she'd been leaning over him. Heaven knows how long he'd lain there.

Granger sighed and swallowed the last of the coffee. He hadn't seen her close up until then. All he'd seen was her blond hair, cut short for a woman, and that the multicolored garment she wore barely reached her knees.

He'd been shocked at first to see that much bare flesh. Until he'd left the hospital and realized that she wasn't the only woman dressed like that. Apparently his mind hadn't remembered that women wore such brief clothes.

Obviously, she didn't recognize him. Granger assumed she didn't know who he was, or that he had been a prisoner in the hospital. Somehow he had to find out the truth before she discovered that fact.

He'd been startled by the odd sights he'd seen when he'd left that place...lamps that glowed red and green in the middle of the street, strange-looking vehicles sweeping past him at an alarming rate, guided by men and women who wore strangely colored spectacles on their faces.

Since his memory no longer served him, he expected things to appear strange to him. There was so much he couldn't remember or understand. He knew how to take care of his personal needs, like using the toilet and shaving, yet the facilities and instruments he'd used in the hospital were completely unrecognizable to him. He'd had to be shown how to manipulate them.

Cups that made no sound when they fell, and water that tasted more pure and clear than he'd ever known, just about everything he touched or tasted seemed unfamiliar.

Nothing, however, had prepared him for the sight of Corie Trenton's face when he'd recovered from his attack. Sea green eyes had gazed down at him with a mixture of concern and fear, while the most desirable mouth he'd ever seen spoke words he barely understood.

Granger lifted his head toward the ceiling and closed his eyes. He had lost so much of his memory. An entire lifetime. He might get it back, the doctor's had told him, and then again he might not.

The one thing he struggled to understand was why he'd been drugged and kept a prisoner in a hospital room. It didn't make sense. He was still pondering on the mystery when he heard footsteps on the stairs.

Corie Trenton walked slowly toward him, that same deep concern in her beautiful eyes that he'd seen before. Granger felt a stirring of interest and quickly suppressed it. He had no time for such thoughts. She was most likely his enemy, and if he was to find out what had happened to him, he needed a clear mind, uncluttered by any lustful ideas.

He almost smiled, realizing that at least that part of him could still respond to the right stimulus. And in that remarkably brief garment that revealed her long, shapely legs, Corie Trenton was, indeed, quite a stimulus.

Under other circumstances he might have been tempted to spend a few pleasant hours discovering exactly which intriguing spot on her body would melt her resistance.

Much as he liked the idea, however, he knew better than to cloud his mind with passion. She could either help him unravel the puzzle and give him back his life, or she could lead him back to rot in that cold, white prison. He would do well to remember that if he was to survive this nightmare.

Chapter 2

"Do you have a car?" Corie asked, as she took a key from her pocket and handed it to Granger Deene.

He didn't answer, but sat turning the silver object over in his palm as if he wasn't sure what it was.

"It's the key to your room," she said, trying not to sound defensive. "I have one for every bedroom."

"Thank you." He dropped the key into his shirt pocket.

"Do you have a car?" Corie asked again, as he rose to his feet. "You'll need to pick up wallpaper and paint, and shelving, stuff like that. And you'd better buy some clothes. You can't wear that outfit all the time. I'll put it on my credit card and you can repay me when you get your money."

If he had any money to get, she added silently.

Granger looked at her as if she'd asked him to go to the moon. "I really wouldn't know what to buy."

He probably wasn't feeling up to it and didn't want to admit it, Corie thought. "Never mind," she said, "I'll go in the morning. Just give me your sizes and I'll pick up something for you to wear."

He looked down at himself. "I'm about average."

Corie sighed. Typical male helplessness. Though it was hard to think of that word when dealing with Granger Deene. "We'll get your measurements in the morning. Right now you look as though you're about to drop again."

She peered up at him, noting the tan that darkened his leathery skin. This was a man who spent a great deal of time in the sun. She wondered what he did for a living, but decided to hold the questions until the next day. Judging from the way he was looking at her, she wasn't making much sense to him right now.

Remembering her concern earlier, she asked, "Are you hungry? I can fix you a light supper if you are. I don't have too much in the house until I shop tomorrow."

He shook his head in a weary way that told her he was barely holding up. She hoped the work wouldn't be too much for him. If so, she would have to suggest he find someone else to give him room and board.

A business arrangement was one thing. Taking in a complete stranger just because he made her feel like a woman again was quite a different proposition.

"I'm not hungry, Mrs. Trenton, but thank you. I'm just very tired."

"Why don't you just call me Corie? It will make things a lot simpler."

Her skin tingled as his gaze rested on her face. "Very well, Corie. Please call me Granger."

His eyes seemed to mesmerize her. He really did have the most peculiar effect on her. Almost as if he could control her mind if he really wanted to.

She gave herself a mental shake, wondering where on earth that ridiculous thought had come from. Without saying anything more, she led him up two flights of stairs to the large bedroom at the rear of the house.

Her common sense told her that if she intended to rent rooms, she would have to get used to strangers staying at the house. But then her common sense seemed to desert her when faced with Granger Deene's harsh features, which were such a contrast to his courteous manner.

Reaching the landing, she stood aside to let him pass, thankful not to have him following her any longer. His magnetic presence behind her had made her knees tremble all the way up the stairs.

Normally she would have opened the door for her guest and shown him into the room, but she was reluctant to do that with Granger Deene.

"That's your room," she said, gesturing at the door. "I hope you will find it comfortable."

He gave her his level look and said quietly, "I'm sure I shall. Thank you. I am very grateful for your kindness. I promise you, I shall repay you. I will start work on the renovations tomorrow."

She nodded, backing away from him as he took the key from his pocket and turned it over in his hand. "I plan to spend the entire weekend working on the house," she said, "so between us we should get quite a lot done."

"I'm sure we shall. Good night, Corie."

She liked the way he pronounced her name. He made it sound different, old-fashioned somehow. Deciding it was time she left before she got any more fanciful ideas, she flashed him a quick smile. "Good night, Granger."

She fled down the stairs without looking back. As she turned the corner to the next flight, she heard him fumbling with the key in the lock. He had to be pretty tired, judging by the length of time it was taking him. Hoping that he wouldn't be there all night, she went down to the kitchen to clean it up before going to bed herself.

She slept fitfully, waking more than once with her nerves on edge, listening for noises that might or might not have been in her imagination. When she finally awoke to the sunlight peeking through the slats in the blinds, she felt as if she hadn't slept at all.

She showered quickly, one ear pricked for any sounds from the upper floor. Granger Deene had to be sleeping soundly, she decided, when she could hear no signs of movement.

When she made her way down to her roomy kitchen she was surprised to find him standing by the fridge, fully dressed in the same ill-fitting clothes.

He had the fridge door open, and was staring at the contents as if he'd never seen food before.

"You must be starving," Corie said, when he looked at her. "I can cook you some eggs, bacon and pancakes, if that sounds all right?"

Granger let the door close with a soft plop. "That sounds very good." He ran a hand over his bristly chin. "I'm afraid I don't have a razor—"

"Oh, I'm sorry, I should have thought of it. There's one in my bathroom. It's the room next to the stairs on the second floor. Just go in and help yourself, you'll find it in the medicine cabinet."

"Thank you."

"I'm afraid I don't have any shaving cream . . ."

"I'll manage."

His eyes seemed lighter, brighter than she remembered. She felt a small shiver dance down her spine when he looked at her. "I'll cook your breakfast while you're gone," she said, more for something to say than anything.

Granger continued to watch her for a moment, and Corie wondered if he wanted to tell her something. Then he gave a brief nod and left the kitchen.

Gathering her senses, Corie set about preparing the meal. The appetizing aroma of fried bacon filled the kitchen by the time he came back, looking slightly less dishevelled with his dark hair slicked down and combed back from his forehead.

To her dismay he sat down on one of the kitchen chairs at the dinette table, which was cozily tucked away in the alcove of the bay window. He seemed engrossed in the morning newspaper lying there, and picked it up to study the front page.

Wondering how to approach the problem, she waited until the eggs were sizzling in the pan, then said casually, "If you'd like to take the newspaper into the dining room, I'll bring you your breakfast in a couple of minutes."

She had her attention on the pan, so didn't see his expression. But she heard the wariness in his voice when he said, "I would prefer to eat out here with you, if you have no objection?"

"Oh, I'm just having a bowl of cereal," she said quickly. "I don't eat a big breakfast usually."

"Where do you eat your cereal?"

"Right there at the table."

"Then this is where I'll eat mine, if that's all right with you?"

She flipped the eggs onto the warmed plate, aware of an odd sensation of just having lost a battle. "Of course," she said, carrying the plate over to the table. "If you don't mind eating in cramped quarters."

"After some of the places I've eaten in, this is paradise."

It wasn't the words that surprised her, as much as the expression on his face. He seemed disturbed by what he'd just said, and sat staring at his plate for several seconds before picking up the fork she'd laid at his elbow.

He was quiet for so long she began to feel worried about him. She sat playing with the granola in her bowl without tasting a single spoonful. He ate steadily without comment.

When she could stand the silence no longer, she cleared her throat. "What would you like me to pick up for you at the store? Jeans? Shirts? Underwear?"

He flicked his gray gaze at her, gave her a brief nod, then went on eating.

Deciding he didn't like to talk and eat at the same time, she waited another five minutes until he finally pushed the plate away from him with a grunt of satisfaction.

"That was an excellent breakfast," he pronounced, in the same deep, husky voice she'd heard in her dreams last night.

Pushing away her frivolous thoughts, she said lightly, "Thank you. You must have been hungry to enjoy it so much."

"I was. It has been a very long time since I remember eating a home-cooked meal."

Grasping the opportunity, she said casually, "And where is your home?"

In the silence that followed she heard the drone of a helicopter overhead. Granger appeared to have heard it too, for he tilted his head on one side as if trying to distinguish the sound.

"That's the Channel Two news team doing a traffic report," she said, determined not to be put off. "Do you come from the East Coast?"

He looked at her as if he hadn't really heard her. But he must have done as he said fairly quickly, "Philadelphia. I come from Philadelphia."

"Really?" She frowned. "So do I. But you don't sound as if you're from Philly. Were you born there?"

"Yes, I think so."

"You think so?"

"Yes. I mean I was born there."

Wondering exactly what that meant, she studied his face. He looked more rested, though she could still see signs of strain around his mouth and at the corners of his light gray eyes.

"What were you in the hospital for?" she asked abruptly.

"I... had an accident. It left me a little disoriented for a while. But I'm quite well now. In fact," he rose to his feet in a swift movement that surprised her, "I would like to start work now. I want to get the best out of the daylight hours."

Getting to her feet, she gathered up the dishes on the table. "There's not a lot you can do until I pick up the supplies. The grass needs cutting, perhaps you can do that while I'm gone?"

He looked surprised, but gave her a somewhat hesitant nod of agreement.

Carrying the dishes over to the sink, Corie braced herself for the next ordeal. "I'll get my tape measure," she said, "and take your measurements. That's if you still want me to buy you some clothes?"

"Whatever you decide will do just fine," Granger said.

His expression suggested he felt uncomfortable, and Corie wondered if he felt awkward about her buying his underwear. It was rather an intimate undertaking, she thought, feeling her pulse jump at the idea. But she could hardly let him wander around in the same clothes every day.

Trying to make him feel more at ease, she said carefully, "Don't worry about me getting you something outlandish to wear. I'm used to buying men's clothing. I did it all the time for my husband when he was alive."

"I'm sure you did a wonderful job of it."

He still didn't look convinced, and she tried again. "I imagine the police will have a hard time tracking down whoever took your stuff. You may not get it back any time soon, if ever. You're certainly going to need clothes while you're waiting."

"Of course. Please keep a careful record of whatever you spend, and I'll see that you're reimbursed in full."

So it was the money that worried him. Feeling more secure by the second, she hastened to reassure him. "Oh, please don't worry about that. I'll put it on the credit card and by the time it comes through, you'll probably have your own money sorted out. I know how long-winded banks can be when you don't have any identification. I suppose it was all stolen with your money?"

"Yes, it was." He started for the door, saying over his shoulder, "I'll start working on the grass. Where will I find the...?"

His last word was drowned out as Corie dropped the pan in the sink. Assuming he'd asked for the mower, she waved a hand at the window which overlooked the backyard. "You'll find it in the shed back there. It's a bit rusty, I'm afraid. I left it out in the rain for too long, but it still works. You just have to give it a good kick now and again."

Granger started to go out of the door, and Corie called out after him. "I'll bring the tape measure out as I leave and get your measurements."

He said something as the door closed behind him that she didn't catch. She stared thoughtfully after him, wondering what she'd missed. He certainly didn't care for questions, that much was obvious. Was he just naturally close-mouthed about his personal life, she wondered, or did he have something to hide?

Impatient with herself, she finished stacking the dishwasher with dishes. If she started doubting all her guests just because they didn't conform to her idea of normal behavior, she would be a nervous wreck by the time the season ended.

Dropping her tape measure into her purse a few minutes later, she went in search of her handyman.

She found Granger standing inside the garden shed, rubbing the back of his head in a gesture of frustration. The mower still stood in the corner where she'd left it. Frowning at the offending machine, she asked, "What's the matter, won't it start?"

"Start?"

Corie met his puzzled gaze with a shrug. "I was afraid of that. I suppose you already checked to make sure there's gas in it?"

He continued to stare at her as if he had no idea what she was talking about.

The nervous flutter of her pulse was becoming a habit. "I have a can of gas somewhere," she said, trying to ignore the uneasiness churning her stomach. She searched the cluttered shelves, all the while conscious of Granger's hard gaze boring into her back.

Finally she saw the can pushed to the back of the shelf, and moved a coil of hose to one side to reach the gas. Squatting down by the mower, she unscrewed the cap and tilted the can to let the gas run into the container.

All this time Granger stood quietly watching her, saying nothing. She would have dearly loved to know what he was thinking, but knew better than to look up into his face.

The acrid smell of the gasoline made her eyes tear, and she wiped them with the back of her hand. At last the container was full, and she righted the can, screwing the cap back on. "It might start now. Try it again. But perhaps it would be better if you took it out onto the grass first."

Holding her breath she got to her feet, then made herself look at him. For a moment or two he stared at the mower, a look of uncertainty on his face. Then he slowly took hold of the handle and pulled the machine back onto its wheels.

She watched him wheel the mower out to the grass. He made no move to start it, but stood watching it as if he expected the thing to move by itself.

It looked very much as if she'd made a major mistake in agreeing to swap room and board for his help with the repairs, Corie thought dismally. He certainly couldn't be called a fast mover.

The lawn wasn't that spacious, broken up as it was by straggly flower beds. The marigolds she'd planted were choked with weeds, and the single rose bush badly needed pruning. A wooden fence bordered the corner lot. Some of its slats were missing, and at least two of the posts leaned drunkenly to one side, their bases having rotted out.

There was enough work out here to keep a man fully occupied, Corie thought, as Granger continued to study the mower. At this rate, it would take him a year just to get the yard under control.

Deciding she didn't have time to wait around any longer, she hurried over to him. "I'll just get your measurements then I'll leave you to it," she said, reaching into her purse for the tape measure.

Now that she had to get close enough to him to wind the tape measure around his chest, it seemed less like a good idea. "Unless you'd rather do it yourself?" she said hopefully.

Granger's face was expressionless as he said quietly, "I would prefer that you take care of it."

Her heart began hammering like crazy as she moved closer to him. "Lift up your arms," she ordered, doing her best to sound calm and collected.

Very slowly, he raised his arms and stood quite still as she reached behind his back with the tape, pulling the end forward to meet the rest of it in the center of his chest.

Taking a mental note of the measurement, she lowered the tape and measured his waist. She was quite sure he could hear her heart pounding as she dropped the end of the tape.

"I don't suppose you know your inseam?"

His gray eyes regarded her with the intent stare that so unnerved her. "I'm sorry, I don't."

Swallowing hard, Corie crouched in front of him and pressed the end of the tape to the inside of his thigh as high as she dared go. Praying he wouldn't notice her hand shaking, she dropped the tape to his shoe, then shot to her feet. "I think that will take care of it," she said, her voice a little too loud.

"That certainly will," Granger said, quite seriously.

She had to get out of there, Corie thought frantically, before she made a complete fool of herself. "I'll be as quick as I can. Help yourself to whatever you can find in the kitchen if you get hungry or thirsty."

She didn't wait for his response, but turned and practically ran to the garage. She didn't breathe properly again until she had backed the car out onto the road and was heading for town.

Granger watched the vehicle vanish around the corner, then turned back to the strange machine in front of him. It was odd what his mind remembered. Some things seemed familiar, some did not.

Since he didn't remember where he had lived before, he didn't know if he'd ever used a mower. Right now, the important thing was to find out how the damn thing worked, before Corie Trenton came back with her too sharp mind and probing questions.

Thinking of Corie reminded him of his physical response to her touch. Her firm thumb on the inside of his thigh had seemed to burn right through the fabric of his trousers. She had just about driven him crazy. It had taken every ounce of his control not to let her know how she'd affected him. One inch higher and she'd have been in no doubt.

It had been both painful and pleasurable. The sensations she'd aroused in him were familiar, yet he couldn't remember any woman having such an effect on him. He wasn't even sure if he'd ever had a physical relationship with a woman.

Granger still didn't trust her, but he felt certain that she didn't know who he was. At the moment, that was. He assumed she would have to go back to work, and could very well learn about his disappearance then. It would be a simple matter for her to put two and two together.

He considered the possibility of holding her prisoner in the house until he learned what he wanted to know. On the other hand, she could not find the answers for him unless she did go back to that place. Until then he would have to stay close enough to find out exactly how much she did know.

In the meantime, he had to deal with this infernal machine. Squatting down on his heels, he scrutinized the various parts of the mower. He saw a small handle at the back of the machine, and tried turning it, but it wouldn't budge. Then he tried pulling it, and to his immense satisfaction, the thing sputtered, then died.

It took several tries, but finally the engine caught and held, settling into a rather noisy, uneven growl. Grasping the handles, Granger eyed the lawn. It looked shaggy, and had a definite slope on the left side.

Deciding to tackle that first, Granger gave the mower a push. The darn thing was so heavy he could barely move it. A lever caught his eye, close to his thumb. More out of curiosity than anything, he flipped the lever forward.

To his amazement, the machine started forward of its own accord, almost getting away from him. Grabbing the handles, Granger held on while the mower charged down the slope. More intrigued by the minute, he turned the machine and guided it back up the slope with no effort at all. How in thunder, he wondered, had he forgotten such a marvelous invention?

Beginning to enjoy himself, he set a pattern to follow, shearing wide swaths of grass in even rows. The sun felt warm on his back, and the wonderful fragrance of freshly cut grass mingled with the sharp, salty smell of the ocean.

Time passed pleasantly as he trudged back and forth across the lawn, until suddenly, he felt a sharp pain in the back of his head. Afraid that he might fall again, he pulled the lever back on the mower, shutting off the engine.

The rubber handles bit into his curled palms as he grasped them for support. The ground seemed to sway beneath his feet, but this time he managed to stay upright. The vision came without warning, bursting into his mind like an explosion.

He saw the green fields again...long grass...thick smoke...buzzing flies. The acrid smell of burning stung his nose. It was hot, much hotter now, the dense moisture in the air making it difficult to breathe. His clothes felt heavy and seemed to drag him down.

A loud noise shattered the eerie silence, deafening, painful to his ears. He was carrying something in his hand, its smooth wooden handle nestled into his palm. He could feel the weight of it...now he could see it. And he knew what it was. It was a revolver, and he had just shot a man....

Corie turned onto the street, expecting to hear the roar of the lawn mower. A quick glance assured her that the slope had been cut, making her think Granger had completed the chore after all, since she couldn't hear the mower.

The wall of the garage prevented her from seeing the entire yard as she climbed out of the car. Gathering up her packages, she carried them into the kitchen and dropped them onto the dinette table. Then she looked out of the window.

Granger stood in the middle of the lawn, unnaturally still, like a panther watching its prey. He seemed to be staring at something, yet she could see nothing that would command such riveted attention.

Her blood chilled as she watched him. He appeared to be in a trance, held by some invisible demons that imprisoned his mind. Several anxious seconds ticked by, then Granger Deene appeared to shudder. The next moment the roar of the lawn mower destroyed the tranquil peace.

Corie watched him for several more minutes as he guided the mower back and forth across the cropped lawn. Whatever it was that had held him transfixed, it now appeared to have vanished. Even so, she couldn't quite get rid of the image of him standing there with that odd, watchful expression on his face. In fact, it bothered her all afternoon.

The clothes she had picked up at the thrift store for him fitted him perfectly. Too perfectly, she realized, when she saw him dressed in them. The jeans clung to his lean hips and the dark blue knit shirt molded itself to his solid chest, emphasizing his athletic build.

Corie tried valiantly not to notice as she directed him to start on the paint work in one of the upper floor bedrooms. She'd already stripped and washed the walls, and now she was ready to use the new paint and wallpaper.

Excited about the prospect of finally seeing the results of all the hard work, she was nevertheless wary of the man who was helping her achieve her goal.

And the last thing on earth she wanted was to feel any emotion for this mysterious man who had seemingly dropped out of the sky at her feet. He stirred her womanly senses just a little too easily, and she wasn't about to get involved with a man again. Ever.

She might have made a mistake in letting her sympathy get in the way of her common sense, but she didn't have to compound it. From now on, she would stay as far out of Granger Deene's way as possible. Any encounters between them would be kept to a minimum, and she would insist that he ate alone, starting with dinner.

It didn't turn out that way. Somehow, when she brought up the subject, he made it sound as if she would be insulting him if she turned him out of her cozy kitchen into the vast wasteland of the dining room.

"I hate eating alone," he told her, as he sat at the dinette table that evening. "I don't enjoy my own company."

"It would be a lot more comfortable in the dining room," Corie said, as she scraped carrots over the kitchen sink. "This table is so small in here."

"Then let's both eat in the dining room."

She really didn't have an answer to that one. While she was still attempting to think of one, Granger added, "It would give me a great deal of pleasure if you would join me for meals. I really don't want to be alone."

She looked up, alerted by an odd note in his voice. If she didn't know better, she would have said he was afraid to be alone. But that was nonsense. He gave every appearance of being in control of any situation that might arise.

True, the way she had first met him didn't support that theory, but the speed with which he'd recovered, and the fact that he'd shown no sign of weakness since, proved that he was a man of formidable strength and determination.

She was willing to bet that Granger Deene would let no one get the better of him, whether they were his friend or his enemy. And she for one was glad she wasn't his enemy.

She wasn't particularly happy with the idea of sitting in the formal dining room alone with him, however. But then neither did she want to offend him without good reason. She could hardly tell him that he turned her on every time he looked at her. Resigning herself to losing that particular battle, she said reluctantly, "Actually, it would be easier to serve dinner in here, if you don't mind the primitive surroundings."

He swept a glance around the kitchen, then settled his gaze on her warm face. "I find the surroundings utterly charming."

He was looking at her when he said it, sending goose bumps up her arms. She tried to appear unconcerned as she reached into the cupboard for the horseradish sauce. The effort was wasted entirely when she dropped the jar with a loud clatter onto the counter.

In an attempt to cover her nervousness, she said brightly, "I hope you like fresh, steamed vegetables. I don't usually bother with stuff like this when I'm on my own. I normally just open a can, but since I'm cooking for two it's worth the effort."

Aware that she was babbling, she concentrated on getting the lid off the jar of sauce. She almost jumped out of her skin when Granger got to his feet and gently took the jar from her. With a quick twist of his wrist he had the lid off. Without saying a word, he handed the jar back to her and sat down again.

"Thank you," she said feeling ridiculously breathless.

"You're entirely welcome. Is there anything else I can do for you?"

"Er...no, thank you. I have it all under control." Which was more than she could say for herself, she thought ruefully, as she washed the broccoli.

"Something smells absolutely delicious," Granger said, sniffing the air in a way that suggested he was more than ready to eat dinner.

"Pot roast. And I have a lemon pie for dessert."

"You certainly have gone to a great deal of trouble. I'm not sure my work is that valuable."

She waved a hand at the fridge. "No trouble. I bought a frozen pie. It's thawing in the fridge."

She had her back to him, but she could feel the tension in his silence.

Throughout dinner, no matter what she asked him, he seemed to avoid the question, turning her words around so that she was the one doing the answering.

Granger seemed preoccupied, though Corie felt pleased by his obvious enjoyment of her cooking. Wondering if he was worrying about his finances, it occurred to her that no one knew where he was.

"How will the police get in touch with you?" she asked, as he munched on a piece of roast beef with a rapt expression as if he hadn't tasted anything quite that delicious before.

She was unprepared for the reaction she got when he registered the question. Granger choked, dropping his fork onto his plate with a clatter as he reached for a glass of water.

Corie stared at him in consternation while he struggled to get his breath. Finally, he said in a rasping voice, "Why would they want to get in touch with me?"

"To return your things if they find them." Bewildered by his attitude, she added a little defensively, "I didn't mean to upset you."

He shook his head, and took another sip of water before answering. "I apologize. I find the entire matter upsetting, and I tend to overreact. Please forgive me."

"Of course." His soothing tone mollified her somewhat, but the little knot of uneasiness stayed with her. Determined to find out more about him, she tried once more to question him after he'd finished his dinner.

"What kind of work do you do?" she asked him, as she served him a slice of lemon pie. "Will you have trouble finding employment again?"

"I am employed," he said, looking at the dessert as if it had sprung out of the ground. "I'm employed by you, in a manner of speaking."

She sat down, feeling decidedly uncomfortable. "Yes, I know. But that's just temporary, until you get your finances sorted out. I mean after that. Were you working down here or in Philadelphia when you had your accident?"

His gaze met hers steadily. "I was in Philadelphia. And I'm sure I'll be able to find work just as soon as I get everything sorted out."

"What about your car? Was that wrecked in the accident?"

His gaze remained steady. "Yes, I'm afraid it was."

"So, you will have to buy a new one, then."

"I imagine I shall, yes."

Corie pushed her plate away, before she was tempted to have another piece of pie. "You won't get much choice down here. It would be best to wait until you go back to Philadelphia. You can drive mine in the meantime, as long as it's just around here."

She had to be mad, she thought, trusting the man with her car. But then she'd come this far, she might as well go all the way. In any case, the insurance on her old rattletrap was worth more than the car.

"That's very kind of you," Granger said, "but I don't foresee any need to go anywhere at present."

She wondered about that. A little voice nagged her to find out just why he didn't want to go out. But then, if he was still unsure of his health, she could understand why he preferred to stay close to home.

"Besides, I imagine you would need the car to get to work," Granger added, breaking the short silence.

"Oh, no, I prefer to walk. At least while the weather is fine. The lab isn't far from here."

"Lab?"

"I'm a research assistant."

"At a hospital?"

She looked at him in surprise. "Whatever made you think that? No, I work in a laboratory for a group of scientists. Mostly astronomers to be exact. They're working on a project that involves the planetary influences on certain aspects of the world and the life that survives on it. It sounds boring, I know, but it's actually quite fascinating."

He sat looking at her with that amazed expression on his face that was becoming very familiar. "I see," he said, sounding as if he didn't have a clue as to what she was talking about. "And you walk to work every day?"

She nodded. "And back. While it's fine, that is."

"I see," he said again.

There was a long pause, while he seemed to digest this piece of information with a great deal of concentration.

The silence unsettled her. Corie rose to her feet and began stacking the dishes. "Would you like to watch some television while I wash the dishes?" she offered tentatively as she carried them across to the sink.

Granger didn't answer her, and she looked over her shoulder at him. Somehow she knew he would be staring at her again with that odd expression. "It's in the living room," she added, deciding that he had to be learning the language after all, to be confused by so much of what she said. It must have something to do with the pronunciation.

"I would prefer to help you with the dishes. Perhaps I could put them into that machine for you."

"The dishwasher?" She suddenly remembered something. He'd told her he was born in Philadelphia. So he wasn't from some foreign country after all. It didn't make sense. Nothing about him made sense. Including her willingness to give him the benefit of the doubt.

"I really don't need any help with the dishes," she said quickly, "but thank you, anyway. I'm sure you have better things to do than help me."

She saw by the look on his face that she'd offended him. "I have not forgotten my part of the deal," he said stiffly as he rose to his feet. "I will get back to my painting right away."

"I didn't mean..." she called out after him, but the door swung closed behind him, shutting off her voice.

So he was oversensitive, too. "Great," she muttered, as she began stacking dishes in the dishwasher. Now she had to watch what she said to him.

She really had taken on more than she could handle, she told herself, closing the door of the dishwasher with a loud snap. The man was a mystery, closemouthed and secretive, and perhaps a little slow on the uptake. On the other hand, he seemed to be well educated, judging by his speech pattern, and he was certainly polite.

She wondered if perhaps he was hard of hearing, and missed some of the things she said to him. Some men were ridiculously vain about that sort of thing.

The man was a mass of contradiction. On the one hand he seemed so strong, so competent and independent, yet underneath it all he seemed lost somehow, confused and alone. Either way, she was beginning to regret ever becoming involved with Granger Deene.

Somehow, however, she couldn't help responding to that sense of need that try as she might, she couldn't ignore. It had been a very long time since anyone had needed her. And for some strange reason, she felt very strongly that he needed her.

He obviously needed help, though how in the world anyone was going to help him when he refused to say anything about himself, she didn't know.

Maybe it was just as well, she told herself, as she turned on the dishwasher. She was already in deeper than she wanted to be. Perhaps the less she knew about Granger Deene, the better off she would be.

Chapter 3

Granger sat on the edge of the bed, his face between his hands. He had to get himself under control again. He had to think, to sort out the muddled thoughts that chased each other through his mind.

He had just about decided to turn himself in. He didn't know how or why he had killed a man, he only knew he had shot someone and that someone had died.

He'd concluded that he was being held under lock and key because he was a dangerous criminal whose mind had been impaired. Perhaps he had lucid moments, when he appeared to be sane, which was why he could remember little of anything that had gone before.

He'd decided that the hospital must be a criminal facility for the insane. The doctors were simply attempting to treat a mad killer who had to be confined to a single room for the safety of everyone.

Or so he'd thought. Now he wasn't so sure.

Getting up from the bed, Granger crossed the floor to the window. It was dark outside, and he could see little except for the street lamps reflecting on the houses opposite. The orange glow sent ghostly shadows of tree branches dancing across the pavement in the night wind.

Corie had told him that she walked to work every day, so it was reasonable to conclude that he hadn't been mistaken about her working at the hospital.

But if the hospital was in fact a scientific laboratory, engaged in nothing more significant than a study of the stars, then why was he being held prisoner there? Why wasn't he in the hands of the proper authorities?

A car crept slowly past the house, directing twin beams of light to banish the shadows. A black cat streaked across the road in front of the wheels and disappeared into a row of shrubs.

His heart skipped as he watched the red lights of the car disappear down the street. He had seen no mention of his name in the morning paper, but that didn't mean they weren't looking for him.

How his mind played tricks with him. He couldn't remember ever seeing a car before now, yet he must have been surrounded by them all his life.

He still found it difficult to believe he had killed a man in cold blood. He couldn't equate that terrible act with what he knew of himself, and yet deep down he knew it was the truth. He had to know what had happened.

He knew that if he went back to that hospital, they wouldn't tell him anything. They would just pump drugs into him with that infernal needle, and he could spend the rest of his life locked up inside four walls.

He couldn't go back. Not until he had learned all there was to know about himself. And Corie Trenton was the key.

Thinking about Corie gave him a warm feeling low in his belly. He had watched her in the kitchen, stretching her lithe body to reach something from the cupboard, and he'd felt a strong urge to take her in his arms and hold her next to him.

She had a quiet strength about her, a peace that somehow he was sure he'd never known. In the midst of all his turmoil that day, she had been like a salve to his shattered nerves. Her smile had warmed him like the midday sun, melting the frozen fear that he strived so hard to overcome.

He'd watched her eyes when she talked to him, eyes the color of a tranquil ocean, and he'd seen compassion in them, and a desire to help him. He'd sat across the table from her, wanting to see those eyes light up with the heat of passion, ignited by the touch of his hands on her bare skin.

He shook his head, staring out at the still night. Somewhere, sometime, he must have made love to a woman. Yet he remembered nothing. Maybe that was why he wanted to make love to Corie. To rekindle what he knew must be a forgotten pleasure.

His sigh shook his body. He could not let such thoughts invade his mind. She could well be his enemy. She worked at that place, she must learn about him eventually. If so, he would have to force her to tell him the truth.

He would make her learn the answers to his questions. One way or the other, he intended to discover how he had ended up in that God-forbidden miserable room.

And if he discovered that he could be a danger to her, or to anyone else for that matter, he would surrender to the authorities. He wasn't about to do that, however, until he knew for sure.

Crossing the room again, Granger flung himself down on the bed. He couldn't bear the thought of returning to that stifling room. He was used to being in the outdoors, with the earth under his feet and the open sky above.

Even now he could feel the sharp bite of the winter wind as snow whisked around his face, almost blinding him. Beyond the stretch of dry ground he could see mountains rising in front of dark gray clouds, their white peaks bright against the drab sky.

He could see tall firs, their green branches weighted down with mounds of pure white snow. He could see ice forming on a lake, and windswept fields shivering in the icy blast.

He shuddered, and the vision changed, whirling around in his head, along with a sharp pain. Now it was warm, muggy, the grass beneath his feet crackling in the moist heat.

He could see nothing in front of him but clouds of gray smoke, so thick it blotted out the sky. He could feel the vibration of thunder as it rolled across the rocks ahead of him.

He was climbing, sweating, his hair sticky and wet beneath his hatband. He felt the smooth handle clasped in his palm again, and knew he carried a revolver.

A flying beetle buzzed in his face and he swatted it away. He wasn't alone. Other men were around him, shouting, swearing, crying, screaming...from somewhere ahead of him he could hear gunshots. Dozens, no, hundreds of guns shooting at will.

He could hear a strange rhythmic pounding and felt the earth shake with the noise. He heard the clinking of chains, the scrape of metal against a rock.

He saw someone coming toward him through the fog, a face shrouded in the mist. Sweat trickled down his forehead...or was it blood? He didn't know. He only knew he had to kill. He had no choice. Slowly, and with cold deliberation, he raised the revolver and fired....

The fact that she'd upset Granger played on Corie's mind, despite her misgivings about the man. She had, after all, made a deal with him and as such she should honor her part of the bargain.

Perhaps a cup of coffee might do as a peace offering, she thought, as she filled the percolator. The thought of him being upset with her depressed her, though she couldn't imagine why it should matter so much. He was just an employee, and a temporary one at that.

The thought did nothing to lift her spirits, and she carried the tray up the stairs, rehearsing what she wanted to say to him. She hadn't meant to imply that he should be working in the evenings. In fact, she would feel a great deal better if he didn't.

Although he seemed fit enough now, she couldn't dismiss the nagging doubt in her mind that something was very wrong with Granger Deene. He was entirely too tense, too preoccupied with whatever it was that troubled him. He needed to relax, and give himself a break at the end of the day.

Judging by his response earlier, he didn't care for television. She would have to find out what he did like to do for relaxation. Perhaps he liked to read, he certainly seemed enthralled by the newspaper that morning.

Corie reached the landing and paused outside the door of the first bedroom. The smell of paint almost overpowered her. She must remember to ask him to leave the windows open at night to air out the place.

She was about to push the door open when she heard the sound of muttering from inside the room. At first she couldn't distinguish the words, then she heard Granger Deene say quite clearly, "Good God above, it isn't possible."

Her pulse quickened as the knot in her stomach tightened. He had to be talking to himself. Perhaps if she listened, she would learn more about the man she'd been rash enough to invite into her house.

Leaning closer, she strained to hear him. The tray tapped gently against the wooden panel and she held her breath, afraid that he'd heard. Even so, she was totally unprepared when the door opened suddenly, almost toppling her off balance.

Granger stood in the doorway, his hair ruffled, his eyes wild with the heat of desperation. "What do you want?" he demanded harshly.

Corie almost dropped the coffee. Completely unnerved, she thrust the tray at him, slopping the hot liquid over the side of the cup. "I thought you might want this. I'm sorry if I disturbed you."

The light in his eyes faded as he continued to stare at her. After what seemed an eternity, he took the tray from her, looking down at the spilled coffee as if it were a wounded animal.

"You didn't disturb me," he said quietly. "It's my place to apologize. I fell asleep. I was having a bad dream. I heard you at the door, and I wasn't quite awake. Please forgive me for my rudeness."

Corie shook her head so violently strands of hair fell across her eyes. She brushed them back, saying, "Oh, that's okay, I have bad dreams myself sometimes."

His gaze seemed to fasten on her face, holding her breathless. To her surprise he said softly, "You are too nice a lady to be living alone like this."

"I...thank you, but...it's better than..." She was floundering helplessly and didn't know why. Pulling herself together, she said firmly, "I'm getting used to it. It has its advantages."

"I'm sure it does."

She couldn't help wondering if he ever smiled as she struggled to meet that intent stare. She couldn't think of anything else to say, and after a short pause she said awkwardly, "Well, good night then. I'll let you go back to sleep."

"Thank you, Corie. I'll enjoy the coffee."

She nodded, backing away until she reached the landing. He was still watching her as she hurried down the stairs.

Try as she might, she could not get the man out of her mind as she lay in bed that night. No matter how she twisted her body to get comfortable, that intense gray gaze and husky voice tormented her mind until she felt like screaming.

Corie knew nothing about him, except that he was born in Philadelphia and had apparently had some kind of accident. He was unusually reluctant to tell her anything else. She could only conclude that he had something to hide.

Not that it mattered to her, of course. As long as he hadn't robbed a bank, or hurt someone.

She snapped her eyes open as the thought jolted her body. No, he didn't seem the type. But then, neither had Ted Bundy. For God's sake, the man could be a serial killer on the run.

Groaning, she sat up in bed and ruffled her fingers through her hair. She was letting her imagination run away with her. If he'd wanted to hurt her he could have easily done so before now. Besides, no matter how strange he seemed, something told her he wasn't physically dangerous.

Staring into the dark shadows of her bedroom, she thought long and hard about that. Whatever was troubling him wasn't directed at her, but at himself. Something traumatic had happened to him, and he was doing his best to deal with it. Something very personal, something he couldn't discuss with a stranger.

She could understand that very well. She knew how it felt to be alone and lost and to have to deal with pain. She also knew how destructive it could be to keep it all inside. Perhaps if she could coax him into talking about it, she might be able to ease some of that pain.

It surprised her how much she wanted to help him, but he seemed like a nice man who'd had his share of bad luck.

Her glance fell on the clock and she sighed. Past midnight. She would look like a wreck in the morning if she didn't get some sleep. Pummeling her pillow, she settled down and firmly closed her eyes.

Corie woke up some time later with an uneasy thump of her heart. For a moment she couldn't think what had disturbed her sleep. Then she heard it. It sounded like a soft moaning, and it came from above her head. Granger's room.

She lay there for a little while, trying to ignore the urge to go and find out what was wrong. He'd made it very clear he didn't welcome her intrusion in his welfare.

Still, if he was sick, maybe he needed help. He'd recently had an accident; he could be in pain. Making up her mind, she slid out of bed.

Grabbing her robe, she stopped only long enough to pick up some painkillers from the bathroom cabinet, then hurried up the creaking stairs to Granger's room. Outside his door, she paused. The moaning was louder, broken now and then by muttered words.

She tapped on the door, then waited to see if he would respond. Apparently he hadn't heard her, since the painful sounds continued. She knocked louder, still without any reaction from inside the room. After a moment's hesitation, Corie opened the door.

The light from the street lamp fell across the figure stretched out on the bed. Granger's dark hair fell across his forehead as he tossed from side to side. One arm lay across his bare chest and the comforter was on the floor. The sheet seemed to be tangled in his legs, and had been drawn down around his hips.

Corie's mouth felt dry as she stared down at him. He was obviously in the throes of a nightmare. And she didn't need a magnifying glass to know that he was naked.

For a moment she let her gaze wander over his muscular body. How she wanted to run her hand over the smooth slope of his shoulder, trail her fingers across the springy dark hair on his chest, drawing them down to the tantalizing expanse of flat belly left bare by the sheet.

His face was turned toward her, his firm chin faintly shadowed, his eyelashes feathering above his strong cheekbones. His hard mouth muttered words she couldn't understand, and she wondered what it would be like to silence him with her own lips.

Dismayed by her treacherous thoughts, she chased them from her mind. She was reluctant to go any closer to him. Instead she whispered urgently, "Granger, wake up."

"Leave me alone," Granger muttered. "I won't go back to that place."

Frowning, Corie edged closer. His eyes were still tightly shut, and his breathing was shallow, uneven. She reached out to the bedside lamp and snapped it on. Raising her voice, she tried again. "Granger, wake up. It's me, Corie."

He answered her with a groan, then said loudly, "Fall back!" His arm thrashed out, narrowly missing the headboard. Afraid that he would hurt himself, Corie took hold of his bare shoulder and gave it a firm shake.

She felt his muscles flex, and before she could snatch her hand away, his fingers imprisoned hers in an iron grip. Her heart leapt as she stared into his eyes. They seemed to be glowing with that same weird silver color she'd noticed the first time she'd seen him.

He appeared to be looking at her, yet the blank expression on his face told her he could see nothing but the dream that still tormented his mind. "They are looking for me," he said, his voice low and menacing. "They won't take me back. I won't let them."

Shocked, Corie backed away from him, her hand still held fast, questions tumbling through her mind. Had she been wrong about him after all? Who was after him? He could have escaped from somewhere...a prison...or heaven help her, a mental home. If she could just get away from him she would call the police.

She twisted her wrist back and forth, but his fingers only tightened on her. Corie let out a yelp of pain. Granger stirred, his eyes gradually losing their odd glow. As she watched, his gaze slowly focused on her, and she realized that he was finally awake.

In the next instant he released his hold on her wrist and she stepped back, rubbing the bruised flesh with her fingers. She saw his gaze move over her body with a slow deliberation that burned her skin, making her painfully aware of her pink satin robe that barely skimmed her thighs.

She could feel her pulse rapidly beating when he looked her in the eye again and said quietly, "Forgive me. I was dreaming."

Moistening her dry lips, Corie nodded. "Yes. I heard you from my room and thought you might be ill. I came up to see if I could help."

"That was kind of you. Thank you."

"You're welcome." Her heart gradually slowed as he continued to look at her, his eyes filled with an anguish she couldn't understand.

"I hope I didn't hurt you."

She shook her head in denial, ignoring the ache his fierce grasp had caused.

After a long moment, he asked, "I was talking in my sleep?"

She swallowed, then nodded again. "I couldn't hear what you said," she lied. "The words were too jumbled."

He seemed to notice that the sheet was down around his hips and reached for it, drawing it up to his chest. "I'm sorry I disturbed you, Corie. However, I'm not ill, so please go back to bed."

She shook the bottle of pills that was still clutched in her hand. "I brought some painkillers, just in case you were in any pain."

"I'm in no pain. But I appreciate the thought. Thank you."

"Sure." She backed toward the door. "Perhaps you can sleep better now."

"Perhaps."

Very carefully, she shut the door.

Granger watched the door close then let out his captured breath on an explosive sigh. Damn the woman. She was spying on him. He wondered what he'd said while fighting the visions that seemed determined to haunt him.

Whatever it was, he was sure it was incriminating. He didn't believe for one minute that she hadn't been able to understand him.

Granger pulled himself into a sitting position and buried his heated forehead in his hands. He didn't know who his enemy was or where they would come from. He didn't even know why they wanted him.

He couldn't allow himself to trust Corie Trenton, yet every time she came near him she lit hot fires of passion in his belly that threatened to consume him.

Seeing her so close to him, her slender wrist imprisoned in his grasp, that scrap of silk molded to her enticing curves, he'd yearned to spread his fingers over her breasts and down her hips to her thighs.

He might not remember the touch of a woman's skin beneath his hands, but there was nothing wrong with his imagination. And it almost drove him out of his mind.

He had to touch her. He had to find out if that golden skin felt as smooth and velvety as it looked. He wanted to bury his nose in her hair, and capture her mouth with his lips and tongue.

He wanted to smell her fragrance that taunted his senses, hear her sigh as he explored her flesh with his eager hands, and he wanted to immerse himself in the wild glory of her body—being to being, soul to soul.

A groan escaped from his lips, and he drew the sheet over his head to smother the sound. From now on he would have to be on his guard, not only against what he said when either awake or asleep, but also against the urgent demands of his body, which he couldn't seem to control.

He cursed her again for the magnetism he couldn't ignore, and for his own damnable weakness that made him forget even for one instant that she could very well be his undoing.

Corie lay awake in her bed, wondering what she should do. Her first instincts were to call the police. But on going through everything in her mind, her story sounded weak.

All she could base her fears on were words spoken during a dream. For all she knew, Granger could simply be dreaming someone was after him. Heaven knew she had dreamed the same thing herself at times. The police would simply laugh at her.

As for Granger's odd behavior, that could be due to the accident which he said had left him disoriented. To call the police in now and provoke an investigation could very well embarrass them both.

It would be far better to make sure she wasn't making a big mistake before she did anything rash. Feeling only small comfort with her decision, she finally fell into an uneasy sleep.

When she awoke the next morning, it was to hear rain spitting on her window, driven by the blustery wind that swept in from the ocean.

Granger said little during breakfast, seemingly preoccupied with his own thoughts. He looked a little tired, but otherwise healthy and rugged in the dark green sweatshirt and jeans she'd bought for him.

He appeared to enjoy the omelette she'd cooked for him, and in spite of her inner turmoil, she felt a warm sense of satisfaction when he pushed his plate away with a sigh.

"That was an excellent breakfast. Will you be cooking for your paying guests when you open the hotel?"

She laid her fork down and reached for her coffee. "Not at first. I'll be offering just the rooms until I'm established enough to quit my job and do this full-time."

"I am quite sure your guests will have no complaints as far as the food is concerned."

"Thanks, I'll bear that in mind when I have to cook my first breakfasts. My customers may not all be as easy to please as you are."

He watched her while she took a sip of her coffee. "You must not be happy with your work to want to give it up."

Corie shrugged. "I'm happy enough with it. It can be fascinating, though a lot of times I have to admit it's pretty dry stuff."

"What is it exactly that you do?"

Corie thought about that before answering. "I guess you can say I do all the dreary stuff while the scientists have all the fun. I figure out the angle of the stars and the planets at a given time, in comparison to the earth's axis. I chart weather patterns, atmospheric conditions, any unusual activities, such as meteors, space debris from satellites, that kind of thing...."

Her voice trailed off as she noticed Granger's expression. He was looking at her as if she'd just arrived from outer space herself. Trying to think over the conversation, she wondered what she'd said to put that look of astonishment on his face.

After a moment Granger said in a strained voice, "I have never met a woman who could even speak of such things, let alone know the meaning. What is space debris, for instance?"

Now it was Corie's turn to look astonished. "You know, the stuff that falls off satellites when they wear out, or maybe collide with something up there."

"Up there?"

"Outer space. With all that stuff floating around up there, it's a wonder we don't have more of it falling to earth."

She peered closer at him, concerned by his stunned expression. "Are you feeling all right? You're not going to pass out again, are you?"

"No," Granger said carefully. "I don't think so."

"Oh, good, you had me worried there for a moment." Corie took another sip of coffee and swallowed it. "Anyway, as I said, it can be fascinating at times. It's just that I'm always at someone else's beck and call. I want to be my own boss, and call my own shots. I want to make it on my own decisions, not somebody else's."

Appearing to recover from his momentary bout, Granger said quietly, "An independent lady. That's ... very refreshing."

"Not really. More and more women are working for themselves these days. A sign of the times, I guess."

"And their men are not threatened by that?"

Corie looked at him in surprise. "I'm sure a lot of them are, but you'd never hear them admit it. In any case, many women don't have men to support them."

He appeared to think about that, but made no further comment.

She got up from the table, glancing at the clock on the stove. "Would you like some more coffee before we get to work?"

Taking the hint, Granger rose to his feet. "No, thank you. I want to finish the painting in that one room before—"

He broke off as the harsh ringing of the telephone interrupted his words. He looked startled, and swung around as if trying to pinpoint the source of the noise.

"Excuse me," Corie said, "I'd better get that." Again she felt that flutter of apprehension, wondering just why Granger Deene seemed so startled by the ringing of the telephone.

The caller was a market researcher, conducting a survey on breakfast cereals. Corie answered the questions in a distracted way that must have seemed vague to the woman on the end of the line.

All the time she talked, Corie couldn't help wondering if Granger was worried that she would tell someone he was there.

One way or another, she had to find out more about her new handyman, and the sooner the better. If someone was looking for him she would just as soon not have them find him in her house.

The survey finally came to an end, and Corie put the phone down with a sigh of relief. "I wonder why they always call on weekends," she said, crossing back to the table. "I suppose because they know they can catch people like me who'll stand there answering their dumb questions."

She began gathering up the dishes, and after a moment, Granger moved over to the door. "I think I'll finish my painting now, if you'll excuse me?"

"Sure." Actually she was relieved to see him go, she thought after the door had closed behind him. Granger Deene made her nervous, and yet part of her refused to accept the fact that he could be a criminal or a madman on the run.

There had to be some other explanation for his odd behavior, and she was going to find out what it was if it killed her. Unnerved by that last thought, she did her best to put him out of her mind for the rest of that long day.

It wasn't easy. Granger finished the painting within an hour, and Corie had to leave her own work to show him the wallpaper she wanted him to hang.

"Have you ever hung wallpaper before?" she asked him, while he studied the wall.

"I think so," he said. "I mean of course I have, I just don't remember what kind it was."

"Well this is the self-adhesive kind," Corie said unrolling a portion of the paper to show him. "You just fill this trough with warm water, cut the length of paper you need, roll it inside out, then soak it in the water for a couple of minutes."

Granger looked as if he wasn't sure that he'd heard her right. "Then it's ready to stick on the wall?"

"Right. Just start at the top of the wall and smooth it all the way down with this brush." She pointed at the little wooden roller lying on the stool. "When you've got two pieces up next to each other, run that roller down the seams to butt the edges, okay?"

"To butt the edges. Right."

"Don't forget to match the pattern, and leave enough overlap at the top and bottom to trim the edges. The razor's there on the stool."

Granger was looking more confused by the minute but nodded his head. "I have it."

"Good. You do know how to cut out the spaces for the switch plates?"

"Yes, I think so."

"I've taken the plates off the wall already," Corie said a little desperately. "After the paper's hung, just cut little crosses where the switches stick out behind it, peel the corners back, then cut out the rectangle just big enough for the switch to poke through. The raw edges will be covered by the plate when you screw it back on."

"I see," said Granger, looking dazed.

"Right." Corie hesitated, then decided she didn't want to wait around to see what he made of all that. "Call me if you run into trouble, okay?"

"Yes, ma'am."

She escaped before he saw her look of panic. What the hell had she been thinking of, hiring someone to help her redecorate her house when he didn't even know the first thing about hanging wallpaper? She must have finally lost her marbles.

Corie figured she wouldn't get much work out of him, but he had done a good job of the painting, from what she could see. However, she would probably end up repapering the darn room herself, she thought, as she marched back down the stairs to finish stripping the wall in the bedroom next to hers.

By the time the job was done it was almost time to start preparing dinner. She'd planned a quick meal of grilled salmon and salad, and a light dessert of fresh strawberries and cream.

After taking a quick shower, she pulled on a pair of tan slacks and a cream cotton sweater. The rain had stopped outside, but clouds still chased across the sky, promising another downpour before long.

Granger had changed into a pair of dark blue pants and a pale blue shirt. To Corie's surprise and pleasure, he waited for her to approach the table with the dinner plates, then pulled her chair out for her to be seated.

He made her wish she'd lit candles and served dinner in front of the fireplace in the dining room. If nothing else, Granger Deene obviously had good manners.

Seated opposite him at the small table in the kitchen, Corie wondered what he thought about her somewhat provincial life-style and surroundings. Not that it mattered to her one way or another. Tonight she would be the one to ask questions, and she wasn't about to let him avoid the answers any longer.

She waited until he had finished the salmon and had served him the fruit and cream before saying casually, "You never did tell me about your accident. You said it was a car wreck. I imagine it must have been pretty bad since you ended up in the hospital."

He sent her one of his enigmatic looks, then stared down at the half of a strawberry on his spoon as if he wasn't sure he wanted to eat it.

"I didn't say it was a car wreck. I think I said that my car was in Philadelphia at the time."

Corie's stomach did its little nervous dance again. "Oh, I see. Sorry, my mistake. I was just wondering how badly you were hurt and if you were in the hospital for a long time. I hate hospitals myself. I won't go near one unless I'm forced into it. I had my appendix out once and I've never forgotten how it felt, lying in that bed, staring up at the ceiling and feeling as if everyone in the world had deserted me."

There she went, running off at the mouth again, she thought ruefully. She was supposed to be asking the questions, for God's sake, not supplying the answers.

"I know the feeling."

He spoke with such vehemence she was startled for a moment.

"I'm sorry," she said at last. "It must be painful for you to remember."

Once more his eyes regarded her with the same deep, intense look he was so fond of using on her. She could feel a pulse throbbing in her forehead as the silence seemed to go on and on.

An engine suddenly exploded into life in the street outside, and Granger shifted in his chair. "That's just the point," he said at last. "I don't remember."

Frowning, Corie stared at him. "Pardon me?"

"I don't remember the accident. As a matter of fact, I don't remember anything that happened before that, either."

For a moment she forgot the sharp concentration in his light gray eyes. Shock rippled through her, leaving goose bumps shivering up and down her arms.

"But that's awful! What did the doctors tell you had happened?"

His gaze seemed to burn even deeper into her soul as he said quietly, "They couldn't tell me anything. Apparently they found me wandering along a road somewhere, with no identification and no memory of what had happened to me. Apparently I had been robbed."

So many things were falling into place. He had no friends, no family. He "thought" he'd been born in Philadelphia. His odd reactions to her comments, as if he didn't have a clue as to what she was talking about.

"I am so sorry." Forgetting all her doubts, she reached across the table and laid her hand over his. "I can't imagine how that must feel. And then to have all your personal possessions stolen on top of all that. Do you remember anything at all?"

He sat staring at her hand, his bleak expression hardening his harsh features. Then he said quietly, "I remember nothing of my past life. While some things seem familiar, others seem strange, incomprehensible."

He looked up, and the anguish in his eyes touched her heart. "The instrument you used this afternoon, for instance. You spoke to someone through it. To all intents and purposes, I've never seen such a thing before."

"The telephone?" She looked at him in amazement. "You didn't have one in your hospital room?"

"I had nothing in my hospital room, except a bed and a small table with a jug of water on it."

His blunt tone made her jump and she quickly withdrew her hand. He went on looking at his own as if he missed her touch.

What kind of hospital had he been in? she wondered. "Perhaps they didn't want to confuse you."

He looked up then, his eyes narrow silver slits. "I have no idea what they thought. I do know they avoided answering my questions."

"I'm sure they had your best interests at heart. I know it doesn't always seem that way. Especially if you are the one lying in that bed."

"Precisely."

Corie shifted nervously in her chair. With his eyes narrowed like that, and the fierce set of his mouth, once more he looked more than a little dangerous.

His loss of memory could explain some of the incidents that had confused her since she'd first helped him to his feet two days ago. But nothing as yet could explain that look of grim vengeance in his eyes, or the way his fist had clenched when he'd talked about the doctors. At times he even looked at her as if she was to blame for what had happened to him.

Something was wrong here. Very wrong. And Corie wasn't at all sure she wanted to know what it was.

Chapter 4

The day passed slowly as Corie tried to concentrate on her work. Questions bombarded her mind, no matter how hard she tried to forget Granger Deene and his odd behavior.

She felt sorry about his loss of memory, of course. But she couldn't escape the feeling that he wasn't telling her everything.

By that night the tension was beginning to affect Corie's nerves. She'd had a grueling day at the lab, and wasn't in the mood to answer Granger's constant questions about her work.

After he'd repeated a question twice during dinner, she finally lost her temper and snapped at him. "I've told you just about everything I do there. Why is it you can ask questions all night long, but you won't answer any of mine?"

He seemed to go very still. "What is it exactly that you want to know?"

"Whatever it is you're not telling me."

He was silent so long she got nervous. Now that she'd begun the conversation, she was starting to regret having said anything. She could feel the cold bite of Granger's gaze right down to the bone.

"Perhaps it is time we put our cards on the table," he said, pushing his half-eaten dessert away from him.

Corie curled her fingers around the handle of her fork, and did her best to relax the tremors chasing down her spine. Meeting Granger's chilling gaze, she said evenly, "What about?"

"About how and why I am here."

Once more he looked at her as if she were to blame for his troubles. Maybe she'd been right about him being dangerous, after all. She'd been fool enough to be taken in by a good-looking face and a few smooth lines, and now she was about to pay the price. Well, not without a fight, she wasn't. No one was going to get the better of her without a darn good struggle.

She made a move to stand up, but Granger snaked a hand across the table and grasped her wrist. "Not quite so fast, Mrs. Trenton. I have a few questions I want answered."

Dismayed at the formality, she tugged at her wrist. "I have a few of my own," she said evenly.

Her challenging stare appeared to have no effect whatsoever. Instead, Granger seemed to have become even more determined. "So I've noticed. You seem unusually interested in my past."

"No more than anyone would when hiring someone to work for them."

"I think, perhaps, it's a little late for that."

Corie felt a tremor of fear. Lifting her chin, she demanded, "What more do you want from me? I gave you a bed and fed you because I felt sorry for you." She gave her wrist another tug, but he held her fast. "Is this the thanks I get for trying to help someone I thought was in need?'' she added, as her temper began to rise.

"I kept my part of the bargain. I finished the painting and hung the wallpaper in two of your rooms. That should repay you for the food and lodging."

"You are hurting my wrist," Corie said pointedly.

"I'm sorry. I really don't want to hurt you. If you drop the fork, I'll let go."

She hadn't realized she was still gripping the fork. Widening her eyes, she said in disbelief, "You thought I was going to attack you?"

"The thought had crossed my mind."

Opening her fingers, she let the fork fall.

Immediately he let go of her wrist. "I'm sorry if I hurt you," he said, sounding sincere. "It appears to be becoming a habit. I have no wish to do that. All I want is a few answers to my questions."

Rubbing her wrist, Corie said a little defensively, "What kind of questions?"

He leaned back in his chair, eyeing her warily. "About your work, for the most part."

She stared at him in amazement. "My work? But I've told you about that."

"No, you told me what you did. I'm interested in the company you work for."

"I told you that, too. I work in a science lab about ten blocks from here."

"Describe the building to me."

She was beginning to relax a little now that he no longer held her in his firm fingers. Although he wasn't making much sense, as long as he meant her no harm, she would answer anything he asked.

"It's a small white building on the corner of the street. Double glass doors on the entrance, no outside windows.

The rooms aren't very big, mostly offices and a couple of labs. There are only a dozen people who work there.''

She frowned in concentration. ''That's about all I can tell you. The building has no signs outside. It's actually a unit of the main laboratory in Philadelphia. That's where all the big stuff goes on. We are more a record-keeping section, though we do have some scientists working there. They are pretty weird creatures, and most of the work is strictly hush-hush.''

She sat up straighter as a thought struck her. ''You're not a spy, are you? If so, you're asking the wrong person. I just deal with figures and calculations. I have no idea what they do with them.''

''I'm not a spy.'' He sat looking at her, a brooding expression on his face. One hand tapped nervously on the edge of the table. After a long pause, during which Corie felt sure she would suffocate from holding her breath too long, Granger said abruptly, ''I need your help.''

Corie puffed out her breath. ''I thought I was helping you.''

''No.'' With a sudden movement that made her jump, he pushed his chair back. ''I need some real help. I'm going to tell you something that you might not believe at first. I can only ask you to bear with me until I'm through.''

Corie ran the tip of her tongue over her dry lips. ''All right.''

He leaned back in the chair and matched the tips of his fingers together to make a tent. Focusing his gaze on them, he said quietly, ''I told you I was in a hospital. That isn't entirely true. I only thought it was a hospital. Apparently I was mistaken.''

Her heart gave a little skip. ''Not a hospital?'' For God's sake, had she been right about the mental home, after all?

''No. My hospital room was actually a room in the building where you work.''

She could feel her jaw drop. Now he had to be talking nonsense. "I don't understand," she said, wishing he wouldn't keep talking in riddles.

"Neither do I. Which is why I need your help. All I know is that I woke up there several days ago, without any knowledge of how I got there, and with no memory of who I am or where I came from."

"So, your name isn't really Granger Deene?"

He passed a hand across his eyes as if he were incredibly tired. "Yes, my name is Granger Deene. They gave me the name of John Smith, but I remembered my real name. It's the only thing I can remember clearly."

Corie frowned, trying to make sense of it all. "You keep saying 'they.' Who are they? Doctors?"

"I don't know. They were careful not to give me any of their names. All I know is that someone jabbed a needle in my arm every now and again, and I went to sleep. When I awoke my head was fuzzy and I had trouble remembering my name again."

"They didn't tell you anything? They must know how you got there."

"All they told me was what I've told you. They wouldn't answer any of my questions after that. They kept telling me I'd remember everything once I'd recovered my memory."

Corie shook her head in disbelief. "I don't understand. There are no hospital rooms in the lab as far as I know. I can't imagine why you would be there. Are you certain it was the same building?"

Granger slowly nodded his head. "I'm certain. I followed you home from there."

Once more her breath seemed to freeze in her throat. "I beg your pardon?"

"I'm sorry. I know this must come as a shock to you. When I saw you by the front doors, talking to someone, you mentioned that you lived alone. I needed somewhere to stay until I could find out what had happened to me, and I needed answers. You seemed like the right person to ask.''

She finally found her voice. "You followed me home?"

"Yes. I waited until you'd gone inside the house. I intended to knock on your door and ask for a room. But then I blacked out, and when I woke up, there you were."

There she was, all right, Corie thought grimly. In the wrong place at the wrong time, as usual. "What would you have done if I'd told you to get lost?"

"Then," Granger said quietly, "I'm afraid I would have had to persuade you to help me."

His words sent a tiny shiver down her back. "How? By seducing me?"

The second the words were out of her mouth she wished them back. Heaven knew what had made her say them. She'd intended to make light of the situation, not get herself in deeper.

Granger's face changed, and for a moment she thought he was going to smile. "It's a pleasant thought," he said softly, "but I was thinking of a more subtle persuasion."

"Oh." More embarrassed than ever, she said quickly, "I can't tell you much more than you know already. I can't imagine why you were brought to the lab instead of a hospital, and I have no idea why they kept you there, unless it was dangerous to move you—"

She broke off when she saw Granger's grim expression. "Precisely. I want you to find out why I was being kept prisoner in your building."

"Prisoner?" Her heart began thumping again, as Granger nodded.

"I was very definitely a prisoner. Every time I tried to open the door of that room, someone would stick the needle in my arm again and I'd black out."

"If they kept you a prisoner," Corie said carefully, "why did they let you go?"

Granger waited a long moment before answering. "They didn't."

In the long silence that followed, Corie could feel the heavy thud of her heartbeat. "You escaped?"

"Yes."

She didn't know if he would answer her but she had to ask. "You didn't . . . hurt anyone, did you?"

Granger made a sound that resembled a laugh. "Rest assured, I did not hurt anyone. I merely borrowed someone's clothes, and left him gagged with a dinner napkin and tied to the bed."

"Oh, great." Corie tilted her head back and closed her eyes. "I don't know who would want to keep you prisoner. I can't believe it could be any of the scientists, and there is only me and Mike, the guard you saw me talking to, and Jennie, the secretary. What did these people look like?"

"The only one I remember clearly was a man with a slight build, wearing glasses. He had a face like a mouse, he kept twitching his nose."

She almost laughed. Eyeing Granger's husky build she said incredulously, "And this was the man who kept you prisoner?"

"No," Granger said grimly. "He was the one who kept sticking that damn needle into me. I'm sorry, I realize that's not much help, but things were hazy for a while."

"It doesn't sound like anyone I'm familiar with," Corie said, shaking her head. "What about the others?"

"I have trouble remembering what they look like. Perhaps there are people there you don't know about."

She looked back at him, feeling suddenly afraid. "It's possible, but I haven't seen any strange men around the building. But if what you say is true, they are probably looking for you."

"I'm sure they are. I saw one of those cars move slowly by here the other night. It might have been my jailers."

Granger leaned forward, his eyes boring into hers. "I need to know as much as you can possibly find out. Where they found me, what they want from me, where I came from. If I know all that, perhaps my mind will piece the rest of it together."

"I'll do what I can," Corie said, ignoring the little voice that told her she was being a sucker again. "If you were being held prisoner by people I work for and trusted, then I want to know about it. I can't believe they would hold you without a very good reason. I want to know what it is."

Granger's wide shoulders seemed to sag. "So do I."

"Mind you," Corie said carefully, "I can't promise anything. I don't have the authority to go barging into places they don't want me to be in, and everything is guarded by computers."

"Computers?"

She sighed. This was going to be more difficult than she'd imagined. Without his memory the guy couldn't understand half of what she said. He couldn't even remember seeing a telephone before, let alone a computer.

"Machines," she said, waving a hand in the air as if that would help him understand. "You have to have special passes to get into some of those labs. All the programs are coded, though I might be able to get around that. I do have some clout there, having worked for the company for ten years."

He looked at her as if she were talking a foreign language.

Thinking of how confusing all this technology must be to someone who didn't remember anything except his name, Corie said sincerely, "I'm sorry. You'll just have to trust me."

"It's a little difficult to trust anyone under the circumstances. In your case, however, I really have no choice."

It was a backhanded compliment, but she let it go. After all, she felt the same way about him. "It was probably the effects of whatever drug they were giving you that made you collapse on my doorstep."

"I imagine so." Granger studied his fingernails. "It certainly wasn't intentional, I can assure you."

"How do you feel now?"

"Much better, thanks to you." He leaned back in the chair. "I would say I'm in the best of health, except for the loss of my memory." He paused for a moment, then added quietly, "And the dreams."

Remembering how she'd been dressed when she'd gone to him in the night, Corie felt her face warm. "Like the one the other night?"

"Exactly. They come without warning, sometimes even when I'm awake. More like visions than dreams. And always so real." His hand inscribed an arc in the air. "Not only do I see everything clearly, I can smell the burning grass, feel the heavy, damp heat cloying my body, hear the thunder pounding in my head..."

Watching his face, Corie could almost hear it, too. "Do you recognize the place in your dream?"

He opened his eyes and stared at her. "I think I do. I can't remember where or when, but I know I've been to the places I dream about. Except—"

He broke off, and something about the look on his face disturbed her pulse again.

"Except what?"

He shook his head. "It's not important."

"Well, that's a start, anyway. How about people?"

After thinking about it, Granger said, "No, I don't recognize any people. I see one face but I don't know it."

"Can you remember anyone from your past?" She had been dying to ask the next question, but now that the opportunity was there she almost didn't take it. "Like your wife for instance?" she added, as he began to speak.

Granger closed his mouth. He sat staring down at the table for so long, she was afraid that perhaps he was seeing another vision. Then he said slowly, "I don't remember a wife. I don't remember any woman. I could be married, I suppose, or have children somewhere."

Corie wanted to answer him, but she didn't know what to say.

Then he startled her by looking up, his gaze intent on her face. "No," he said, in a firm voice, "I am sure I don't have a wife. If I did love a woman, I would know it." He tapped his chest with his clenched fist. "Right here in my heart. Of that I am absolutely convinced."

His words seemed to burn themselves into her mind. God, what she would give to be loved like that. To belong to a man like Granger Deene, to be so sure of his love that she would know without a shadow of a doubt that they belonged together and nothing could ever change that.

She felt a sudden fierce longing that took her breath away, then a voice in the back of her mind brought her back to reality. No man was that trustworthy. No man was immune to the endless temptations waiting for him out there.

Few women were lucky enough to hold a man's love for an eternity. That was fantasy. And this was the real world. She had better remember that, before she went and made a damn fool of herself again.

Once more she met Granger Deene's intangible stare, and steeled herself against the promise that could never be realized.

"I need your help," he said softly. "I have nowhere else to turn. You are my only hope."

Feeling tired now, she got to her feet. "I'll do my best to find out what's going on. Whoever they are, I just hope they haven't got the police out looking for you, or we'll both be in big trouble."

Granger stood up, a fierce frown darkening his face. "I don't want to cause trouble for you. If there is danger—"

"Don't worry," Corie said, with a good deal more confidence than she felt, "I can take pretty good care of myself. I learned the hard way."

He looked down at her, his face troubled. "I don't want you to take any unnecessary risks for my sake. Just find out what you can without causing any trouble for yourself. Perhaps you can give me something to work with and I'll be able to manage the rest myself."

"We'll see." She picked up her plate and reached for his, but he forestalled her.

"Please allow me to do this tonight," he said, taking the plate from her hands. "I've watched you do this, and it doesn't look too difficult. If I keep working with all these strange gadgets perhaps I'll eventually remember them again."

In spite of her reservations, Corie grinned. "That's the spirit. And after you've finished, I'll reintroduce you to the wonders of television. You should get a real big kick out of that."

By the time Corie went to bed that night, she felt even more confused about her houseguest. It seemed that they had reached an uneasy understanding, the best they could expect under the circumstances.

Part of her warned that he could be all her worst fears poured into one. Yet an even stronger part of her insisted that he wasn't dangerous and meant her no harm.

Granger had been mesmerized by the television, sitting glued to the screen while she ran a couple of loads of wash. He'd seemed shocked by much of what he saw, and she was beginning to understand what it must be like for him to re-member nothing of his life before now.

Forty years wiped out literally overnight, and to wake up in a strange town surrounded by unfamiliar and even frightening objects, had to be traumatic to say the least. It must be like moving to another planet.

Staring at the darkened ceiling, Corie drew the covers up to her chin. She still couldn't believe anyone had kept Granger prisoner in a room at the lab, let alone the people with whom she worked, but she was determined to find out. He was so confused about everything, he could have simply imagined the whole thing, as the doctors had told him.

Yet something about the situation was very strange. As far as she knew, there were no doctors at the astronomy lab. And if there were, why weren't they where they belonged, in a hospital, not a research lab?

Corie turned on her side, trying to get more comfortable. If Granger was telling the truth, it was possible she could be innocently involved in something criminal.

Besides, she couldn't ignore the anguish in his mesmer-izing eyes. She wanted him to recover his lost life. More than anything, she wanted to know who he was and where he came from. And though she hated to admit it, she wanted desperately to know if Granger Deene had a wife.

She hadn't quite fallen into a deep sleep when she heard his voice above her again. He was shouting, though the words were too muffled for her to hear them properly.

She resisted the urge to go up to his room again. The last thing she wanted was for him to think she was using his nightmares as an excuse to go to him.

Praying he wouldn't hurt himself thrashing around the bed, she made herself stay where she was, her pillow over her ears to shut out the torment of his voice.

She overslept the next morning, after shutting off the alarm and drifting back into an exhausted sleep. When she awoke again, it was over half an hour later.

She showered quickly, sifting through the possibilities of a fast breakfast. Finally deciding on scrambled eggs and bacon, with perhaps a bowl of cereal thrown in, she dressed in a light blue cotton shirtdress and slipped into her sandals.

She'd just have time to make breakfast, she thought, eyeing the clock. Today Granger would have to eat the meal by himself.

The tempting smell of bacon wafted up the stairs as Granger made his way down to the kitchen. He was hungry, and tired. He hadn't slept well, tormented by the dreams that were becoming an almost constant occurrence.

He didn't know when he'd decided to trust Corie Trenton. Not that he had much option, since she was the only one who could give him the answers he needed. But he was convinced now that she knew nothing about his predicament, and she seemed willing enough to try to find out the truth. Though whether it was to satisfy herself or to help him, he wasn't really sure.

His main worry was that she could be taking a risk, though he had no way of knowing if she would be in any kind of danger. In fact, she could very well put him in danger, by inadvertently alerting his former jailers of his whereabouts.

Granger reached the bottom of the stairs and paused, preparing himself to face Corie in the kitchen. He could hear her moving about in there, crashing dishes around as if she were in a hurry.

He hoped she hadn't been disturbed by his restlessness in the night. The dreams had been so realistic, to the point now where he was almost certain that they were actual memories, and not dreams at all.

He was afraid to hope for too much. Afraid that his memory was actually returning. For if that was so, he had to face a truth far more devastating, far more preposterous than anything that had happened to him so far. A truth that would be impossible to overcome, unless Corie Trenton could help him.

Slowly he walked toward the kitchen door, the delectable smell of the bacon reminding him of his empty stomach. One thing he did know. Whatever he might have done in the past, he was certain he had broken no laws. So whoever had kept him prisoner in that barren room, had done so for their own ends.

Whatever those ends were, he had no idea. But he was going to find out. And he didn't care much how he went about it. If he had to use force, he would do it. But somehow, someway, he was going to know how he had arrived in that bed, and by whose hand.

Corie looked up as Granger walked into the kitchen. In his freshly laundered shirt and jeans, his hair still damp from the shower, he looked ruggedly appealing. Granger Deene was a good-looking man, Corie thought, feeling a tug at her heart.

She looked away, caught off guard when he bade her good-morning in his deep voice. "I was just about to scramble your eggs," she said, stumbling over the words in her confusion. "You timed it about right. Your cereal's on the table, and the paper's there too, if you want to look at it."

"Thank you. It smells good." He sat down on the chair and reached for the paper. "Have you read it?"

"No, I haven't had time." Whisking the eggs around in the pan, she added, "I won't have time to eat breakfast with you this morning. I overslept. I'll grab something at the office."

"You get breakfast in the office?"

He sounded surprised and she flashed him a quick glance. He was concentrating on enjoying the cornflakes she'd poured for him, and didn't seem to notice her hesitation.

"It comes from a machine. Doughnuts, pastries, coffee... not too nutritious, but they fill a hole."

"You get breakfast out of a machine?" He shook his head, and swallowed another spoonful of cereal. "Machines that take you from one place to another, machines that allow you to talk to someone who isn't there, machines that can show you stories of what's happening all over the world, machines to wash your clothes, cook your food and even serve you breakfast. It's a wonder a man can find work in this world."

Corie grimaced. "I hadn't thought about it quite like that, but I guess you're right. And you haven't seen the half of it yet. Wait until you see what a computer can do. That machine can even think for you."

"I'm not sure that's such a good deal for the future of mankind. If machines can think, one day they might very well end up governing the world."

"God, what a gruesome thought." Corie dished up the scrambled eggs and added the bacon to the plate. Expertly catching the toast as it popped up, she dropped the pieces on another small plate and carried everything to the table.

"Though I guess without disease," she added, "or old age, or temperament to worry about, machines might do a better job than men at that. They couldn't do much worse."

Granger directed his intent stare at her. "There is one small exception."

She felt a flutter of awareness as her eyes met his. "And what's that?"

"Reproduction. Since machines can't multiply in the way humans do, eventually they will wear out, unless they have men to make more."

"Unless the machines know how to make machines," she said a little breathlessly.

He studied her for a moment longer. "You are a remarkable lady, Corie Trenton. I admire your intelligence. It is rare in a woman."

She would have liked to argue that point, if she'd had the time. Instead, she set his breakfast down in front of him and asked, "Would you like some orange juice? I have frozen, but it tastes like fresh squeezed."

"Frozen orange juice?" He shook his head. "In the middle of summer?"

"In the freezer. Another machine. I do have some thawed out, though. I'll get it."

She glanced over her shoulder as she reached the fridge, feeling a small shiver run down her spine when she saw him watching her. She might as well be stark naked, the way he made her feel so darn exposed.

Trying to get her mind off his blatant sexuality, she said lightly, "If I call you, will you answer the phone?"

When he frowned, she lifted her hand to her ear. "The telephone?"

His brow cleared. "Yes, of course. I just pick up the handle and listen, right?"

"Just make sure it's the right end. You talk into the end with the cord, and put the other end over your ear." She almost smiled, thinking how ridiculous it seemed to be explaining something so simple. Though of course, it couldn't be simple to someone who couldn't remember ever seeing a phone before.

"I'll try and remember," Granger said solemnly.

She poured the orange juice, almost spilling it as a thought struck her. "Wait a minute. That may not be such a good idea. Someone else could be calling the house. If a strange man answers there could be awkward questions."

"Couldn't you just say you were taking in boarders already?"

She shook her head. "I've got a better idea. I'll let it ring twice and hang up. Then I'll call again. So if you hear two rings, then a long pause, then it starts ringing again, you'll know it's me. Okay?"

He pondered on that for a moment. "But what if someone needs to get in touch with you? You'll miss the call."

Corie flipped her hand in the direction of the living room. "No, the answering machine will pick it up. I'll get it when I get home."

His look of astonishment almost made her laugh out loud. "You have a machine that answers a machine," he murmured. "Fascinating."

"I have to run." Corie glanced at the clock and groaned. "I'll have to take the car, it's too late to walk now. But you won't need it for anything today."

"I can't drive it anyway," Granger reminded her dryly.

"Oh, right." She hesitated at the door. "Since you've finished papering the bedroom, perhaps you could get started on the one next to it? That needs painting and papering, too. I've left the materials in the room, just do it the same way you did the other one. The paper's a different color but it's similar to the one you used yesterday."

"I'll get to it as soon as I've done the dishes," Granger said, picking up his fork. "This looks delicious, by the way."

"Thanks." She hesitated, then added, "I'll do my best to find out what I can. Just don't expect too much, okay? They are pretty closemouthed in that place."

The look he gave her was unlike anything she'd seen from him before. It was a level look, unwavering in its intensity as always, yet somehow it seemed to convey warmth, an almost intimate sharing of a bond, that left her breathless.

"Please take care, Corie."

She nodded, feeling a catch in her throat. "You too. I'll call if I find out anything." She left then, before he saw in her eyes what was happening in her heart. "Damn," she whispered fiercely as she started the engine. She didn't need this. She couldn't fall for him. Not after everything she'd gone through. She knew nothing about the man, for God's sake. What she did know didn't seem too promising. She wasn't even sure she believed all that stuff about him losing his memory.

Granger Deene was a smooth talker. He could have been making all that up just to con her into feeling sorry for him and giving him somewhere to stay.

The engine caught and held, and she slid the gear into Reverse. She didn't really believe that. His confusion over all the machines was genuine, she'd stake her life on it.

Okay, so he'd lost his memory. But what about all that stuff about being held prisoner, in the very building where she worked? Now *that* didn't make sense.

One way or another, she had to get to the bottom of this. And once she did, Corie vowed as she backed the car out onto the road, she would give Mr. Granger Deene the answers he wanted, then she would send him packing. The last thing in the world she wanted was to get involved with another charmer.

Mike was seated at his usual position at the desk when she entered the building a few minutes later. It occurred to her to wonder how Granger had got past him on Friday night. Then she remembered that Mike had been watching a ball game on the monitors, instead of focusing on the hallways as he was supposed to do.

She could hardly blame him. Mike was a retired cop, and his days spent seated at a desk watching a steady diet of people passing to and fro through the hallways had to be extremely dull by comparison.

She nodded to him as she hurried across the lobby, and he answered with a casual wave of his hand. Letting herself into her office, she wondered how big a pile of work would be waiting for her. Thank God it wasn't a Monday.

Mondays were always a pain. A couple of the scientists often worked over the weekend, leaving her a pile of research to sort through and take care of that would take her the best part of the week.

Corie didn't believe in working weekends. She was a firm believer in giving mind and body a proper rest in order to function at top capability when it became necessary. Science was an exact field. One mistake could cost thousands, even millions of dollars. Or even lives.

Thinking of lives reminded her potently of Granger Deene waiting anxiously in her house for some word that might give him back his memory. Wondering how to begin, Corie booted up the computer and began scrolling through the tasks she still hadn't had time to get to.

The usual stuff rolled up her screen. "Calculate degrees of angles produced by lineup of Jupiter in conjunction with Uranus, taking into account the easterly jet stream crossing the Continental Divide."

Symbols and abbreviations drifted past her eyes while she contemplated the problem at hand. Somehow she would have to find out if there was a room such as Granger described. That should at least tell her he was telling the truth about being held prisoner there. She could think of no other reason for there to be a bedroom in the building.

Watching the lines of print drift by with half an eye, Corie noticed a mention of the new star, Specturne. It had been recently discovered and named by an astronomer connected with the Smithsonian Institute.

There had been a lot of excitement about it at first, and Corie had been thrilled to be part of a new discovery, even if the work had been tedious. Then the find had taken second place to the new breakthrough of a possible cure for muscular diseases. As far as Corie knew, the only person with any interest at all in Specturne was the astronomer who discovered it.

Someone, however, must have an interest, since she'd been instructed to calculate new data on the star. Glancing at the code name, Corie saw that Dr. Boyd Richards, one of the chief scientists at the lab, had ordered the information.

The head office must have decided to reopen the file, she thought, scrolling past the name again. She'd get to it later. Right now, all she was interested in was locating that darn room.

Her mind drifted back to Granger, and she wondered if he was busy at work on the walls. She could just picture him, muscles rippling as he swept the paintbrush carefully up and down the woodwork, his hard mouth tight with concentration.

Oh, how she wanted to feel the pressure of that mouth hard and demanding on her own. The sudden longing took her by surprise, heating her from her thighs to her breasts. God, how long had it been?

Years. It had been years since she had been even remotely interested in sex. Funny, but she hadn't really missed it until now. Maybe it was the long abstinence that made her weak every time Granger looked at her. Maybe it was simply the fact that she missed the intimate connection with another human being, and that was why she longed for his hands to touch her, caress her, and send her wild.

Or just maybe, it was the way he looked at her, seduced her with his eyes, breathed her name in that husky voice, or moved across the room toward her creating sparks of animal magnetism as he drew closer. Maybe all of that was the reason she wanted to feel his body naked and hot against hers.

"Damn, damn, damn!" She pounded the desk in frustration. What the hell was she doing fantasizing about a man who could be at best married, and at worst a hunted criminal? The sooner she found out what was behind his crazy story, the sooner she could get him out of her life.

Because whether she liked it or not, Granger Deene could be a dangerous man. In every aspect of the word.

Chapter 5

Fiercely concentrating on the task at hand, Corie decided to have a word with Mike. If anyone knew the layout of the building, it would be the security guard.

Making her way down the corridor, Corie saw Professor James Butler ambling toward her. The scientist was a pleasant little man, always ready to exchange a word or two, more often than not a bad joke about the weather.

Today, however, he barely gave her a nod of recognition before scuttling past her, heading for the security door that led to the labs.

Frowning, Corie wondered if she'd done something to upset him. Her pulse quickened when she wondered if perhaps he was upset over something that had happened last Friday. Such as a prisoner escaping, perhaps?

Thinking about it now, it seemed so crazy. The scientists she worked for were all respected in their field. They couldn't possibly be involved in anything so bizarre as holding a man prisoner in a room and pumping him full of drugs. It was just too weird to even consider. Granger Deene had to be mistaken. Or lying.

Corie paused at the end of the hallway. Mike was seated at his desk, a newspaper propped up in front of him. Every now and again he glanced up at the monitors above his head, checking on the movement in the hallways.

As Corie approached, she could see on the monitor screen the slight figure of Professor Butler scurrying down the passageway to the labs. She watched him reach the doors, slip his ID card into the slot on the wall, then wait. After a moment a green light glowed above his head, and he pushed the door open, letting it swing closed behind him after he'd passed through.

Mike's voice made her jump. "Corie, how're you doing?"

She shrugged. "Busy. I was working on the house."

Mike shook his shaggy gray head. "That house'll be the death of you, Corie girl. Took on too much when you bought that one, I reckon."

She laughed. "It keeps me out of mischief." Glancing casually up at the monitors, she added, "I don't know how you sit there glued to those monitors all day. It must send you cross-eyed."

"Nah, I'm used to it." Mike closed one eye in a conspiratorial wink. "Besides, I keep one of 'em tuned to the soaps and the ball games. Passes the time, if you know what I mean."

Corie nodded, her gaze intent on the monitors. "You know, I've worked here for almost a year, yet I have no idea what lies beyond those security doors. One day I'll have to get them to take me on a tour of the building."

"Wouldn't take you too long," Mike said, smothering a yawn. "There's only the two labs and a couple of offices."

Corie did her best to keep her tone casual. "And a day room, I guess?"

Mike squinted at her. "Day room?"

"Yes, you know, a room where the big brains can sit and relax, maybe lie down for a quick nap. . . ."

Mike's hearty laugh rang out across the lobby. "If there is, they're doing a good job of hiding it. I've been through every inch of this building and I've never yet seen a room like that. If I had, I might have used it on my break sometimes, instead of dropping off in this darn chair."

"Maybe we should suggest it," Corie said, trying to ignore the uneasy fluttering in her stomach. Granger had seemed so positive. And no matter how much her instincts warned her to be careful, she couldn't bring herself to believe he was deliberately lying to her.

Could there be a chance that such a room existed without Mike's knowledge? It was worth a shot to find out.

"I suppose you have to check inside all the rooms every day," she said, pretending to be interested in an elderly couple walking past the window outside.

"Yeah, all except the labs. I just look through the windows of those babies. No one gets in there, not even me, unless it's an emergency. Top secret stuff, I suppose. I just hope they're not planning on blowing up China or something. I don't want to be around for the Third World War."

"Me, either," Corie murmured, her mind only half on the conversation. Somehow she would have to get into the labs to see if the room that Granger described actually existed. That promised to be tricky.

"I'd better get back," she said to Mike, who was scanning the monitors with a bored expression on his craggy face. "I have a ton of stuff to do."

Mike nodded, and lifted a hand in a distracted way. "Talk to you later."

She left him still watching the monitors, and made her way back to her office, turning over the problem in her mind of how to get into the labs without being seen.

It would seem the best time would be either lunchtime, when everyone took a break, or at the end of the day, after everyone had gone home. But then Mike did his rounds to make sure everyone had left before setting the alarms for the night. It would have to be during the lunch hour. Which would be in two hours. Corie sat with her chin on her hands and considered the possibilities. Once more her mind drifted back to Granger, wondering how far he'd progressed with the decorating.

She couldn't forget how he'd looked in the night, naked and sweating in a rumpled bed, his face tortured by the dreams that wouldn't let him rest. Neither could she forget the ache she'd felt as she looked down on his powerful body.

Just thinking about it brought back the longing. She needed to get this whole situation taken care of, and as soon as possible. If she could just get into the lab...

The phone rang, startling her out of her reverie. With Granger's face still on her mind, she thrust out her hand, sending her empty coffee cup flying as she snatched up the receiver.

Her heartbeat slowed when she heard the voice of Dr. Richards, the scientist in charge of the Specturne project. Assuring him that she would get the data he requested to him as soon as possible, Corie righted the cup, staring at the spilled dregs on her desk.

She barely heard the scientist hang up. Now she knew how to get into the lab.

The next two hours passed quickly, as Corie worked on the list of tasks in front of her on the computer. Before she knew it, the green figures on the digital clock clicked to twelve noon. It was time for lunch.

She waited another ten minutes before entering the lunchroom. Only two people were seated at the tables, the rest having apparently gone out to eat. Mike sat in the corner, his nose buried in a mystery novel. Professor Butler was at his usual table by the window, eating his packed lunch.

Corie was extremely thankful that it was Professor Butler who brought his lunch every day. Had it been the short-tempered, gruff-voiced Dr. Ivan Spencer, another chief scientist, she would have found it far more difficult to put her plan into action.

As for his partner, Dr. Richards, he could look quite intimidating when annoyed. More than once she'd been stung by one of his caustic remarks.

After buying a ham sandwich and an apple from the dispenser, Corie filled a paper cup from the coffee machine. Carrying the brimming cup carefully over to the table, she sat down next to Professor Butler.

He looked up in surprise, his face turning red at the sight of his unexpected visitor. "Miss Trenton? Is there something I can do for you?"

Corie gave him a wide smile. "I hope you can help me, Professor Butler. I have to make some calculations on the new star, Specturne, and I was wondering if you had the altitude list on the project?"

Professor Butler shook his head violently, almost dislodging his glasses. "Oh, no, I'm sorry, I don't. I'm not sure...that is...I don't think—"

Corie froze. *A man with a slight build, wearing glasses. He had a face like a mouse...* Could it possibly have been this nervous little man who had pumped a dangerous drug into Granger? It didn't seem feasible, and yet...

Gathering her thoughts, she leaned closer. "It's all right, I'll manage. I'll leave you alone to enjoy your lunch." She pushed back her chair and rose to her feet, reaching for her coffee.

Her fingers caught the edge of the cup, and it tipped, sending a stream of hot black liquid into Professor Butler's lap. He yelped and jumped to his feet, slapping at his white coat as if there were a bug crawling up it.

"Oh, geez, I'm sorry," Corie said, dabbing at the puddle on the table with her napkin. "That was really clumsy of me."

"No matter," the professor muttered. "I just hope I can get the stain out of this."

"Here, give it to me." Corie reached for the buttons of his coat and began undoing them. "I'll take it down to the washroom and rinse out the spot in cold water before the stain has time to set. By the time you've finished lunch I'll have it back to you as good as new."

"No, really... Please... don't bother," Professor Butler stammered, doing his best to prevent Corie from stripping him of his coat.

"No bother at all. I insist." Corie finished unbuttoning the man's coat, in spite of his fluttering attempts to stop her. Dragging it off his shoulders, she said firmly, "Now you just sit down there and finish your lunch. I'll be back in a jiffy."

Without giving him a chance to answer, she fled across the room with the coat in her arms, conscious of Mike's astonished gaze following her from the room.

She had ten minutes at most, then she would have to be back in the washroom to rinse out the coat. Checking for the ID card, she found it firmly pinned to the inside top pocket. Fumbling with the catch, she finally got it unfastened, then looked around for somewhere to hide the coat until she could return for it.

The waste bin seemed the only place, and she stuffed it inside. The hallway was still empty when she looked out, and she raced down to the security door. Her hand shook as she slid the card into the slot on the wall and waited impatiently for the green light.

When it came she almost missed it in her excitement. Pushing the door open, she slipped inside and let it close with a soft thud behind her.

Her heart was banging so hard she felt sure she would pass out. Quickly, she crossed the lab to the door at the rear. Her biggest fear now was that one of the scientists had been too engrossed in his work to leave the building for lunch.

She let out her breath on a slow sigh when she opened the door and found the small room empty. It was obviously an office. A computer sat on the desk, and a small cabinet lurked in the corner of the room. Two chairs accompanied a low table in front of a television set, while a monitor, tuned to the hallways, hung from the wall. There wasn't even room for a bed.

Corie tried to calm her jumpy pulse as she sped across the floor to the lab next door. Holding her breath, she wound her way between the long, narrow tables crowded with microscopes, Bunsen burners, and an assortment of instruments and utensils.

When she reached the door her heart sank. It was firmly locked.

Biting her lip in frustration, Corie turned away and sent a desperate glance around the lab. In the corner of the room on her right a couple of white coats hung haphazardly from a peg on the wall.

Not really expecting too much, Corie dashed across to take a look in the pockets. Her heart skipped a beat when her fingers closed around a ring of keys. It seemed to good to be true, but it was worth a try.

With her fingers crossed, she darted back to the door and fitted one of the keys into the lock. It wouldn't budge. She tried a second key and this time, with a smooth click, the door opened.

With a soft, triumphant, "Yes!" Corie looked inside the room. There were just two pieces of furniture. The white walls seemed to glare at her as she stared at the small table and unmade bed. It must have been left just as Granger Deene had last seen it. The dinner napkin still lay on the crumpled pillow.

Closing the door again, Corie locked it with trembling fingers. He'd been telling the truth. But why in God's name would anyone want to keep him locked up in a room at a laboratory? It just didn't make sense.

There was no time to worry about it now. Once more she sped across the room and slipped the keys back into the pocket of the coat.

As she passed through the first lab again she glanced at the open door of the office. Had it been open when she'd come in, or closed? Trying desperately to remember, she approached the office. The door had been closed. She was almost positive.

She reached for the doorway, glancing at the image on the monitor. Her stomach jolted when she saw the two people walking down the hallway toward the security doors. The scientists were already back from lunch.

Granger paced back and forth across the bedroom, the paintbrush forgotten in his hand. His head ached, filled as it was with sights and sounds that were nothing more than a jumbled mass of confusion.

The pictures he saw in his tormented mind had nothing in common with his surroundings. Yet everything in his visions were so familiar. Far more familiar than anything he had seen since the day he woke up a prisoner in that barren hospital room.

True, the images were distorted. No more than flashes of time, split seconds of motion, swift glimpses of scenery, fractured explosions of noise and suffocating smoke. Yet he knew now that what he saw was real, or had been real to him at some time. And what he saw filled him with a fear such as he'd never known before.

He'd tried to erase the visions by working at maximum speed. Half the room was painted already, and it would take him only an hour or two to finish. By the time Corie arrived home from work he should be all cleaned up and ready to hang the paper in the morning.

Thinking about Corie gave him further pangs of anxiety. Could he really trust her? She was one of them, and could easily be arranging for his capture at this very minute.

If so, as much as it would hurt him, he would have to deal with her the way he dealt with all his enemies. Swiftly and without mercy. That's if he lived long enough.

If what he suspected was true, they couldn't afford to let him go free. He could imagine what turmoil his presence would create. He still found it impossible to believe. Maybe his mind was crazy after all.

He looked at the watch Corie had lent him. Twelve-thirty. He realized he was hungry and went down to the kitchen to find something to eat.

He was standing by the refrigerator when the strident peal of sound seemed to scream in his ear. This time it was no vision. The sound came from the living room. From the telephone. It rang once, twice, then silence.

He stood transfixed, waiting for it to ring again. When the shrill ring came again, he crossed the floor swiftly and snatched up the receiver. Pressing the end of it to his ear, he raised his voice. "Can you hear me?"

"You don't have to shout," Corie's voice said in his ear. "You'll break my ear drum. Just speak normally."

She sounded surprisingly close to him, as if she were standing right there next to him. Startled, he pulled the receiver away and looked at it, half expecting to see her image.

He heard her say something else and slapped the phone back to his ear. "I'm sorry, what did you say?"

"I said, have you eaten lunch yet?"

"I was just about to eat something."

"I just wanted you to know..."

She paused, and something in her voice made his heart begin to thump. "Yes?"

He waited, then heard her say softly, "You were right, Granger. I found the room where they held you. I almost got caught, I had to hide in a broom closet until they'd gone past."

He closed his eyes briefly, relieved that at least he hadn't imagined that room, and thankful beyond measure that Corie had not been discovered.

"There's something else," Corie added, before he could speak. "I found a list of supplies on Helen Grant's desk. She's Richards's secretary. I searched her desk before she came back from lunch. Guess what I found?"

Realizing the risks she had taken, his throat closed up. "What?" he asked gruffly.

"I found an invoice from an ambulance company, for transporting a patient from Philadelphia to Cape May. I also found a receipt for a prescription drug. It had been sent down from the main lab in Philadelphia. I didn't recognize the name so I looked it up."

Again she paused and he waited, heart racing for her to continue.

Finally she spoke, in a voice tight with disbelief. "It's a drug used in experiments on animals to test their memory span. When given in high enough dosage, it suppresses the memory altogether."

His mind raced, grappling with the significance of her words.

"Granger," Corie said urgently, "you didn't lose your memory. For some reason I can't possibly imagine right now, they deliberately suppressed it. You must know something they don't want you to remember."

Now he knew. He didn't know how, why or when, but he knew it had happened. And the knowledge left him speechless.

Very carefully, he rested his finger on the button and cut off Corie's voice. Slowly, he replaced the receiver and walked to the window.

Outside, white fluffy clouds skimmed across a pale blue sky. The sun shone through the branches of the trees, sending shifting patterns across the window panes, and the wind rustled the green leaves, making them dance on the slender limbs.

Faintly he could hear the wild song of the birds, and the muffled shouts of children playing somewhere in the distance. A silver-haired man in shirtsleeves walked slowly down the street, his weight supported by a cane. A boy passed the man, balanced on a two-wheel machine, waving his hand and shouting to an unseen companion.

It all looked so normal.

No wonder they wanted him under lock and key. But he had no intention of spending the rest of his life a prisoner, a guinea pig for their experiments. He would die first.

Closing his eyes, Granger lifted his chin. Raising his fists he shook them at the fates that had played such a cruel joke on him. Gathering his breath he let it out in one, mighty, echoing howl of anguish. "No!"

"I'm sorry we got cut off this afternoon," Corie said, as she unloaded the bag of groceries into the fridge. "I couldn't call you back because that miserable Dr. Richards was on my tail. He's been bugging me all day to get a report out to him. That's why I was late."

"I was beginning to get worried," Granger said, from his seat at the table. "You said you would be home at 5:30. It's an hour past that now."

She glanced at him. He looked strained, drawn, as if he hadn't slept in weeks. Remembering the dreams that disturbed him, she could understand why he looked haggard. But the tension that seemed to keep him coiled like a panther ready to spring seemed even more pronounced.

"I'm sorry if I upset you," she said, closing the fridge door. "I know it must be a shock to find out that someone has been tampering with your mind. But now that we have the proof you can go to the police and—"

"No!"

She stared at him, the feeling of dread numbing her mind once more. "But you have to tell someone. What they did was criminal, no matter how they try to justify it. You can't use drugs like that on a human being without their consent. It's still in the experimental stages. I'm quite sure it's not approved—"

Granger got abruptly to his feet. "I'd prefer not to deal with the authorities." Apparently sensing her dismay, he added softly, "I appreciate your concern, Corie, but I have to deal with this myself. In any case, I have some good news. Now that I am no longer under the influence of the drug, my memory is returning. I think that within a few days, I shall be able to remember everything."

"That's wonderful," Corie said hesitantly. "But I still think you should prosecute them, or at the very least find out why they did this to you. There doesn't seem to be any doubt that the scientists are involved, and obviously it goes all the way back to the head office in Philadelphia. Of course, if you remember whatever it is they don't want you to remember, then I guess you'll know why they drugged you."

"No doubt I shall. Then I shall have to make a decision." He closed his eyes briefly in a gesture of despair, and her heart ached for him. "Until then," he added, "I hope you will allow me to continue our arrangement. I am rather anxious to see the renovations completed."

In spite of her reservations, her pulse leapt. "You can stay as long as you want," she said rashly. "I'd like to see the house finished, too. Though I'm afraid there's a great deal of work still to do."

"I like to be busy," Granger said, moving toward the door. "It helps me to think more clearly. So if you'll excuse me, I'll finish cleaning up in the bedroom so that I can start with the wallpaper in the morning."

"Sure. I'll give you a call when dinner's ready."

He gave her a long look, and again she had the feeling he wanted to tell her something. Then he gave a slight shake of his head and disappeared.

Her feeling of uneasiness increased as she prepared the lasagna and salad she'd planned for dinner. She hadn't had time to dwell on her discovery that afternoon, her mind kept busy by the reports that she'd promised to deliver before she left.

But now, the more she thought about the situation, the more implausible it seemed. It would appear that Granger Deene had somehow stumbled on a secret that the scientists were desperately anxious to conceal.

Presumably they had lied about finding him wandering along the road. Why hadn't they simply sworn him to secrecy, if it was important enough to go to these lengths? Granger seemed like an honest, upright citizen, surely he would have been happy to comply if his country's security was at stake.

The fact that the scientists had gone so far as to apparently kidnap him and risk his life by giving him unapproved drugs that affected his mind, suggested one of two things.

The secret they were so anxious to keep hidden could be something that would get them all in grave trouble if it was discovered by the proper authorities. On the other hand, if the secret was ethical, the scientists could consider that Granger Deene could be a dangerous threat to mankind if he remembered what he had learned.

Corie's heart skipped. Either way, she was in dead trouble. The very fact that she had given shelter to Granger, no matter how innocently, put her firmly in the middle of this mess. Part of her wanted desperately to believe that the scientists were the guilty party. Yet her mind refused to accept that such trusted, respectable professionals would go to such terrible lengths without a darn good reason.

Then there was Granger's obvious reluctance to go to the police with this bizarre story. Admittedly, they might have trouble believing him, but she had the proof. She had seen the room with her very own eyes, and right now, tucked inside her purse was a copy of the receipt for the drug.

Of course, if Granger was the enemy, so to speak, the last thing he would do would be to contact the police. Which made it look more and more as if she were harboring some kind of criminal. And a very dangerous one at that, if the scientists had risked killing him in order to keep him quiet.

Corie rinsed the lettuce under the tap, her mind going in crazy circles. What she should do was go to Dr. Richards and tell him that Granger had wandered into her house. She could pretend she knew nothing about him having been kept prisoner at the lab.

But then the scientist would wonder why she was telling him about her houseguest. Dr. Richards was not the kind of man she could talk to about personal subjects. In fact, he discouraged any conversation unless it was directed entirely on her work.

No, he would know at once that she knew more than she was saying. And she could hardly tell him she'd been snooping in unauthorized territory. She could lose her job.

And what if Granger was merely an innocent bystander who had stumbled onto a dangerous secret by accident? What if the scientists were engaged in something criminal, weird as it sounded? She would not only be putting Granger's life in danger, but also her own.

Tearing bite-size pieces of leaves from the lettuce, Corie dropped them into the bowl. She could lose a lot more than her job, she thought gloomily, if she didn't do something about this.

She frowned, taking out her frustration on a tomato as she chopped it into pieces and added them to the lettuce. Granger had said he was beginning to get his memory back. She would ask him what he had remembered. If he was willing to tell her, she would be inclined to believe he was innocent. If he refused, then she would really have something to worry about.

"Is there something I can do to help?"

Granger's deep voice seemed to vibrate down the length of her back. She dropped the knife, and it clattered onto the counter, spinning around until the blade pointed straight at her belly.

Hoping it wasn't a bad omen, she picked it up. She had to force her voice to sound casual when she answered him. "Thanks, but I have it all under control. Why don't you sit down and read the paper? Or have you read it already?"

"I've read it."

Out of the corner of her eye, she saw him wander over to the window and look out.

"You must be tired of being cooped up inside the house," she said carefully. "It was such a nice day. Perhaps when it gets darker you might want to go for a stroll along the seafront. It should be safe enough then."

He spun around to look at her, his gaze sharpening. "They are looking for me, then?"

She shrugged, concentrating on scrubbing the mushrooms. "If they wanted to keep you in that room, they must be concerned about your whereabouts now."

"Do you think the police are looking for me?"

The edge to his voice deepened her apprehension. "If they are," she said quietly, "they are not doing a very good job. This is a small town, I imagine I would have heard something by now."

He didn't answer, but turned back to look out of the window. As she sliced the mushrooms, she thought about what she'd just said. If the scientists were involved in something sinister, they wouldn't want the police to know about it. On the other hand, if Granger was in possession of a sinister secret, they wouldn't want that to get out, either.

Frustrated with the back and forth nature of her thoughts, she tossed the salad with more vigor than was necessary. Pieces of vegetables flew across the table, but she hardly noticed. One way or another, she had to learn more about what was going on. Only then could she make a decision as to what to do about it.

Dinner that evening was tense, to say the least. Granger was preoccupied, answering her comments with one word answers. Feeling the need of something to relax her, Corie had opened a bottle of wine.

Granger drank only one glass of it, while she refilled her glass twice. By the end of the meal she was feeling a little more mellow, her mind finally relaxing from the upheaval of the day.

She offered Granger more wine, but he shook his head. "No, thank you. I rarely drink."

"I'm happy to hear that. There have been more families destroyed by drunks than any other reason."

"Including your own?"

Surprised at his intuition, she said sharply, "How did you know that?"

He shrugged. "Your reaction when we first met. You made it very clear you detested a drunk. I merely wondered if you had a personal reason."

She stared down at her plate, remembering how unsympathetic she'd been over Granger's condition at the time. "I'm sorry," she said ruefully. "I must have sounded like a heartless witch."

"No." He leaned back in his chair, his steady gaze on her face. "Just immensely hurt."

She uttered a short laugh. "I grew up with a drunk. My father was rarely sober. On his bad days he would take out his frustrations with a belt buckle across my back. That was after he'd beaten my mother senseless."

The words sounded so empty in the quiet room. So few words to convey the pain and terror she'd accepted as part of her life for so long.

"I'm sorry," Granger said softly. "Some men cannot hold their liquor. It affects their brain. They don't know what they are doing. Often they attack the people they love the most."

She looked up, the bitterness making her voice sharp. "And that makes it all right?"

He moved his hand, as if he wanted to touch her, then withdrew it again. "Of course not. But sometimes it helps to understand."

"All I understand is that I lived in dread of hearing my father sing when he came through the front door. He always sang when he was drunk. That was right before he lost his temper over something trivial and slammed into us."

Something in his eyes changed, became softer as he looked at her. "I do understand," he said quietly. "I wish I could say something to make it better for you."

She shook her head. "It was over a long time ago. I married the first man who asked me, to get away from my father. My mother died shortly after that."

"And you were not happy in your marriage?"

"I thought I was." Carefully she ran a finger around the rim of her glass. "We had problems, of course. Who doesn't? I met Tony in college. He was studying to be a pediatrician, and after we married I worked to put him through medical school."

She stared at the golden liquid in her glass, feeling the familiar pain. "I wanted a baby, but there was never enough money at first. Then, when Tony finally graduated, he wanted time to settle into his career. He kept on making excuses why we shouldn't try for a baby, until finally he told me he didn't want children, period."

"That must have been a terrible shock to you."

She looked up, grateful for his sympathy. "It was. Oh, he gave me all the good reasons why we shouldn't have kids. We had become used to our life-style after waiting so long. Children would alter all that. We would lose our friends, we were too old to change, it wouldn't be fair to the kids to have older parents than their friends' parents."

She lifted her hands in a gesture of resignation. "I finally gave up trying to change his mind. I tried to accept our life for what it was. I told myself I was content with our marriage, we had a lot to be thankful for. We loved each other, we had a nice house, money to go places, do things . . . the affluent life Tony had always wanted."

"But it wasn't enough for you."

"No," she said in a low whisper, "it wasn't enough." She paused, remembering the ache of loneliness. Shaking off the regret that would always haunt her, she added, "And then Tony died. A heart attack. It happened suddenly. Neither of us knew he had a heart problem. All that rich living was too much for him, I guess."

"I'm sorry," Granger said again.

Corie straightened her back. "I had to go through his papers after his death. That was when I discovered that for the last three years of his life he'd been having an affair. I knew the woman. She was his secretary, and I never even suspected. I had trusted him implicitly, and loved him too much to see what was going on right under my nose."

For a long moment there was complete silence between them. Then Granger said softly, "You must have loved him very much."

Corie shrugged, unable to answer for a moment.

"He was a very stupid man," Granger said. "Had I been blessed with such a love, I would never have let you go."

She managed a tremulous smile. "That's sweet. Thank you." She didn't know how he had managed to get past her defenses. She hadn't spoken to anyone about Tony's affair, though she had soon become aware of how many people already knew what she had been too blind to see.

Seeing the quiet sympathy in Granger's eyes, she was glad she had told him. For now she could look back rationally, and without the pain that had once cost her many a night's sleep.

Deciding it was time to change the subject, she remembered her intention to question him. This seemed like a very good time.

"You said your memory was returning," she began, watching his gaze grow wary. "What have you remembered so far?"

He shrugged. "Not a lot. Mostly brief flashes of scenes."

"You don't remember anything about your past life? Your family, for instance? I would think they would be the first people you would think about."

Granger reached for his fork and started twirling it around in his strong fingers. "I don't think I have any family. At least I don't remember. I must have had parents at some time, of course. I seem to remember they died, though I don't know how.''

"Who brought you up, then?"

"I grew up in a home of some kind. A military school, I think."

She looked at him in surprise. "You were in the military?"

"Yes," Granger said slowly. "The army."

Corie's heart speeded up again. "Do you know what happened to you? The accident?"

He shook his head, his fingers twirling the stem of the wineglass. "I'm afraid that's still a blank."

She couldn't make up her mind whether the fact that Granger was in the military incriminated him more, or whether his line of work could be a motive for his capture by the scientists.

"There must be someone out there anxious about your whereabouts. What about a wife, and children?" Damn the wine, she thought. She hadn't intended to ask that.

"As I said before, no wife or children. I'm certain of that."

So he didn't have a wife, after all. She couldn't help wondering why he wasn't married. He was a very attractive man. That inner strength she could sense beneath all the confusion in his mind was very appealing.

She had the feeling that he could take charge of any situation and see it through. The kind of man who wouldn't let anyone get the better of him. A man who would stand up for what he believed in, and refuse to be intimidated by convention or popular belief. A man who would not give his heart lightly, but once he did, would honor the commitment to his dying day.

As much as he desperately needed information, he was concerned that she not take risks for him. And she couldn't forget his statement that had he loved a woman, he would know it.

Damn it, she couldn't believe that he was anything but an honest, respectable, innocent man who'd had the bad luck to stumble into something evil through no fault of his own.

But if that was so, that meant she was working for some kind of criminals. It was up to her to discover exactly what was going on at the lab. Even if she had to take risks to find out.

Chapter 6

"I want to help you," Corie said, making up her mind. She rose from the table, her plate in her hand. "I believe you're the victim of something corrupt."

Granger got slowly to his feet, and the sudden heat in his eyes took her breath away. "I don't want you to get into trouble on my behalf. You have taken enough risks already. From now on I'll handle this myself."

She could feel her heart speeding up as she met his determined gaze. "I work at that place. I have a right to know what I'm involved in."

"Not if it means trouble for you. I won't allow you to do that."

"You can't stop me."

Through the long pause that followed, Corie could hear someone's radio playing across the street. She was only half conscious of the sound. All she could think about was the intense longing she saw in Granger's warm gray eyes.

"Corie," he said huskily, breaking the tense silence. "I appreciate your trust, and your willingness to risk your own well-being in order to help me. But I beg you, leave this alone. You don't know what you are dealing with."

Her lips felt dry, and she ran the tip of her tongue over them. "And you do?"

"I think so. Don't ask me to tell you, I can't right now. I'm having a tough time believing it myself. And it's better that you don't know."

He leaned forward, resting his hands on the table. "Trust me a little further, if you can. I swear that I will tell you just as soon as I have it all straight in my mind."

She nodded, her heart pounding so hard she could hardly breathe. "Are we in danger?"

"Not at the moment. At least, you are not all the time you don't know the truth."

Once more she could feel herself being drawn under the spell of his intense gaze. She put the plate down, and steadied herself with her hands on the table as she leaned closer to him.

"I want to know the truth," she whispered. "I want to help you."

Very slowly, he lifted his hand and drew his fingers down her cheek. His touch gently grazed her skin—the touch of a man who knew what it was to work with his hands. She shivered inside, a pulse hammering in her throat as she thought about those fingers caressing her body.

Cupping her chin in his hand, Granger said softly, "You are a gracious and lovely lady. How I wish that things were different."

His words shimmered in her mind like precious gems. Somewhere in the midst of that bemused haze the warning voice made itself heard. She tensed, drawing away from him.

For a moment his grasp on her chin tightened, then he said quietly, "Perhaps it is just as well, Corie. I could not be satisfied with one kiss. Once I tasted your lips I would want more, and that wouldn't be fair to you."

Shocked by her reaction to that statement, she jerked away from him. His face was full of regret as he dropped his hand. "I'm going to take your suggestion and go for a walk," he said, moving away from her. "I need time to think."

Her confusion was momentarily forgotten in her alarm. "Granger, please be careful. If they are looking for you—"

"I'll be careful." He paused at the door and looked back at her, the sorrow on his face tugging at her heart. "Thank you for the wonderful meal."

"You're welcome." She summoned a smile from somewhere. "Don't be too long, or I'll worry."

Once more his hot gaze seared her skin. "I'll be back soon, I promise."

"Wait." She hurried into the living room and found a piece of paper. After scribbling her telephone number down she handed it to him. "Just in case something happens," she said unsteadily. "If you get lost or something. Just dial zero for the operator and when a voice answers, ask for that number. Tell them you want to call collect. And here's the key to the front door, just in case I'm in bed when you get back."

He stared down at the scrap of paper in his hand. "They have telephones on the street?"

She nodded, her throat tight. "You'll see them. If not, ask someone."

She hated to let him go out there where anything could happen to him. But she understood his need to be out in the fresh air, alone with his thoughts. She needed time to think herself. "Just be careful," she repeated.

He gave her a slight nod, then turned and made his way down the path to the gate.

She closed the door, leaving it open just a crack to watch him until he had turned the corner. Then she made herself go back to take care of the dishes. There was nothing more she could do for him right now.

But tomorrow, she vowed, no matter what Granger said, she was determined to find out just why a bunch of so-called respected scientists had done such a terrible thing as to mess with an innocent man's mind.

And when she did find out the truth, she was going to see that the people involved paid for it, no matter who they were. Even if it did go all the way up to the head office in Philadelphia. Whatever the consequences might be.

Granger stood at the edge of the water on the darkened beach, watching the silver-tipped waves curl and crash into a foaming cloud of spray before spreading gently out to reach his feet.

He wanted Corie Trenton. He wanted her so badly his body caught fire every time he looked at her. How he longed to take her in his arms and know the fascinating pleasures of her naked form.

He must have known women before. He could not have reached this age without satisfying himself with a warm, willing body. Yet he could not remember the cool, smooth touch of flesh against flesh, or the heat of sinking himself into the very core of passion.

He wanted to know. He wanted to taste the thrill of what he instinctively knew had to be the most intoxicating sensation known to man, the mating of two willing and passionate human beings.

Lifting his burning face to the star-sprinkled sky, he uttered a soft groan. He certainly knew what it was to feel the hunger of that need. And he knew, without a shadow of a doubt, that he wanted to relive that experience with only one woman. Corie.

She had risked so much for him that day, without really knowing why she was doing so. He had thought of women as soft creatures, helpless and in need of protection. Corie had a fierce independence that he greatly admired, a strength and determination equalled by any man.

Yet he knew that deep inside her she was hiding pain, a deep hurt that had not been resolved. He could see it in her eyes when she looked at him, wanting what he needed so badly to give her, yet afraid to trust, afraid to reveal her thoughts and follow her feelings.

He wanted to erase that pain. He wanted to see her eyes fill with passion to match his own. Yet he could not. He could not offer her anything more than the moment, and he knew that for a woman like Corie, it would not be enough. He had no wish to add to her pain.

A rush of water swept over his feet, snapping him out of his tormenting thoughts. Turning his back on the restless ocean, he trudged across the sand toward the lights of the town. There was still so much he couldn't remember. So many gaps he couldn't fill in, so much he had to relearn about himself.

He wasn't at all sure he wanted to know all of it. There didn't seem much he could do about it, anyway. It looked very much as if he were destined to run for the rest of his life, always looking over his shoulder. And he could not subject Corie to that kind of danger much longer.

Reaching the boardwalk, Granger turned in the direction of Corie's house. The street lamps cast shadows ahead of him, spilling dark shapes that lengthened as he left the glow behind him. The breeze played across his back, cooling his heated skin beneath the knit shirt.

He had made a bargain with her and he would keep it. Once the work had been done, he would leave. And if, for any reason, he felt that his presence created an immediate danger, he would leave before the work was finished.

Her safety was the most important consideration. He could not involve her further in his problem, and she would surely become involved if it was discovered that she had given him shelter. He had no idea where he would go or how he would survive. But he would not stay and endanger her life, too.

Turning the corner, he glanced up at the window he knew to be her bedroom. A light glowed behind the drawn curtains, telling him she was still awake. His heart ached at the thought of leaving her. How he longed to go to her now, slip into her warm bed, and blot out all his troubles with the touch of her body beneath his.

He reached the gate and stood for a last, long moment, until the cool, salty breeze chilled his skin. Only then, did he let himself into the house and climb the stairs to his bedroom.

Corie heard him pass her landing, her body tense, her mind hovering somewhere between relief at his safe return and a tingling expectation that she knew was foolish.

She didn't want him to make any moves. Sure, she fantasized about him, but that's all it was, fantasy. It had been a long time, after all. She knew, only too well, the futility of falling for a man. Especially one as unconventional as Granger Deene.

Not only did she not know much about him, he didn't know much about himself. What kind of security was that? The only thing she did know was that he was mixed up in something very strange and possibly dangerous.

So no matter how much her hormones told her that he was an appealing, provocative male with the most seductive eyes she'd ever seen, she would simply have to ignore her feelings. Period.

Turning on her side, she buried her face in her pillow to smother her groan. It wasn't easy, knowing that he lay in bed directly above her, knowing how he looked with the sheet tangled around his naked hips.

"Grow up, Corie," she whispered into the pillow. A man like that was not for her. She was better off on her own.

She lay awake a long time, chasing her thoughts away every time they dwelled on the man upstairs. When she finally dozed off her mind refused to rest. She dreamed of a man without a face, pursuing her relentlessly through swirling fog and treacherous swamps.

She awoke with a start, aware of a strange noise somewhere outside her room. Granger was once more shouting in his sleep. He sounded urgent, desperate, his voice harsh and commanding.

This might be a chance to learn more about his past, she thought, slipping out of bed. The street lamp cast enough light to find her robe and she quickly wrapped it around her, then crept from the room.

Once more she climbed the stairs, jumping with every creak. Granger had stopped shouting now, but she could still hear his muttering from inside the room.

Shivering on the landing, Corie leaned closer to the door, straining to hear the muffled voice. Only a word or two here and there was audible, and she couldn't tell what he was talking about.

Giving up, she was about to turn away when his voice rose. She could feel her scalp tingling as she heard the words quite clearly now.

"The rebels have us surrounded! We can't let them take the hill!"

Briefly she closed her eyes. It had to be Vietnam. She'd heard so many stories about the mental anguish of men who survived that terrible war. Apparently his most painful memories were the first ones to surface.

She made her way down the stairs again, her heart aching for the tormented man. How sad that out of all his life, the things he remembered most clearly were the dreadful experiences he must have gone through more than twenty years ago.

More determined than ever to help him now, she looked forward to the next day, when she could do something more concrete than lying in bed worrying about him.

Granger was still in bed when she left for work the next morning, apparently exhausted from his nightmares of the night before.

Corie spent the morning catching up on all her reports, so that she could have the afternoon free without fear of interruption. The date on the receipt for the prescription drug had been a week earlier, and she wanted to monitor all the events that had happened that day.

After feverishly working at the computer all morning, she finally had the last report finished and sent to the labs. After a quick lunch, which she brought back to her desk, she sat down in front of the computer again and brought up the files she'd worked on the week earlier.

Her scan of the labels didn't seem to suggest anything unusual. Two reports on climatic activity in the Western Hemisphere, a series of calculations on the lineup of the planets, and a report on the whereabouts of Specturne.

Corie frowned, staring at the screen. She checked the date next to the label again. There was no mistake. Her original file on Specturne had been opened a week ago. Yet she had not worked on the star project for months, until the day before, when she'd opened a new file. Someone had pulled up the data on her screen and altered it for some reason.

Reaching for the top drawer of her desk, Corie pulled it open. Regulations required her to keep a backup copy of her work. The floppy disks were kept in the main bank vault, along with other important records from the labs.

But according to Corie's philosophy, she could never be too careful. She always made her own personal copy of her work, and kept it on a floppy disk in the back of her drawer.

Sliding the disk into the computer, she brought up the files. After printing a hard copy off the original Specturne file, she ran the opened file again from the hard disk. It took a matter of moments to discover that the calculations had been altered.

Staring at the two sets of figures, Corie's mind worked furiously. Who would go to all the trouble of altering her files? Obviously someone who didn't want her in possession of the correct calculations for some reason.

But why didn't they just erase the information if it was classed as top secret? Probably because they didn't want her to know there was any special significance to the project.

Dr. Richards had asked for the report yesterday. The calculations were to assess the star's current behavior, and any future predictions as close as were possible.

It didn't seem feasible that he would be the one to deliberately alter her file. Yet, if she was to believe Granger, a lot of bizarre things had been happening at the lab lately.

Confused, she struggled to make sense of it all. She couldn't imagine what on earth Granger Deene could possibly have in common with a remote star that no one as yet was sure was going to be around for long. Specturne's behavior was unpredictable, and it was the general consensus that it would simply disappear into another galaxy eventually.

It had to be coincidence, that was all. Nevertheless, she decided, as her pulse quickened, it wouldn't hurt to check it out.

Nerves tingling, she ran the calculations through the program. Every now and again the star was positioned in a direct line between Jupiter and Earth. It had been determined that when this happened, for reasons as yet unexplained, a beam of light penetrated the atmosphere, hitting the earth for the space of five seconds.

Approximately a month later, the star would again be in line with the planet, producing the same phenomenon. Roughly six months after that, the process was repeated. This had happened twice so far. At intervals of six months, the star beamed its light to Earth twice within the month.

Corie remembered the excitement the first time the scientists had discovered the evidence of the beam. She had been the one assigned to determine the point of impact—a remote, uninhabited island in the Pacific. Everyone had been amazed that the beam had hit land at all, with all that water around.

The scientists' findings were still under wraps, classified information. After that, Corie had heard no more about it. Not much had been said about the star's second appearance, and she assumed that since there appeared to be no spectacular results, the Powers That Be had simply lost interest.

Until, apparently, a week ago.

Staring at the screen, Corie's pulse quickened. *The star's current behavior.* According to her own report, there had been a lineup with Jupiter a week ago.

Using the altered statistics on her hard disk, Corie ran the calculations through the program. The predicted location of the beam's target showed an area of dense jungle in Thailand.

Her heart began to thump as she changed the directory to the floppy disk with the original information. The floppy drive hummed and buzzed, then offered up the information.

On June 12, Specturne's beam had collided with Earth at a point somewhere in the United States.

Her fingers were unsteady on the keys as she typed out another command. The answer seemed to jump out at her. *Pennsylvania.*

She had heard the rumors, of course, but she hadn't believed them. The concept had been too wild even to consider for one moment. Yet somehow, she knew, even as she typed in the command what she would see.

Granger's voice echoed in her mind, harsh and commanding, shouting something in that odd, sometimes stilted, old-fashioned way he had of speaking. *The rebels have us surrounded.*

The words appeared on the screen in front of her, looking so mundane, she almost laughed. Specturne's beam of light had hit an open field. Near a place called Cemetery Hill... on the battlefield of Gettysburg.

Granger awoke with a start, knowing instinctively that he was alone in the house. His glance at the clock told him he had slept late. Corie would be at work by now.

He showered quickly, stopping only to swallow down a bowl of cereal before starting work on the house. The dreams of the night before still tormented him. He remembered almost all of it now.

Only the last piece was missing, the events that led up to him waking up in a science laboratory in a small town on the New Jersey coast.

And that was only a small part of it. How the rest could have happened, he couldn't even begin to imagine. Maybe when he could remember all of it, he would understand more about what had happened to him.

Right now, he wanted to get as much work done on the house as possible. Sooner or later they would track him down, and he did not want to be in Corie's house if and when that happened. He had to protect her at all costs.

He worked quickly, sweating with the exertion as he smoothed the pale blue striped paper onto the walls. With grim determination he kept his visions uppermost in his mind, hoping to find the missing pieces.

He wasn't having much success, but at least it helped to keep his mind from dwelling on Corie, and the pain he knew he would suffer when he had to leave her.

When the telephone rang downstairs he had no idea it was so late. He had been so absorbed in his thoughts he had completely forgotten about lunch. Pounding down the stairs, he heard the pause after the second ring, and just reached the living room as the telephone began ringing again.

Snatching up the receiver, he took a steadying breath. This time he remembered to keep his tone soft as he said cautiously, "Corie?"

Her voice sounded strange when she spoke in his ear. "I just wanted to know how things are there."

"Things are very well. I have finished two of the walls and have started on the third. The wallpaper looks very nice, it should be a pretty room when it's finished."

"Thanks." She hesitated and he frowned, alerted by the tense pause.

"Is something wrong?" he asked sharply. "You're not in any trouble are you?"

"No, no, I'm fine. It's just... I was just wondering if you'd remembered anything else. You were talking a lot in your sleep last night and I thought—"

"You heard me?" He hadn't meant to sound so sharp. Cursing himself for his impatience, he added quietly, "I'm sorry if I disturbed you."

"I... You didn't. I wasn't sleeping very well myself. I couldn't hear what you said, of course."

He wondered if she heard the relief in his voice when he said, "I'm sorry, Corie. I'll let you know if and when I remember anything of any significance. Meanwhile, please don't worry yourself on my behalf."

"All right." She paused, and he had the odd feeling she desperately needed to tell him something. Then she added, "I'll be home by 5:30, unless I'm loaded down with new reports. I'll see you then."

She hung up before he could reply. He stared at the receiver a long time before replacing it. Something was wrong, he could sense it.

His pulse jumped as he pictured someone standing next to her, forcing her to talk to him in order to make sure he would be there when they arrived to pick him up.

He shook his head, chiding himself for his runaway imagination. Of course Corie was nervous. She had a strange man in the house who yelled and shouted in his sleep all night long. It was a wonder she hadn't thrown him out before now.

Feeling the pangs of hunger, he wandered into the kitchen to find something to eat. He couldn't let his mind play tricks on him. He had enough problems as it was.

He still couldn't believe it was possible. But this was almost the 21st century. Anything was possible. The world had come a long way in the last hundred years or so.

He would just have to accept what had happened and deal with it as best he could. He would not tell Corie the truth. She would think he was crazy. And just maybe he was.

Corie sat at her desk, her chin propped in her hands. Rumors, that was all they had been. Wild stories made up by the jokesters who would do anything for a laugh.

After all, time travel was something you read about in fantasy novels, or watched on a screen in a darkened movie theater. Things like that just didn't happen in real life.

And yet, somehow it all fell into place. She had first heard the rumors while working in the main lab in Philadelphia.

Whispers heard at the water fountain or in the ladies' room, about the top secret project the scientists were working on—research into traveling through time.

After all, the believers had earnestly argued, scientists had conquered the barriers of sound, space and light, why not time?

She had been one of the skeptics, of course. Good old down-to-earth Corie Trenton, deeply entrenched in scientific fact and scornful of illogical fallacies that had nothing to do with the real world.

She had been working on the Specturne project at the time and was too fascinated with the marvels of new discoveries in a world yet unexplored to pay much attention to the ridiculous speculation.

Corie reached for a pencil, and began aimlessly doodling on the yellow pad in front of her. Now that she came to think about it, shortly after her report on Specturne was finished was when she'd been offered the surprisingly lucrative post at the Cape May branch. To get her away from the main office?

Her pencil dug into the paper as she added a chimney to the uneven house she'd drawn. She couldn't accept that. The position had been posted on the bulletin board. She'd seen it and applied. There had been no other applicants, she'd been told, since no one wanted to move to a remote coastal town to live.

It had seemed like the perfect answer to her, after everything that had happened. Peace and quiet, and the chance to start a new life. Then again, her bosses knew about her personal problems. They could have predicted she would jump at the chance to leave town and start again somewhere new.

Well, if what she suspected was a fact, she could say goodbye to peace and quiet. Granger Deene would be as hot as a chili pepper, and she would be as much involved as he was.

She felt a chill when she thought about the lengths the scientists had gone to in order to make him forget what had happened to him. What were their intentions, for heaven's sake? Did they think they could keep him drugged for the rest of his life so he wouldn't know where he came from?

The sinister thought intruded, despite her best efforts to prevent it. Just maybe, they were simply keeping him quiet until such time as it was possible to get rid of him without any questions being asked.

In the meantime they would be able to study his reactions, he would be invaluable to the project. And what then? Destroy him when he was no longer any use to them?

There was no one she could go to for help, Corie thought desperately. Who would believe her strange story? Any proof she might have would be destroyed long before the proper authorities could step in. Whoever the proper authorities might be.

This could be a national secret, not just a scientific one. If so, both she and Granger Deene were in deep trouble. The worst part of all this was not knowing for sure if Granger knew what had happened.

What was it he'd said? *Don't ask me to tell you, I can't right now. I'm having a tough time believing it myself. And it's better that you don't know.*

If he had been zapped from the past, how could he possibly comprehend what had happened to him? But then Granger was an intelligent man. It was possible that he already knew, and was keeping it from her. In which case, it was time they both put their cards on the table.

The only way she was going to help him, if, God willing, she was able to help him, was if they both were completely honest with each other. It was time she found out exactly how much Granger did remember.

* * *

Corie broiled a steak for Granger that evening, her mind jumping with the possibilities of how to deal with the subject. She had already decided that she would tell him everything she knew, in the hopes that he would do the same for her.

He sat quietly in the kitchen while she cooked, while she chatted about anything that came into her head. Realizing now that he would not comprehend much about what went on outside the walls of the house, she was careful to mention only things he would understand. It wasn't easy.

She had always maintained that problems were better solved on a full stomach, and so she struggled through the meal, determined to make light conversation until her head ached with the tension.

Finally, Granger put down his fork. "You are a remarkable cook, Corie. That had to be the best steak I have ever tasted."

She managed a smile as she thanked him. Now that the time to talk had arrived, she wasn't sure where to start. "It's more likely that you've forgotten the food you've eaten in the past," she said lightly. "But I appreciate the sentiment."

He studied her face for a long moment. "What happened, Corie?" he said at last.

She shifted uncomfortably in her chair. "What happened when?"

"Today, at the laboratory. I can tell something is wrong. If it concerns me I want to know what it is."

Unable to escape his intense gaze, she said hesitantly, "I did some checking on the computer this afternoon. I was looking to see if anything unusual had happened about the time you would have arrived at the lab."

He was very still now, watching her closely. "And?"

"And," she said carefully, "I found some information on a new star that has recently been discovered. Its name is Specturne."

"A new star," he repeated, his expression suggesting he didn't have a clue as to what she was talking about.

Giving up the attempt to go slowly, Corie leaned forward and said urgently, "Granger, you must tell me what you have remembered. It's vital."

She could see a pulse beating in his jaw as he looked at her. "You know," he said simply.

She nodded, her heart hammering against her ribs. "I don't know how, yet. I only know it happened."

His shoulders sagged as he slumped back in his chair. "I thought I was crazy."

"I thought I was, too." Corie shook her head, still grappling with the improbability of the whole mess. Trying to actually put it into words made it seem so outlandish. She felt as if she were acting a part in a play, speaking words she couldn't really believe in. Yet the words had to be said.

"I believe you were zapped from Gettysburg, on June 12. The scientists must have been waiting for the beam, they predicted where it would hit. Imagine their surprise when you popped up out of nowhere."

"I imagine it must have been quite a shock," Granger said dryly.

"I'm sorry." Corie tried to suppress her excitement. "I know how tragic and horrifying this must be for you. But the scientific side of me is in awe of this whole crazy thing. Imagine me, talking to the very first time traveler from the past. It just boggles my mind."

"Forgive me if I don't share in your enthusiasm," Granger said, giving her one of his purposeful looks. "The question now is, how do I get back?"

Corie looked at him unhappily. "I don't know the answer to that, Granger. I wish I did."

"But you can find out?"

She stared at him, realizing how much she would miss him. Up until that moment, the concept of sending him back hadn't occurred to her. Of course he had to go back. He belonged in another time, another world. "If it's possible," she said, already feeling the ache of loss beginning to spread, "I'll find the answer somehow."

She could see the apprehension in his eyes when he slowly nodded. "Thank you."

She wanted to reach out and touch his face. Her arms ached to hold him, to comfort him, to reassure him. Her rush of tenderness was so overwhelming, she felt a tear forming, and blinked it back.

Damn, she thought, doing her best to compose her face. When had that happened? It was just as well he didn't belong here in her world. She didn't need these kind of complications. Not now. Now that she'd come to terms with her life and what she wanted from it.

Aware that Granger had said something she hadn't heard, she pulled her thoughts together. "I'm sorry," she said quickly, "I was thinking about how I can tackle this problem."

"I asked if this computer of yours can find a way to send me back."

She had to stop thinking about herself now, and concentrate on his needs. "I don't know," she said honestly. "I can only tell you I'll try everything I know. The problem is, I'm no scientist. I just do the research. I'm limited to what I can do, unless there is a way I can get into Dr. Richards's classified files. The more I think about it the more I'm convinced he's involved in all this."

"I don't want you taking any risks," Granger said sharply. "I won't be responsible for placing you in danger."

"I may have to take risks if we are to find a way to send you back." Corie got to her feet and began stacking the plates. "The important thing is not to let them know where you are. Even if they find out I know what's going on, they won't necessarily know that you are in my house."

"And what happens to you if you succeed in sending me back? Afterward, I mean."

She shrugged, and carried the plates to the sink. "Once we have achieved that, once you are safely back where you belong, there won't be much point in them doing anything to me."

"But you will know what happened." Granger said, standing up. "You could tell the world."

"And who's going to believe me? Think about it."

He didn't answer, but looked at her in a helpless kind of way that started the ache again. In an effort to ignore the pain, she dumped the plates into the sink, then pulled down the door of the dishwasher.

"How much have you remembered?" she asked, as she began stacking the plates in the racks. "Perhaps if we know what happened when you were zapped, it will help us figure out a way to get you back."

"I remember pretty much everything, up to a point." His expression changed and he stood quite still, as if struck by a thought.

Corie stared at him, her heart beginning to thud again. "What is it?"

"Is it possible that in this . . . transition . . . the days could have been altered?"

"I'm not sure what you mean."

Granger stared at her thoughtfully. "You said that I arrived in this place on June 12."

"Yes." Briefly, Corie explained about Specturne, knowing much of it would go over his head.

"But that's impossible," Granger said slowly, after she had finished speaking. "I remember very clearly being in Gettysburg on June 30. It's one of the last things I do remember."

Chapter 7

Corie stared at Granger in confusion. "Granger, look at the date on the newspaper. Today is only the twenty-first of June."

"Yes, I've seen it. But I know I was there on June 30." His gaze rested intently on her face. "We are...were... engaged in civil war at the time. In 1863. There is...was a division between north and south."

"Yes," Corie said, beginning to feel light-headed. "I know. The Civil War was a very important event in American history."

He seemed surprised about that. "You have studied it?"

"Everyone has. It's a requirement in the classroom."

He nodded, obviously pleased at the thought.

Corie felt her grasp on reality slipping away. This whole situation seemed more like a very long, very realistic dream. It was hard to believe she was standing there having a conversation with a soldier who had actually fought in the Battle of Gettysburg.

PLAY
ONE MILLION
BIG BUCK$
ONE MILLION
AND YOU COULD WIN THE
$1,000,000.00
PLUS JACKPOT!
YOUR PERSONAL GAME CARD INSIDE . . .
SILHOUETTE

IT'S FUN! BIG BUCKS IT'S FREE!

HOW TO PLAY

It's so easy...grab a lucky coin, and go right to your BIG BUCKS game card. Scratch off silver squares in a STRAIGHT LINE (across, down, or diagonal) until 5 dollar signs are revealed. BINGO!...Doing this makes you eligible for a chance to win $1,000,000.00 in lifetime income ($33,333.33 each year for 30 years). Also scratch all 4 corners to reveal the dollar signs. This entitles you to a chance to win the $50,000.00 Extra Bonus Prize! Void if more than 9 squares scratched off.

Your EXCLUSIVE PRIZE NUMBER is in the upper right corner of your game card. Return your game card and we'll activate your unique Sweepstakes Number, so it's important that your name and address is completed correctly. This will permit us to identify you and match you with any cash prize rightfully yours! (SEE BACK OF BOOK FOR DETAILS.)

FREE BOOKS PLUS FREE GIFTS!

At the same time you play your BIG BUCKS game card for BIG CASH PRIZES...scratch the Lucky Charm to receive FOUR FREE Silhouette Intimate Moments® novels, and a FREE GIFT, TOO! They're totally free, absolutely free with no obligation to buy anything!

These books have a cover price of $4.25 each. But THEY ARE TOTALLY FREE; even the shipping will be at our expense! The Silhouette Reader Service™ is not like some book clubs. You don't have to make any minimum number of purchases–not even one! The fact is, thousands of readers look forward to receiving six of the best new romance novels each month and they love our discount prices!

Of course you may play BIG BUCKS for cash prizes alone by not scratching off your Lucky Charm, but why not get everything that we are offering and that you are entitled to! You'll be glad you did.

Offer limited to one per household and not valid to current Silhouette Intimate Moments® subscribers. All orders subject to approval.

EXCLUSIVE PRIZE # 3K 237463

BIG BUCKS

$

TWO WAYS TO WIN BIG BUCKS!

1. Uncover 5 $ signs in a row ...BINGO! You're eligible for a chance to win the $1,000,000.00 SWEEPSTAKES!

2. Uncover 5 $ signs in a row AND uncover $ signs in all 4 corners ... BINGO! You're also eligible for a chance to win the $50,000.00 EXTRA BONUS PRIZE!

HURRY!
This jackpot must be claimed!

Scratch here →

LUCKY CHARM GAME!

Claim 4 FREE books AND A FREE Mystery Gift!

YES! I have played my BIG BUCKS game card as instructed. Enter my Big Bucks Prize number in the MILLION DOLLAR Sweepstakes III and also enter me for the Extra Bonus Prize. When winners are selected, tell me if I've won. If the Lucky Charm is scratched off, I will also receive everything revealed, as explained on the back of this page.

345 CIS AH4C
(C-SIL-IM-07/95)

NAME _____

ADDRESS _____ APT. _____

CITY _____ PROV. _____ POSTAL CODE _____

THE SILHOUETTE READER SERVICE™: HERE'S HOW IT WORKS

Accepting free books places you under no obligation to buy anything. You may keep the books and gift and return the shipping statement marked "cancel". If you do not cancel, about a month later we will send you 6 additional novels and bill you just $3.21 each plus 25¢ delivery and GST*. That's the complete price, and – compared to cover prices of $4.25 each – quite a bargain! You may cancel at any time, but if you choose to continue, every month we'll send you 6 more books, which you may either purchase at the discount price...or return at our expense and cancel your subscription.

*Terms and prices subject to change without notice. Canadian residents add applicable provincial taxes and GST.

0195619199-L2A5X3-BR01

"BIG BUCKS"
MILLION DOLLAR SWEEPSTAKES III
P.O. BOX 609
FORT ERIE, ONTARIO
L2A 9Z9

MAIL▷POSTE
Canada Post Corporation / Société canadienne des postes
Postage paid | Port payé
if mailed in Canada | si posté au Canada
Business | Réponse
Reply | d'affaires
0195619199   01

If he had fought in the battle. Her heart skipped a beat. "You said you were there on June 30?" she said slowly. "I don't understand how you could have been, unless there was some kind of time warp when you were hit by the beam. What's the last thing you remember?"

Granger went back to his chair and sat down, propping up his head with his elbows on the table. He sounded very tired when he finally spoke.

"I remember falling asleep in my tent on the night of June 30. Though I can't help feeling that there is something else. I'm almost certain I awoke the next morning, still in my tent, but when I try to remember what happened then everything becomes hazy...confusing."

The strain on his face was so distinct, so painful to see that Corie said quickly, "Don't worry abut it now, Granger. Give it time and it will come back to you. I've learned that much. Just tell me what you do remember."

He nodded, and after a pause, began speaking again. "I am a cavalry officer in the Union army, under the command of General Buford. Things haven't been going very well for the North. We had made camp on McPherson's Ridge, just outside of Gettysburg.

"We knew the rebels were somewhere in the area and advancing. We were facing the possibility of having to defend the ridge. Buford had sent word to General Reynolds, requesting further orders."

Lifting his head, he looked at her across the room. "Most of us weren't too concerned, though. Buford didn't think it would be more than a skirmish and we'd seen plenty of those. I doubt if many people have heard of Gettysburg, much less know where it is. It's a very small town."

She knew he'd seen her swift change of expression. He frowned at her, saying sharply, "What is it?"

"Granger," Corie said, "the Battle of Gettysburg is one of the most famous battles to come out of the Civil War. It changed the entire course of the war."

His eyes widened as he looked at her. "You've heard of it then? You know about it?"

Corie smiled. "Everybody's heard of it. The battlefield is a national shrine."

Granger rose to his feet, moving slowly, as if walking in his sleep.

Corie tensed as he approached her, his gaze fixed firmly on her face. He paused in front of her, his hands reaching for her shoulders. She could hear the tension in his voice when he said harshly, "I don't know why it hasn't occurred to me until now that you know the answer to this question. Tell me, Corie. Which side won that battle?"

"The Federals. It was their first significant victory."

He looked almost afraid to ask the next question. "And the final victory of the war between North and South?" She smiled up at his anxious face. "We still have a United States of America, Granger," she said softly. "The Union army won the Civil War."

A fierce blaze of delight lit up his face. Lifting his chin, he let out a shout of triumph, then before she could stop him, he planted a firm, joyous kiss full on her lips.

It was over before she could really appreciate the impact of his embrace. One second his lips had been warm and hard on hers, the next he had let her go. Moving away from her, he said quietly, "I'm sorry, I shouldn't have done that."

"It's okay, forget it. Under the circumstances I'm surprised you didn't go around breaking all the dishes or something."

She grinned at him, determined not to let him know how much his kiss had affected her. He didn't have to be so darn apologetic, did he? "Look, this has been a big shock to both of us. We can't do much more about the situation now, so let's just try to put it out of our minds. Maybe if we sleep on it we'll both be able to think more clearly tomorrow.''

She turned back to the sink, and began rinsing the forks. If she stood looking at him much longer, she thought ruefully, he'd know exactly how much she ached to be in his arms.

"Since we got through with dinner early," she said, after an awkward pause, "I think I'll start the papering in the second floor bedroom. If you want to watch television, please go ahead."

"Corie—" He broke off, muttered a low curse, then added, "I have only a few spots to finish in the room I'm working on. I'll attempt to get that done tonight so I can start fresh with the next room tomorrow."

"Thanks, that would be great." She flashed him a quick smile then snatched the grill out of the oven and shoved it under the faucet. The rush of hot water almost drowned out the sound of the door closing behind him as he left the room.

For some crazy reason she felt like crying. She couldn't afford the luxury of letting her feelings show. She was not about to make a fool of herself. Once she worked out how to send him back, he would be gone from her forever.

Even if he was forced to remain in the present, she knew very well he wouldn't be able to stay with her. It would be too dangerous for both of them.

Besides, she told herself as she scrubbed furiously at the grill, what had happened to her resolution not to get involved again with a man? That was considering he was the least bit interested in her.

Judging by his quick apology earlier, he seemed very anxious not to give the wrong impression. He'd kissed her because he was excited at finding out that his side had won a long and terrible war. Nothing more.

Corie carefully rinsed the grill under the faucet. Thinking about that brought up all kinds of questions. What if she sent him back? Would he remember what she had told him? How ethical was it, she wondered, to tell a man who was involved in a struggle of that magnitude the outcome of events?

Staring at her reflection in the base of the grill, she pulled a face. It looked as if there would be more than one problem to deal with before all this was over and she could go back to her normal life. If anything would ever feel normal again after knowing Granger Deene.

A few minutes later she stood looking around the large bedroom, facing the task of papering the ceiling. So far she had only painted ceilings, this would be the first time she had attempted to paper one. But the room was so big, she was convinced it would look cozier with a papered ceiling.

She'd chosen a paper with a faint peach stripe on a cream background, which would blend in with the aqua-and-peach wallpaper. She'd fallen in love with it the minute she'd seen it at the store. The trick now, was to get the paper up there without doing too much damage to it.

Dragging a wide plank of wood to the corner of the room, Corie set it up between two chairs, resting each end on the seats. She'd already filled the trough with water and cut out the first strips of paper. Now all she had to do was wet the rolls down and smooth the whole thing onto the ceiling.

It had sounded so simple when she'd read the instructions. Balanced precariously on the plank, she looked down at the roll of paper floating in the warm water.

It would be impossible to reach it from where she stood. Muttering to herself about her own stupidity, she climbed down again and grabbed the edges of the paper. Water streamed from the strip when she lifted it. Little puddles formed on the floor as she clambered back on the plank holding the sticky, wet length of paper in her hands.

Tilting her head back, she eyed the corner of the ceiling. It looked to be a long way away. She gritted her teeth in concentration, and laid one end of the soggy paper against the edge of the wall. She had to get underneath the paper to smooth it against the ceiling, which meant drawing the length of it over her head and down her back.

Maneuvering into a secure position was difficult, but she managed it. The paper slid sideways and she straightened it, then smoothed it with her fingers against the ceiling until it held. Supporting the weight of the remainder of the strip, she looked for the brush. It lay on the plank at her feet.

She would have to stoop to reach it, which meant letting go of the paper. She cursed herself for not tucking the brush inside the waistband of her jeans before she got started. Now she would have to bend down and hang on to the paper at the same time.

Her efforts were rewarded by the wet paper slapping her on the head. Grabbing up the brush with one hand, she grimly held onto the paper with the other and straightened her back. Once more she went through the procedure, this time with the brush firmly tucked inside her waistband.

She had pulled on a pale lemon cotton sweater when she'd changed out of her office clothes. Now she was beginning to wish she'd picked out something more expendable. The sweater was fairly new, and wouldn't look too attractive with wallpaper paste dabbed all over it.

It was too late now, she decided. She had to get the paper onto the ceiling before it dried out, or she'd have to start all over again.

Once more she tapped the paper firmly onto the ceiling and smoothed it out. So far so good. Moving slowly backward, feeling her way on the plank one careful step at a time, Corie drew the brush down the length of paper.

Her efforts seemed to be working this time, since the paper clung to the ceiling. She had almost reached the end of the strip when she noticed the other end beginning to peel away from the wall. Before she could save it, the entire sticky mess plopped down and wrapped itself lovingly around her head.

With a growl of frustration, Corie peeled the paper from her hair. A slight sound behind her startled her, and she turned her head. Standing in the doorway, a slow smile spreading over his face, was Granger Deene.

"You look as if you could use some help," he said, gazing up at the wet ceiling.

She hadn't heard him come down the hallway. Unprepared for the sight of him, she was totally defenseless against the rush of emotion she felt when she saw him. It was the first time she'd seen him really smile. It did things to his face she wouldn't have imagined.

He'd tucked the blue shirt she'd bought for him into the waistband of his jeans. His face was tilted up at her, and Corie couldn't seem to look away from the tempting triangle of tanned skin below his throat. She could just imagine pressing her lips into the musky warmth of his neck. The thought made her go hot and cold.

"I can manage, thanks," she said, trying to find enough breath to sound normal.

"Why don't you let me do it?" Walking toward her, he held out his hand for the paper. "I seem to have a knack for this job."

Corie shook her head, determined not to give in. She just wished he'd leave her alone to get on with it. Her face felt sticky, and heaven knew what her hair looked like. Plastered down on her head, no doubt. She resisted the urge to lift her hand up to find out. She'd rather not know.

"I'll get the hang of it," she said, doing her best to straighten out the length of limp paper. It seemed to have a life of its own, and fought her efforts to tame it.

Granger folded his arms across his chest in a typical male pose of smug superiority. "Well, if you're quite sure..."

"I'm sure."

Darn the man. He seemed determined to stand there and watch her make a fool of herself. Turning her back on him, Corie once more lifted the edge of the paper and slapped it against the ceiling.

It hung for the space of a second or two, then gracefully peeled away again.

"Perhaps you need to soak it again," Granger said helpfully.

He sounded as if he was struggling to hide his amusement, and Corie fumed. "I think I'll just dump this piece and start again with a fresh strip," she said tartly.

"For heaven's sake stop being so stubborn and let me do it for you. Here." Reaching from behind her, he took hold of the offending strip of paper.

She had no idea why she was being so immature. It had something to do with her making an idiot of herself in front of the one man she wanted to impress, and it had a lot to do with the knowledge that she was falling for the guy when she knew full well that nothing could ever come of it.

Whatever it was, her fragile hold on her composure snapped. Attempting to drag the paper from his hands, she snapped, "I could manage a lot better if you weren't standing behind me giving me orders."

Her sharp tug on the last word tore the paper right across the middle. Glaring at the ruined strip, she puffed out her breath. "Now look what you've done. Well, that settles that, I guess. Now I'll have to start over—"

She never finished the sentence. Granger dropped the torn paper and took hold of her arms. Ignoring her muffled protest he pulled her off the plank to the floor.

"I'm not going to stand here arguing with you," he said firmly, "so just hush up and let me do this. Go and make me some coffee if you want something to do."

"Now just wait a cotton-picking minute." Temper blazing, she shook a finger at him. "This is the twentieth century, and you can't come in here giving me orders as if I'm your slave. Women are equal to men in this day and age, and you'd better get used to the idea or you are going find yourself extremely unpopular."

He stared at her for a full minute, while she stared back at him, struggling to control her ragged breathing.

"Is that so?" he said at last, his voice dangerously quiet.

"Yes," Corie snapped recklessly. "That's the way things are now."

"Times seemed to have changed in more ways than one."

Something in his voice made her check her next retort. His gaze dropped to her mouth, and her heart skipped a beat.

"Though I'm sure there are some things that haven't changed," Granger said softly.

Before she could move he'd taken a step closer. The breath rushed out of her body as he wrapped his arms around her and pulled her against his hard chest. She saw the glint in his gray eyes just before he brought his mouth down on hers, successfully silencing any protest she might have made.

She wasn't about to protest. This was what she'd wanted from the moment she'd sat him down in her living room that first night. No matter how hard she'd try to fight it, some part of her had always known it was inevitable.

He had appeared out of nowhere in her life, and soon he would leave it. She knew that. But the short while that he would spend in this time and space belonged to her. And she was going to make the most of it.

Forgetting all her reservations, she returned his kiss, determined to enjoy it body and soul and to hell with the consequences. She'd deal with her pain later.

As if sensing her resolve, Granger shifted his position, drawing her even closer, his hand in the small of her back to bring her into his hips.

It was a not too subtle way of letting her know how much he wanted her. It blew her mind to know that her excitement was matched just as fiercely by his.

He lifted his head, the fire in his gaze melting her soul. "I've wanted to do that ever since I first set eyes on you," he said softly.

"What were you waiting for?" Her feeble attempt to make light of the fact that her entire body was trembling apparently failed.

Granger brushed her lips lightly with his. "I wasn't sure if you'd take a carving knife to me. You can be quite a little spitfire when you're provoked."

"You should see me when I'm really mad."

His smile faded as he gazed deep into her eyes. "Corie," he said softly, "I want you as I've never wanted another woman. Yet I can promise you nothing. You must know that."

"Yes, I know that."

"I don't want to bring you more pain. You've had more than your share already."

Abandoning the last of her doubts, Corie tangled her fingers in his hair. "Let's not worry about tomorrow, Granger." Gently she drew his face down to hers, and touched his lips with her own.

Immediately his response caught fire, and he made the kiss last, teasing with his tongue and lingering on her mouth until his breathing became harsh and labored. When he drew back, her skin tingled as he looked down at her. Never had she seen such a look of pure, naked need on a man's face.

His voice was husky with emotion when he spoke. "No woman has ever kissed me like that before."

She smiled up at him, feeling an exhilarating sense of power. "You've never kissed a modern woman before."

His answering smile played havoc with her pulse rate. "I hope that doesn't put me at a disadvantage. How do modern women like to make love nowadays?"

"I imagine the same way they did then. It depends on the woman."

His expression grew serious. Gently, he drew a finger down the side of her cheek, then rested his knuckles against her throat. "Corie," he said softly, "I don't know...this is a different time, a different age, I don't want to...behave in a way that might offend you."

She couldn't believe the depth of her love for him as she looked up into his face. It was as if she'd been waiting for him all of her life, preparing for this one special moment when all her dreams and fantasies exploded into glorious reality.

His hunger for her burned in his eyes, yet he held back, concerned about her feelings, her sensitivities. She couldn't possibly love anyone more than she did this man at this moment.

"Granger," she said, her voice trembling with her emotion, "time doesn't change the way a man and a woman make love. The instinct is born in us, and when two people need each other, they express that need by pleasing each other. It's as simple as that."

"And as complex." He lifted his hand and smoothed his fingers over her hair. "I only know that right now, I want to make love to you, Corie. I want to know the secrets of your body, and give mine to you. I want to join with you in the rituals that are as old as time itself, and I want to sleep tonight with you in my arms, and as you say, forget about tomorrow.''

She felt her throat close, preventing her from speaking. Instead, she took his hand and led him from the room. He followed behind her, his breathing harsh in the quiet of the hallway.

She reached the door of her bedroom and opened it. Then, turning to him, she said quietly, ''There is one thing I must know, Granger. You said you remembered everything, up until the last day. Did you . . . Is there a wife waiting for you somewhere?''

Looking down at her, his face shaded from the light, he seemed almost intimidating. His eyes once more appeared to glow with a silver sheen, and his harsh features looked almost cruel in the shifting shadows. He was unlike any man she had ever known before, and she felt a moment of misgiving.

Then he spoke, in the soft voice she had come to know so well. ''There is no one, Corie. I swear. I am a military man. There was never enough time for more than a brief relationship.''

She didn't want to dwell on the brief relationships. It was enough to know that he belonged to no one but her, at least for now. Tomorrow would eventually come, but right then, she could rest in the knowledge that she would be hurting no one but herself.

Without another word, she led him into the room.

The two men seated in the corner of the nightclub sat quietly talking, taking care not to be overheard. Dr. Boyd Richards, a tall, gaunt man whose black mustache made his features look even more austere, scowled at the glass of beer in his hand.

''I can't imagine where he could have gone. We've combed this town from one end to the other. We know he didn't take a train or a bus out, and he can't drive. Unless he went out on horseback, and I'm damned sure someone would have noticed him if he had. He must still be in town somewhere."

"But where?" Dr. Ivan Spencer fingered his gray beard. "Even if someone took him in, it would not take that person long to realize his...condition."

"Not unless he's been clever enough to hide it." Richards shook his head. "Even so, anyone with half a brain could tell there's something radically wrong somewhere. There are so many ways he could be tripped up. When you think about it, it's damn amazing he's been able to function at all for this long without attracting a hell of a lot of attention."

Spencer looked worried. "You think he's regained his memory yet?"

"Without a doubt. Without the drug there's nothing to prevent him from remembering everything. He knows where he came from by now. It's probably driving him crazy."

"What if he goes to someone for help? He was in the army, he'd know where to find the White House. It's been there since the beginning of the nineteenth century."

"The possibility did occur to me." Richards swirled the beer around in his glass, trying to contain his apprehension. Damn that idiot, Butler, he thought savagely. He should never have let the fool administer the drug. He should have done it himself. But then Butler was expendable if there had been a problem.

"We could be in serious trouble," Spencer said, his voice shaking. "We should have notified them when it happened."

"And have the entire scientific community descend on him like locusts? Here we had the perfect opportunity to study what happens to a human body when it travels through time. I wasn't about to let anyone else in on that."

"It isn't ethical," Spencer mumbled. "He is a human being. I think we should let them know what's happening."

"We can't let them know what we've been doing. You know the government would never sanction our studies. We've had to use a cover-up in order to get the financing as it is."

"And that's fraud," Spencer said unhappily.

"Exactly. I'm still investigating the possibility that Specturne isn't a star at all, but some kind of space vehicle. If that's true, imagine the potential of capturing such a craft. It could put science ahead a thousand years. And my name in the history books."

He took a swig of beer and smacked the glass down on the table again. "We can't inform them about anything. We would lose it all. All that we've sacrificed and worked for. Our only way out of this is to find the bastard, and try to send him back where he belongs. Which is what we intended to do anyway, eventually."

"You think he can be returned?"

Richards hesitated. "I think it can be done. Whether it can be done safely, I don't know."

Spencer looked startled. "He got here in one piece."

"True. But we don't know exactly how it happened. We only know that it did. So far the procedure has always been spontaneous. There could be all kinds of variables that we are not aware of. If we set this thing in motion, it could set off all kinds of complications. If so, there is no way of knowing if our traveler could survive the trip."

"So, what are we going to do?"

"First," Richards said grimly, "we have to find him. I'm convinced he's still here in town somewhere. If that means going from door to door, questioning everyone, we will do it. Thank God we had the good sense to get him out of the lab in Philly. Can you imagine how difficult it would have been to find him in the city?"

"I'd say impossible."

"Right. Anyway, once we have him in our custody again, we'll run our experiments on him, then we'll try to send him back. From the latest reports we know that when the star returns within the month, it always hits the same place. If the reverse procedure works, he will disappear. We will never know if he makes it or not, of course, but at least we will have done our best to rectify the situation. It's all we can ask for."

Spencer stared gloomily across the room. "What if someone did take him in, and knows about it all? He could have told someone and asked for help. What do we do then?"

"We can't take the risk of anyone being in possession of that information." Richards met his colleague's worried gaze, and added quietly, "We will have to cross that particular bridge when we come to it."

Spencer flicked his tongue over his lips. "You mean—?"

"Whatever it takes. In the meantime we'd better start hunting for him in earnest. If we don't get him back before the end of next week, we're stuck with him for another six months. That's if Specturne ever returns after this trip."

"If he does make it back to his time, you know he could very well create a sensation if he tells them what happened."

"Who's going to believe a story like that?" Richards shook his head. "In any case, he won't remember anything. We've found out that the time frame is bounced back several days when the beam hits. It's like crossing the international date line, we lose time in the transition. We make it up when we cross back. If he gets back he'll arrive before he left, so to speak. He won't remember anything."

"I hope you're right," Spencer said, sounding unconvinced.

Richards shrugged. "I know I am."

"How can you be so sure?"

"Because," Richard said patiently, "if someone had caused a sensation like that more than a hundred years ago, I'm quite sure we would have heard about it."

Spencer stared at him for a long moment. "Yes, I suppose we would. The more we discover about this situation, the stranger it becomes."

Richards nodded his agreement.

"But then," Spencer persisted, "what if we don't get him back? What if the procedure doesn't work? What if he has to stay here for the rest of his life?"

"Then," Richards said deliberately, "I'm afraid that our first time traveler will have a short life. After all, accidents do happen."

Spencer shook his head violently. "No, not that. I won't be part of that."

"I don't want that either," Richards said. "But I'm not about to allow everything I've slaved for all these years to be snatched away from me just when I'm on the brink of the greatest discovery of mankind."

He lifted his glass and drained the last of the beer. "Anyway," he said, as he set the glass down again, "think about it. Who in the hell is going to miss him?"

"Corie," Granger whispered, "you are a beautiful woman."

She shivered, although his gaze roaming her naked body seemed to burn her skin. She had looked at herself in a mirror so many times, yet never until now had she felt beautiful. He made her feel beautiful. The look in his eyes when he gazed at her made her feel like the most gorgeous woman ever to grace the earth.

She lay at his side, the shaded light from the bedside lamp casting a soft glow across his body. He had undressed her slowly, with none of the haste he must have felt raging inside. He had stood patiently while she'd taken off his clothes, though she'd heard his sharp intake of breath now and then.

Even now, he seemed content just to look at her, while her heart raced with impatience, her breasts aching to be touched.

"Corie," he breathed again, and at last he moved his hand, his fingers gently tracing a path from her throat down to the valley between her breasts. "I am afraid to touch you, for fear that I will wake up from this wonderful dream and find myself back in my tent."

"You are not going to wake up, Granger." She reached out a trembling hand and flattened her palm against his chest, enjoying the sensation of soft dark fuzz beneath her fingers. "Not yet, anyway."

"I'm very happy to hear that." Propping himself up on one elbow, he watched his finger continue the path down to her belly. "I am not nearly as anxious to go back now."

A quiver of grief caught her unawares. Determined not to dwell on his leaving, she pulled his mouth down to hers. His kiss blotted out all thoughts beyond the touch of his hand and the feel of his body straining against hers.

It was as if he'd suddenly let go of his hold on his patience. He lifted his mouth from hers and looked deep into her eyes. "Are you sure, Corie?"

She nodded. "I've never been more sure."

Once more his mouth covered hers, while his hand explored her body. Tremors of excitement fanned out from his touch, spreading the rising pressure of need that seemed to possess her mind.

The hard contours of his body felt hot beneath her searching fingers, and she cried out as his lips nuzzled at her breast. She felt his chin gently graze her tender flesh, and the sensation created new shivers of pleasure to torment her.

She had never wanted a man the way she wanted this one. The smooth skin of his back beneath her hands, the pressure of his rough thigh on hers, the clean fragrance of his body, the hush of his voice as he whispered her name, everything about him excited her beyond thought or reason.

His knowing hands sent her mind reeling with the force of her passion. Her body seemed beyond her control, arching impulsively as his fingers found an exquisite source of pleasure.

Yearning to give back the incredible sensations, she drew her hand down to his belly, her pulse leaping at the sound of his harsh voice muttering his response. "That is so good."

"I want you," she whispered back, and his mouth found hers again, no longer gentle now, his tongue probing with the fierce demands of a man beyond control.

He shifted his hips, his shoulders lifting as he braced himself on his hands. "Now, Corie, now."

"Yes, now." Again she cried out as he slipped inside her, his body filling her with a drowning heat that spread the intense pleasure all the way up her body.

She clung to him, feeling the strength of him, that indomitable power of his body, rejoicing in the knowledge that at last, she had broken the reserve that had held him in control for so long.

Moving with him, her hips in rhythm with his, she rode with him on the ever rising crest of passion, until his shuddering body strained with the grasping need for release.

She was close now, very close. But she wanted to wait for him, to soar with him to that elusive essence of sheer contentment. Again he stretched his body, his head thrown back, his back arched, while the muscles in his arms knotted with the effort.

Digging her fingers into his strong back, she wrapped her legs around him, holding him deeper inside her for one last final driving effort. Together their bodies met, held for one interminable second, then with a mingled cry, shuddered into the sweet, final surrender.

Granger lay in the darkness, still feeling the rapid beat of his heart. Corie lay in his arms, breathing evenly, though he knew she was awake.

Thoughts chased through his mind. Wild thoughts, crazy thoughts, so many conflicting emotions. He wanted to stay. Oh, how he wanted to stay. Yet his duty lay in the past. For now he remembered it all. That last morning.

There was still a chance that he could be wrong, of course. Only Corie could tell him that. And it was entirely possible she didn't know the answers. But he had to at least try to find out if what he suspected was true.

"Are you awake?" he whispered.

"Yes." Her reply came back softly in the darkness. "I don't want to go to sleep."

He knew how she felt. Neither did he. He wanted this night to last forever, and never have to face tomorrow. "Feel like talking?"

"Sure." She snuggled closer to him. He felt the sweet pressure of her breast against his chest, and his body stirred in response. Steeling himself to remain passive, he said quietly, "There's something I want to ask you."

He felt her tense, and hoped he wasn't raising any false hopes. "About the battle in Gettysburg," he added quickly.

"Oh." He felt her body slump a little, but she added casually enough, "I don't know all the details, of course, but I'll try. I've been to the battlefield and seen all the movies and displays about the battle, so I do know something about it. What do you want to know?"

"You said that the North won the Civil War, and that Gettysburg had a bearing on that victory."

"Yes." She paused, as if reluctant to say anything further, and he wondered if she knew the reasoning behind his questions.

"In what way?" he prompted, every bit as unwilling as she was to pursue the discussion.

"From what I remember, there were several incidents. The most significant, I believe, was when General Lee ordered General Ewell to attack the Union army on Cemetery Ridge on the afternoon of July 1. It wasn't a firm order, and for some reason, General Ewell decided not to attack.

"By the time Lee arrived at the camp, the reinforcements were in place. The North held the ridge, and changed the course of the battle. Gettysburg was the turning point in the war. Had the South won that battle, they might well have won the war."

He couldn't answer for a long moment. In the distance a faint rumble of thunder warned of a storm at sea. The ominous sound seemed to echo in his heart. "And no one knows why Ewell delayed the attack?" he asked carefully.

Corie took her time answering. "I don't think so. According to the history books, he was sick that afternoon, and there was some confusion about the position of the Union army. I don't think anyone knows for sure what happened. I do know that a lot of people blamed him for turning the course of the war."

So now he knew. No matter what his feelings were, one way or another, he had to go back. He had no choice. After all, he was a military man. As always, his duty to his country came before everything else. And his duty lay with the Union army, in a tiny town called Gettysburg, somewhere in Pennsylvania, on July 1, in the year 1863.

Chapter 8

Corie awoke some time in the night, feeling strangely content and at peace. Granger held her in the circle of his arms, her face against his chest, which gently rose and fell in the relaxation of deep sleep.

She could find no way to describe her feelings. The wild, raw longing for him had been appeased, and she knew a deep sense of fulfillment that was warm and satisfying in a way she'd never known before.

Yet beneath it all, the pain was only just beginning. This was all she'd ever have. Unless his feelings for her were deep enough to hold him here in the present.

But how could she expect him to do that for her? He didn't belong in this time, and it was up to her to find a way to send him back. She must do her utmost to send away the only man she would ever love.

She raised her head to look at his strong profile, etched clearly against the light from the street lamp outside the window. Her heart ached with love for him.

As she watched him, he stirred and opened his eyes. "Hi," he said softly. "Having trouble sleeping?"

She shook her head. "I'm enjoying watching you sleep."

He smiled, and she felt the warmth of it deep in her soul. "Was I talking again?"

"No, you looked very peaceful." God, how she was going to miss him. Before he came into her life, she'd been more or less content. That was before she realized how much she was missing. When he left her alone again, he would leave behind a cold, dark empty space that would never be refilled.

"What are you thinking so hard about?" Granger whispered, drawing his fingers down her cheek.

Abandoning her troubled thoughts, she snuggled closer to his warm, naked body. "I'm thinking about kissing you again."

"I'd say that's a very good thought. And it can easily be arranged." With his hands on either side of her face, he drew her up until he could cover her mouth with his.

Once more she was lost in his embrace, and the enchanting power of his touch.

She slept soundly after that, and awoke with daylight flooding the room. A quick glance at the clock on the bedside table told her she'd overslept again.

Granger stirred as she leaned over him and planted a kiss full on his mouth. "I'm late, so you'll have to get your own breakfast this morning."

"Sorry," he mumbled. "That was my fault, keeping you awake half the night."

She grinned. "It was worth it. But now I'll have to scramble to make it to the office."

His arms came around her for one last hug and a long, deep kiss that almost made her forget about work altogether.

But she had a job to do, and an important one. Somehow she had to find a way to get him back to his own time. And somehow she had to be strong enough to let him go.

Seated at her computer several hours later, Corie wearily studied the screen in front of her. She had gone through everything she could find on the Specturne project. After all the calculations had been computed, her reports stated little more than the dates that Specturne appeared, and the expected point of impact of its beam.

Any further information about the star was being held under classified information, and in order to learn any more she would have to break into the records. An almost impossible task without being discovered. And if they did catch her, Granger's life could be in danger. It was a risk she didn't want to take.

Staring at the screen again, Corie ran both hands through her hair. According to her calculations, the star was expected to make the return trip in nine days.

She leaned forward, her interest caught by the date. If the star arrived as scheduled, its beam would contact earth on July 1. What had Granger said? *I remember falling asleep in my tent on the night of June 30. Though I can't help feeling there is something else. I'm almost certain I awoke the next morning, still in my tent...*

The next morning. July 1. Was that why the star returned each time? To return things to normal? If the beam produced a time warp when it hit, it was feasible to assume that nature was reversing itself and replacing the time lost.

Her pulse raced as she considered the theory. If she was right, then it seemed entirely possible that if Granger stood directly in the path of the beam on Specturne's return, he should also be sent back to where he belonged.

It was worth a try. If it didn't work she'd have to think of something else. But right now it was all she had, and she was going to go for it.

Her mind buzzing with a hundred details that would have to be taken care of, she almost bumped into the gaunt figure of Dr. Richards when she left the office later that afternoon.

She tried to edge around him, but he barred her way, standing in the doorway of the lobby making it impossible for her to pass him.

"Ah, Miss Trenton, yes, I wanted a word with you. Do you have a minute?"

Corie stared up into his almost black eyes, frantically hoping her expression looked more innocent than she felt. It was hard for her to imagine that this man could be responsible for risking Granger's life with an experimental drug, let alone consider the possibility that he intended to do away with Granger altogether.

Nevertheless, she wasn't about to give the man the slightest hint that she knew what was going on. Bracing herself to meet the arrogant gaze, she said, "I'm rather late for an appointment, Dr. Richards. Perhaps tomorrow...?"

"This won't take a moment." To her dismay, the man took hold of her arm and led her down the hallway back to her office. Opening the door, he ushered her inside and closed the door behind him.

Corie's heart began to thump uncomfortably as she watched the scientist's cruel face. Did he suspect that Granger was hiding in her house? How could he know that? Her mind raced with possibilities, while Dr. Richards continued to study her with a thoughtful expression.

"Miss Trenton," he said at last, making her jump. "I wonder if you would help me in a little project?"

Feeling a leap of relief, Corie answered promptly. "I'll be happy to, Dr. Richards. How can I help you?"

Richards placed his hands behind his back, his cold gaze fixed on her face. "I'm trying to discover the whereabouts of a friend of mine. I'm rather anxious to get in touch with him. The problem is, I've mislaid his address, and I was wondering if you would help me locate him."

She tried her damnedest to keep a cool attitude. She couldn't imagine what he was getting at. This could be a trap, she warned herself. If so, she'd have to be on her toes, or she could walk right into it.

"He's not listed in the telephone directory?" she asked, as casually as she could manage.

"He has an unlisted number."

"I see." She pretended to think for a moment. "How about the city directory?"

The scientist pursed his lips. "He has recently moved into the area. He's not listed in the directory."

She could feel a chill spreading down her back as she stared up at him. "Then how can I help you?"

For answer, Dr. Richards withdrew something from the top pocket of his jacket. "I have a picture of him. This is a small town, and I thought that if you happened to see him, you could let me know."

She nodded, striving for a blank expression as she gazed down at the photo of Granger. He was sitting on the edge of a bed, looking at the camera with the same bewildered expression he'd worn the first time he'd seen her television. It took all her willpower not to let her sudden rush of tenderness show on her face.

"Nice looking man," she said cheerfully. "If I should see him I'll tell him you're looking for him."

"No!"

She looked up, faking a startled expression. "Isn't that what you want?"

Richards stared at her, his face registering suspicion. "No, I want to surprise him. My friend loves surprises. If you could just watch where he goes, and let me know where he is living, I'll be able to pay him a surprise visit."

"Oh, I bet he'll just love that," Corie said recklessly.

"I'll pay you for your trouble, of course," Richards said, narrowing his eyes. "I'll make it very worth your while to find him for me."

Corie stared down at the photo again. "Well, I'll certainly do my best to locate your friend, Dr. Richards. You obviously are very anxious to surprise him."

"Yes, I am." Richards took the picture back and thrust it in his pocket. "Well, thank you, Miss Trenton. I won't keep you from your...appointment any longer."

Thanking him, Corie escaped from the room, determined not to let him see how much he'd unnerved her.

She was still shaking when she arrived back at the house a few minutes later. She had taken the car again and this time she was thankful for the security of being locked inside the vehicle, instead of having to look over her shoulder all the way home, as she surely would have done had she walked.

Even then, she looked around carefully before climbing out of the car. Not that it mattered if anyone followed her or not. Her address was on record at the lab; she would be easy enough to find if anyone wanted to do so.

Praying that Granger wouldn't open the door and give away his presence to anyone who might be watching for him, Corie fumbled with the key in the lock. It seemed an eternity before she finally got the door open. Practically falling inside, she slammed the door firmly behind her and leaned against it to recover her composure.

"What's happened?" Granger said sharply from above her. "You look as if you've just seen a ghost." He was standing near the top of the stairs looking down at her.

She would have laughed at the comment if she hadn't been so unnerved by her encounter with the menacing Dr. Richards. "I've just had a chat with our head scientist," she said, moving away from the door.

Granger began walking down the stairs toward her, his face taut and wary. "What happened?"

Corie dumped her purse on a chair and perched on the arm. "What happened was that he showed me a picture of you. He asked me to watch out for you, and if I saw you, to follow you home. Then I was to tell him where to find you."

Granger swore softly. "Do you think he suspects you?"

Corie shrugged. "I don't know. He could suspect everyone at the lab. I'm afraid he's going around asking everyone to keep an eye out for you. He's telling this story about wanting to surprise a friend whose address he has conveniently lost."

"Why would anyone do that for him without good reason?" Granger said, sitting down on the couch opposite her.

Corie gave him a grim smile. "Lots of people would, if they were offered enough to do it."

Granger lifted his eyebrows. "He bribed you for the information?"

"Me, and probably a dozen other people. I think the way he put it was that he would make it very worth my while."

Granger pressed a thumb and forefinger to his forehead. "What did you tell him?"

"I said I would be happy to watch out for you. What else could I say?" She frowned, leaning forward to peer at him. "Do you have a headache?"

"It will pass." He lowered his hand and gave her his rare smile. "You don't think he knows I'm here?"

Corie dropped onto her knees in front of him. "No," she said softly, "I don't think he knows. And he's not going to. As long as you don't go outside the house, no one will ever know."

"I can't stay here forever," Granger said slowly. "Sooner or later I have to leave here. As long as I'm with you I'll be putting you in danger, too. They can't let you go free knowing what you know. Once they find that out they will have to get rid of you, too.''

She looked up at him, feeling the chill of his words. "You believe they would kill you?"

He shrugged. "What else can they do?"

She didn't tell him she'd come to the same conclusion. "Well, they won't get the chance," she said, with a note of belligerence.

Something in her voice must have alerted him. He looked down at her, his eyes wary. "You sound very sure of that."

Raising herself up enough to reach him, Corie pressed a warm kiss on his mouth. Immediately he closed his arms around her, hugging her close.

"I missed you," he whispered, his breath tickling her ear.

"I missed you, too. I thought about you all day."

"I was worried you'd do something crazy and get yourself into trouble."

"Well, I didn't." She sank back on her heels and looked at him in triumph. "I didn't have to take any risks."

He took her by the shoulders and gave her a gentle shake. "Are you going to tell me why you're so damn proud of yourself?"

Doing her best to hide the pain the words would cost her, she scrambled to her feet and sat down next to him on the couch. "I don't want to get your hopes up, but I think I know how to send you home."

Her heart ached when she saw the grave expression on his face.

"Tell me," Granger said, his voice suddenly weary.

Briefly, and as clearly as she could, Corie explained about the movement of Specturne. "It's just a theory," she hastened to add, after he'd listened intently. "I'm not sure about anything, of course. You could be sent even further forward in time, or you could end up in a different time period in the past. Anything could happen."

He stared at her for a long moment. "But you think it might work," he stated flatly.

"I think it's your only chance."

The stark silence that followed her words seemed to linger far too long.

"I see," Granger said, at last.

She needed to reassure him, to take away that still, resigned look in his eyes.

"I do believe it could work," she said, a little desperately. "I think the return of the star is nature reversing itself back to normal. In which case, you should end up where you left, when you left."

He looked at her for a long moment, then he reached for her hand. Tracing the tips of her fingers with his thumb, he said gently, "I don't want to go back, Corie. What I want is to stay here with you."

Her rush of joy robbed her of speech. Granger was silent for several seconds, and watching his melancholy expression, Corie felt her newfound happiness ebbing away. When he spoke again, his words filled her with a pain she'd never known before.

"I have to go back. I wish to God I didn't have to, but I have no choice."

Her hopes dashed, she could only gaze at him in misery. He lifted his head, his gray eyes filled with pain. "You know I wouldn't leave you unless it was imperative that I go back."

She nodded, trying to find her voice. "You don't have to explain," she whispered. "I understand."

"No, you don't." He let go of her hand. Getting to his feet he moved over to the fireplace. With one arm resting on the mantelpiece, he stared into the empty grate.

"You have a right to know," he said, speaking in a voice so low she could hardly hear him.

Her heart began thumping painfully as she watched him. All she could think of was that he'd lied to her about having a wife waiting for him. If that were so, the pain she felt now would be nothing compared to the anguish she would suffer knowing he had deliberately betrayed another woman.

"You don't have to tell me," she said desperately, preferring not to hear his confession.

"Yes, I do." He turned to face her, and clasped his hands behind his back. "I have to go back for one reason and one reason only. If I am not in Gettysburg on the morning of July 1 to carry out an order that was given to me, the entire course of history could be changed."

This was not at all what she'd expected. Staring at him, her mouth suddenly dry, Corie whispered, "What do you mean?"

Granger closed his eyes briefly, as if struggling with some elusive memory. When he looked at her again, he seemed to have reached a decision of some kind.

"I know why General Ewell did not attack the ridge that afternoon," he said. "I remember what happened, just before the light blinded me."

She stared at him, bewildered by his words. "The light? You mean the beam?"

Once more he crossed the room, and sat down on the chair in front of her. "I'll start with the beginning," he said, "and I'll try to make it brief."

She watched him, the ache in her heart intensifying as he paused, then finally began speaking, in a slow, quiet voice as if he were reciting a poem.

"We had spent the night on McPherson's Ridge, outside of Gettysburg. The next morning, on July 1, we clashed with the rebels. We were driven back through Gettysburg, and we retreated to Cemetery Ridge, where we were expecting reinforcements."

Corie's pulse quickened as the familiar details were repeated by the man who had lived them. Even now, she felt that same sense of unreality as Granger's quiet voice described the battlefield as it was then.

"It was hot and sticky," he said, "and we were sweating like pigs in our uniforms. The flies were everywhere, stinging our eyes and buzzing in our ears. Everyone was on edge. We'd been driven back, our unit depleted by the dead and wounded, and the reinforcements hadn't yet arrived. They were trickling in far too slowly, and we knew if Ewell attacked, we would have no defense."

He paused, and she waited, while the shadows grew longer in the quiet living room. Finally, he spoke again. "In a last-ditch effort to save the ridge, it was decided to send a spy into the enemy camp. We planned to feed the rumors that the reinforcements had already arrived, and that two cavalry units were firmly entrenched in the surrounding woods. We hoped to stall Ewell long enough for the rest of the troops to arrive."

Corie gasped. "Then that's what happened! No one really knew for sure why Ewell delayed the attack. Now we know."

She saw Granger's expression change and slumped back in her chair. "Of course, we can't tell anyone."

Granger leaned forward, and the fire of determination in his gaze made her flinch. "Corie," he said harshly, "if I don't go back, it won't have happened. I was the man chosen for that assignment. I was on my way to Ewell's camp when a blinding light hit me in the eyes. The force of it knocked me off my horse. The next thing I knew, I was lying in a bed in a cold, bare hospital room, wondering where I was and how I got there."

The impact of his words hit her slowly. "You are saying that if you hadn't spread the rumors, Ewell might have attacked earlier. In which case, he would have had an easy victory. There would have been no battle at Gettysburg.''

He nodded. "And if what you say is true, without that Union victory, the entire future of the United States of America could have been changed."

Corie felt sick as she stared at him. "You don't know that. It's anybody's guess. No one could possibly predict the outcome. It's entirely possible the chain of events wouldn't have been altered by your absence. Maybe Ewell wouldn't have attacked earlier, even if he hadn't heard the rumors. They say he wasn't well, they say—''

"Corie, I can't take that chance. Please understand. I am a military man. No matter what my personal feelings are, I must go back and carry out my duty."

She wasn't thinking straight. She knew that. But somehow her mind wouldn't let her accept what he was saying. "But we know from the history books what happened. You can't change history."

"Exactly." He reached out his hand and brushed her cheek with his fingers. "Which is why I must go back."

He rose swiftly, his arms reaching out to enclose her. Holding her trembling body close to him, he gently stroked her hair. "Believe me, if I had any other choice, I would stay."

She couldn't speak. Part of her knew he was right, but that was the practical part. A much bigger part of her, the part that loved him, cried out in pain, demanding to know why he didn't feel deeply enough for her to stay.

She stood quietly in the comforting circle of his arms until her tumbling thoughts calmed down and she regained some semblance of control. Somehow she had to get through this. Somehow she would survive.

Drawing back, she looked up at him and managed a tremulous smile. "We will have to go back to Gettysburg, to the spot where you arrived."

He looked worried. "I'm not sure I could find the exact spot."

"But I can. Or at least, very close, thanks to modern technology. Certainly close enough to see the beam when it hits."

A shudder shook her body and she paused, waiting for it to pass. "The shaft of light will last for five seconds. That's all the time we will have for you to reach the beam and stand inside it."

"And if we don't get there?"

She shrugged, unwilling to think beyond that. "It could be another six months before Specturne returns. If ever. Even if it does, there is no guarantee that it will hit the same time zone or place in the past. We can only guess."

"What is your closest estimate?"

She considered that question. "From what we know, Specturne appears to be on an uneven orbit. There is a slight variation in the direction of the beam. The last time it visited it hit an island in the Pacific. This time it hit Pennsylvania. The only similarity so far is the fact that it has hit twice in this time period."

Her voice cracked, and again she paused. "But it's unpredictable. We don't know if it will appear in this time period again."

She pulled away from him and walked to the window, wondering how she was going to tell him the rest without breaking down. "It would seem that if the direction and the distance remains the same, then whatever happens out there would repeat the same pattern. But we can't be sure. In other words, this is probably your only chance to leave here and return to the right place and time."

"And once I do, there will be no coming back."

She turned and looked at him. "No," she said steadily. "There will be no coming back. Not unless Specturne returns in the exact same orbit. At this point, it seems unlikely. There are so many factors involved. The slightest variation could change its orbit."

The look he gave her threatened to break her control. "I understand," he said quietly.

The ache in her throat made it difficult to speak. "I wish I did," she said brokenly.

He crossed the room in quick strides and reached for her. He held her so close she could feel the vibration of his heartbeat against her breast. With his lips against her forehead he whispered, "How long do we have?"

"Less than a week." She swallowed, then went on painfully, "We will go to Gettysburg on June 30, and book into a motel. Specturne is expected to direct its beam in the early hours of the morning of July 1. If all goes well, you should arrive back at the same moment you left."

He brushed her forehead with his lips in a soft kiss. "We have a few precious days left to us. Let us make the most of them. If they are all we'll ever have, I want to remember them for the rest of my life."

Her eyes filled with tears as she looked up at his face, so dear to her now. She held them back, determined not to waste time in crying. There would be time enough for all the tears she could shed after he had gone.

For now she would fill the hours they had left together with love and laughter. She would do her damnedest to give him the wonderful memories as her final gift to him.

His kiss was a bittersweet mixture of pain and pleasure. As he deepened it, Corie forced her mind to blot out the bleak future, and lost herself instead in the sensuous magic of his touch.

Long after Granger had fallen asleep that night, Corie lay staring into the darkness, unable to sleep with the dismal ache that refused to go away, no matter how hard she tried.

How could she live without him now? It would have been better if she'd never known him. At least then she wouldn't have known what she was missing. She would have simply gone on with her life, unaware that a very special part of living had eluded her.

Turning her head to look at him, she was immediately ashamed of her thoughts. How could she deny herself, even for one moment, the happiness and joy that Granger had given her? Those memories would last her for a lifetime. How could she trade them for the dull, boring existence she'd known before he burst into her life and changed her forever?

Granger stirred, murmuring something she couldn't catch. Her heart seemed to overflow with her love for him. How she wished he could have loved her enough to stay. Yet how could she deny him his need to obey the instincts that had been driven into him? He was a soldier.

She remembered something he'd said before they'd made love for the first time. *I am a military man. There was never enough time for more than a brief relationship.*

But this wasn't quite the same as a man going off to war with a promise to come back to her. This was a man going far beyond her reach, with the certain knowledge that she would never see him again. And there was nothing she could do to change that. Unless . . .

The idea hit her so sharply, she wondered why she hadn't thought about it before. Why couldn't she go back with him? She had nothing keeping her here. No family, no real friends.

She had left her friends behind in Philadelphia, and they had gradually lost touch. Too busy with their own lives to worry about someone they never saw. There hadn't been time to make new friends at the shore.

No one would miss her. Except the people at the lab. She could just quit, tell them she was going back to Philadelphia.

The more she thought about it, the more appealing the idea became. To go back in time, to find out exactly what life was like then. To meet the people she'd read about, experience the events that up until now had been no more than stories in books. It was the chance of a lifetime.

It wouldn't be easy, of course. She'd have a lot of adjustments to make, and there would be many things she'd miss about the twentieth century.

Again she raised her head to look at Granger. She loved him enough to do it, though. She loved him enough that no matter where he went, or how strange and uncomfortable her life might become, as long as she was with him, she could live happily by his side.

Her heart skipped a beat as she thought about her decision. She longed to tell him what she'd decided. But she knew he would do his best to talk her out of it. She had to pick the right moment.

Excited and terrified at the same time at the prospect, she fell into an uneasy sleep, only to wake up feeling tired and unrested the next morning.

She hated the thought of leaving Granger to go to the lab. "I could stay home and bug you all day," she said, more than half-serious as she dished up the pancakes she'd cooked for him.

"You can't do that. It might look suspicious, and we can't take the chance of anyone finding me here before I have the chance to leave." He softened the words with a smile, but they still hurt.

She told herself that his leaving had to be his priority. Even so, she wished he didn't have to sound so anxious to go. The next instant she reminded herself that this was no simple journey from one country to another.

This trip was fraught with possibilities, none of them pleasant. Of course he was anxious for the outcome. He must be eaten up with anxiety at the thought of what might happen. She knew exactly how he must feel.

He pulled her close as she was preparing to leave for the lab. "Please, be careful," he said, kissing her brow. "I don't want anything to happen to you."

She made light of it, laughing up at him, although her nerves jumped at the thought. "Don't worry, I'm not going to let anything happen to me. You need me to get back home again."

"I need you for a lot more than that."

For once his kiss failed to comfort her, and she had trouble hiding her uneasiness as she looked up at him. "At least we'll have the weekend together. Now I'd better go, or I'll really be late."

He lifted a hand and traced her lips with his finger.

"Promise me you won't do anything foolish?"

"Like what?"

"Like trying to find out more than you're supposed to know."

She went up on her toes and dropped a light kiss on his willing mouth. "You worry too much. Get on with the papering, it will take your mind off our problems."

"Now who's giving the orders?"

She grinned. "Women are allowed now." She made herself pull away from him and open the door.

"I was right about one thing," Granger said behind her, as she stepped out onto the porch.

"What's that?" Only half paying attention, she scanned the street up and down to make sure no one was spying on them.

"There are some things that haven't changed, thank the Lord." He gave her a lecherous look and blew her a kiss from the doorway.

She smiled back at him. "You're right. Women still know how to please their men."

"I can guarantee that."

Seeing him standing there, with a lazy half smile on his face, she longed to run back to him, close the door on the outside world and spend the day making wild, passionate love with him.

"Granger," she said softly, "it depends a lot on the man, too. I'll see you tonight."

"I'll look forward to it."

He closed the door, and already she missed him. She'd given herself enough time to walk to the lab that morning, needing to feel the fresh salty breezes from the ocean on her face.

The sky looked threatening as she marched along the boardwalk, reflecting its steel gray face in the choppy waves that smacked against the shore.

The air felt thick and heavy with moisture, suggesting the onslaught of a storm, and she wished now that she'd brought the car. It looked as if it might turn out to be a wet day.

Granger must be getting cabin fever, she thought, as she watched the sea gulls swooping low over the beach, complaining loudly with hoarse cries at the lack of leftovers.

For a man who was used to the outdoors, he must be thoroughly sick of being cooped up within the walls of a house day and night.

A poster caught her eye as she rounded the corner of the street. It showed a colorful picture of a Ferris wheel standing in the midst of various rides and booths, with the sea in the background.

Corie paused in front of it, a slow smile spreading over her face. Wildwood was at least six miles away. Miles of boardwalk crammed with people this time of the year, if the weather was good. It would be easy to get lost in the crowds.

The more she thought about, the more excited she felt. It

was just what they needed. A place where they could forget their problems and just enjoy the fun and excitement.

Another thought struck her and she almost laughed out loud. How would a man from the mid-nineteenth century deal with a late twentieth-century extravaganza like the Wildwood boardwalk? It would be very interesting to find out.

She could hardly wait until the end of the day when she could get home and put the idea to Granger. Two whole days of the weekend to enjoy, before she had to come back to work. She was going to make the most of them.

She would take her camera and get some pictures, something concrete to take back in time with her, to remind him of his brief stay in the future.

Cold fingers knotted in her stomach when she thought about leaving behind everything that was familiar to her. How would she cope in that strange world where everything she had taken for granted would not yet exist?

She stared at the monitor of her computer. How could she live without computers, televisions, telephones, cars, washing machines, much less modern plumbing?

Panic almost drowned her as she struggled with her doubts. She couldn't do it. Yet, if she didn't, she would lose Granger forever. Did she really love him enough to give everything up for him? It was a question she'd better know the answer to before she took that step, she warned herself.

Because once she'd let go of her existence in the twentieth century, she would be forever trapped in the past, forced to live out the rest of her life in an alien world. There would be no turning back.

Chapter 9

Granger stood back to survey his day's work with a sense of deep satisfaction. The bathroom had been a challenge after the comparative ease of plain bedroom walls. But then he always enjoyed a challenge. And now he was pleased with his handiwork.

He liked the wallpaper's design of pale aqua seashells, and the slight silver sheen to the paper was something he'd never seen before.

This was a colorful world, this twentieth century. Everywhere he turned, he discovered new wonders, new miracles that people from his time had never dreamed could be possible. How he wished he could take some of it back with him, to show them what life could be like with the technology and experience accumulated in 130 years.

He laid down the brush on the footstool, smiling at the thought. Introducing marvels to people unprepared for such revelations would probably cause a major upheaval. He would most likely be considered a magician, or even an evil sorcerer with magical powers.

He'd more than likely be hung from a limb of the nearest tree, which was the way people usually dealt with strangers they didn't understand.

His smile faded. He could never tell anyone about his strange experience. Who would believe him, anyway? All he could do was to go on with his life as if all this had been a dream. Although he knew without a doubt, that as long as he lived he would not forget the woman who had given him the most precious gift of all, and for a brief moment in time had made him feel a passion unequalled by anything he'd ever known before. Or ever would again. The lingering memory of her voice as she whispered to him in the dark would haunt him to the end of his days.

The sound of a key in the front door startled him out of his thoughts. He'd lost track of time, and now Corie was home and he was unprepared.

Running a hand through his tousled hair he hurried down the stairs to greet her. She stood in the hallway, gazing up at him, her face alight with a glow that took his breath away.

He leapt down the last two steps and caught her up in his arms, swinging her off her feet as his mouth sought hers. Her lips were warm and pliant under his, and the fire in his body took hold.

Lifting his head, he smiled down at her. "Hi," he said softly. "I missed you."

She started to speak and impatiently, he smothered her answer with his mouth. Her soft curves pressed against his chest and belly, and he longed to feel the smooth, cool touch of her naked body.

Her fragrance teased him with a seductive promise when she curled her fingers in his hair, and she strived to fit her soft body closer to his. He had trouble breathing when he finally lifted his head.

"I have to shower," he said thickly. "I've been working up a pretty good sweat."

She grinned up at him, the light gleaming on her small, even teeth. "Want me to wash your back?"

He lifted an eyebrow, his pulse racing at the thought. "In the shower?"

"Sure. Haven't you ever showered with anyone before?"

He brushed his lips across her tempting mouth. "Sweet lady, I have never been inside a shower before, remember? I must admit, it's a very pleasant alternative to tin baths and cold, muddy rivers."

She laughed, and he was certain he'd never heard a more beautiful sound in his life. Taking him by the hand, she gave him her mischievous smile. "Oh, you have no idea how pleasant it can be. Come with me and I'll show you."

Right then he would have gone with her into the devil's dungeons. Somehow she seemed different tonight. Light-hearted, perhaps even excited. He wondered what had happened to change her mood.

He felt a moment's depression as he climbed the stairs behind her. She seemed to have recovered from her grief at his leaving.

He soon forgot about his dejection a few minutes later though, when Corie stood with him in the steaming spray from the faucet above their heads.

The sight of her naked body, with water cascading over her shoulders and down her full breasts, made his body ache with longing. Her wet hair molded to her head, gleaming in the soft light, and her eyes were closed in her upturned face. Her hands rested tormentingly on his chest, her palms covering his taut nipples.

Lifting his hand, he adjusted the spray lower, and she opened her eyes. He watched her expression change, softening as she smiled at him. Tiny drops of water trickled down her breast, and he stooped to catch them with his tongue.

He felt the shudder that rippled through her. The vibration of it seemed to leap between them, like lightning between the clouds.

He had no patience this time. All he'd thought about all day was the memory of their lovemaking. The intense sensations that had rocked his body still tingled in his blood.

He wanted to feel those sensations again. He wanted to hear her soft cries, and answer her with his groan of pleasure. He wanted to feel her body moving beneath him, giving as well as taking, while he brought them both to the rapture of that final shuddering release. And he wanted it now.

Even as he closed his arms around her, he cursed himself for his impatience. This was a woman who deserved to be pleasured, to be caressed and stroked, until she, too, felt the desperation of the wild hunger that overwhelmed him.

Before now he had taken his pleasure when it was offered, a brief moment of satisfaction soon forgotten in the tumult of war. But this was different. This woman was different. Now he wanted to please her even more than he wanted to please himself.

He felt her wet, naked body shiver against him once more, and again the sensuous friction almost shattered his resolve. Putting her away from him, he opened the door of the shower and reached for a towel.

She spoke not a word, but simply stood there watching him with a sultry promise in her eyes that sent his temperature soaring. Quickly, he wrapped the towel around her and stepped with her out of the shower.

He set her on her feet and took a shuddering breath. "I want you."

"I know." She caught her bottom lip between her teeth for a brief second, then gave him her sweet smile.

He could wait no longer. With a swift movement he swept her up in his arms and carried her into the bedroom. Gently he laid her on the bed and removed the towel from her enticing body. For a long moment he allowed himself the sheer pleasure of looking at her, then slowly lowered himself onto the bed beside her.

He was more knowledgeable now of what pleased her, and he took his time, exercising a tight control on his own needs. She responded quickly, her body coming alive in spasms of pleasure as he stroked and gently probed until he sensed she was close.

The setting sun cast a soft glow across the bed, filtered by the flimsy drapes. He watched her face as he brought her to the edge of her climax, and then beyond. When she uttered her final cry, her body arching against his hand, he felt a deep sense of wonder and fulfillment that almost matched his own release. It amazed him that he could feel so complete just by pleasuring her.

But now it was his turn. His body quivered at her touch, and the control he'd held on to for so long snapped like a weighted bough. The heat of his hunger unleashed into a fiery storm of touch and taste, kiss and caress, until he could restrain himself no longer.

The moment he sank into her warm body, the driving need began, filling his mind and his soul with a fierce, hot yearning that had to be satisfied. He felt her fingers digging into his back with an exquisite pain, her silky thighs clamping around his hips in passionate bondage.

Now he was close...so close. His back arched as he drove harder, deeper, striving to release his body from the torment. His hoarse cry mingled with hers, then finally, he was free, soaring with pounding heart and aching limbs to that moment of euphoria, before drifting with her to that quiet place where he could rest at last.

"Granger."

Corie's soft voice aroused him from a doze. How long had they been lying there, content in each other's arms? Some time, judging by the fading light and the growling in his stomach.

She must have read his thoughts, as she turned her head and gently nipped his shoulder with her teeth. "You hungry?"

"Yep." He cupped her breast, loving the soft weight of her warm flesh. Leaning over her, he gave her a firm kiss. "Ravenous, in fact."

"It's way past dinner time."

"I know. My stomach is reminding me of that."

"I can hear it." She sat up, pushing her silky hair off her face with both hands. "How about we order in a pizza?"

Puzzled by the unfamiliar term, he frowned. "Pizza? What's that?"

She burst out laughing. "You haven't lived until you've tasted pizza. I'll order it. What would you like on it?"

He fell back on the pillow with a mock groan of despair. "I don't even know what it is, much less what I want on it."

"Typical male." Lightly, she punched him on the arm. "All right, I'll order a supreme. That way you get a little of everything."

He watched her climb out of bed, his heart stirring at the sight of her naked body. She turned to look at him, laughing down at him with that mischievous look he found so appealing.

"Don't look so worried," she said, tugging the covers from his body. "You'll like it, I promise."

He sat up and made a grab for her, but she sidestepped out of his reach. "I'm going to put on some clothes and order the pizza. It will take about half an hour to get here so you have plenty of time to make yourself decent."

Blowing him a kiss she left the room, and he sat for a moment hugging his knees, his mind still spinning with the thrill of their passionate union.

How could he have lived so long and not known how beautiful lovemaking could be? How could he have lived so long without meeting a woman who could set him on fire the way Corie Trenton did so easily?

Perhaps it was just as well that he hadn't met her in his own time and world. If so, he would have had to make some difficult choices. As it was, the choices were already made. He wasn't surprised that the thought failed to comfort him.

Corie put down the phone, smiling in anticipation of Granger's reaction when she sat a pizza down in front of him. It was hard to imagine an adult never having seen one, let alone eat one. She couldn't wait to see his face.

Hearing him on the stairs, she turned to face him. He was wearing jeans and the dark blue shirt she'd bought for him. She'd pulled on white jeans herself, and added a denim, sleeveless shirt.

They looked like a typical modern American couple, she thought, watching him move toward her. Her gaze fell on his bare feet and she shook her head. "We have to get you some sneakers," she said, "you can't go around in bare feet, and those shoes you borrowed will look odd with jeans."

"I am going to look odd no matter what I wear when I return to the battlefield," Granger said grimly. "I'd like to know what they did with my clothes."

Corie stared at him. "I never thought about that. They have to be somewhere. I hardly think the scientists would destroy something of that value. I'll have to look for them when I go back on Monday, though I doubt they would risk keeping them in the lab."

"I don't want you taking any risks—"

She interrupted him with an impatient wave of her hand. "I know. I promise I'll be careful. But in any case, I wasn't talking about how you look when you go back."

Her pulse skipped as the thought hit her that she would look even more strange in her modern clothes. There wasn't a lot she'd be able to do about that.

Granger was looking at her with his familiar puzzled expression. "I don't understand."

For a moment she'd forgotten what it was she'd said. "Oh, I was talking about tomorrow. I have a surprise for you, but you'll need sneakers if you're going to walk the boardwalk with me."

"And what exactly is a boardwalk?" he asked carefully.

She grinned at him, pleased with her idea. "You'll see. The boardwalk is not exactly a modern invention, but what modern technology has put on it will grab your attention. I think you'll find it very intriguing."

Granger looked unconvinced. "What about the work on the house?"

"Never mind the work on the house. We've both earned a rest." Emphasizing her point, she flopped down on the couch. "Besides, you need to get outside and get some fresh air into your lungs. You'll need to be in excellent shape for your trip back."

He came and sat down beside her, his face creased in worry lines. "I thought we'd decided that it wouldn't be safe for me to go outside. What if someone sees me and recognizes me from the picture your Dr. Richards is passing around?"

"We won't be walking around this town. We're going to Wildwood, and it's at least six miles away. No one will think of looking for you there, and besides, there will be so many people, no one is likely to see you in that crowd. I'll buy you a baseball cap and sunglasses."

She laughed at his astonished expression. "You'll see tomorrow. Just trust me."

His face changed, registering a warmth that she could feel right down to her bones. "I do trust you, Corie. I don't know what I would have done without you. You are probably the only woman in my life I have ever been able to trust."

"Except for your mother." The words had slipped out before she'd given any thought to what she'd said. He'd told her he'd grown up without parents, for pity's sake. How could she have forgotten that? "I'm sorry," she said quickly, "that was incredibly thoughtless of me."

He reached for her hand, and rubbed his thumb across her fingers. "There's no need for an apology. I never knew my parents. From what I've been told, my mother died giving birth to me. I was her first child. Apparently my father drowned while attempting to cross a swollen river to find a doctor. I was taken into an orphanage and later sent to a military school. That's about all I know."

"Your parents didn't have any family?"

Granger shook his head. "According to the records, there were no living relatives to claim me. Or none that cared to take on the added responsibility of a baby."

Her heart ached for the lonely life he must have had. Lifting his hand to her mouth, she pressed a light kiss on the back of his fingers. "I'm sorry," she said softly.

"It wasn't a bad life. Military school was hard, but it taught me a lot of valuable lessons."

She studied his face, wishing she knew more about the kind of life he led. "Did you enjoy being a soldier?"

"It's all I've ever known, since I was old enough to handle a gun." He paused, obviously dwelling on the question. "I suppose I enjoy being important to someone," he added quietly. "I never had that as a child. I enjoy being responsible for the men in my command, of having someone look up to me for guidance and knowledge.''

''You must be very proud of what you've achieved.''

''Proud?'' he shrugged. ''If I'm proud of anything, it's the fact that my country relies on me to protect its people to the best of my ability, and to maintain the rights that we believe in.''

Tears dimmed her vision as she looked at him. ''That's an impressive testimonial,'' she said softly.

''This is an impressive country. No other country in the world offers the freedom that the American people enjoy. That kind of liberty is hard won and even harder to maintain. It is well worth fighting for. And dying for, as many men have proved.''

She felt her throat tighten. ''You'll be happy to know, that in spite of all the turmoil that this country has had to suffer over the past hundred years or so, and even though men are still dying to preserve those rights, that freedom still remains.''

His smile spread over his face. ''So I understand. Your newspaper is very informative. It's quite enlightening to read so much about foreign countries. There are many things I don't understand, and some of the phrases and descriptions I read muddle my mind, but underneath it all that one truth still stands out, as clearly defined as it was when the Declaration of Independence was first enacted. This country was, and still is, governed by the people.''

''And so it should be.'' She smiled, pleased by the thought. ''There might be a lot wrong with the way the country is run at times, but the basics haven't changed. That's really all we can ask for in this day and age.''

He looked at her, his smile in his eyes. ''You are a very intelligent woman, you know.''

She laughed, feeling a little self-conscious. ''I'm not sure I deserve that compliment. I'm just well-informed, that's all.

With all the media available to everyone today, there is no reason why everyone shouldn't at least know what is going on in the world.''

"But not everyone can analyze it the way you do, I'm sure."

"Thank you." She glanced up at the clock to avoid the awkward moment. "The pizza should be here any minute. Would you like a beer with it?"

"Beer? That sounds good." He looked around the kitchen, an expectant look on his face. "Where does the pizza come in?"

Now it was her turn to stare at him in puzzlement. "Come in?"

"I assume it arrives by some kind of machine. I just wondered which one."

She laughed, enjoying the idea. "God, I wish it did. No, I'm afraid we still have to do it by the old-fashioned method. I call the pizza shop, they send someone out in a car to deliver it."

"Hardly old-fashioned. If you want food in the house in my time, you have to prepare it yourself. No one will bring it to you unless it's a gathering of some kind where everyone's invited."

"Well, rest assured, no one is going to join us to eat this." She rose to her feet as the front doorbell rang. "And that should be our pizza."

Opening the door, she smiled at the young man who stood waiting with the flat square box in his hand. Thanking him, she handed over the bills, then carried the warm box back to the kitchen.

Granger's expression when she opened the box surpassed her expectations. Staring at the colorful mix of pepperoni, sausage, ham, green and red peppers, and a sprinkling of mushrooms, he muttered, "Great heavens, I've never seen anything like this in my life."

"Sit down and eat it before it gets cold," she told him, pulling the slices apart.

He sat down, watching her take a bite out of her slice before reaching for one himself.

Corie prepared to enjoy herself as she watched him tackle his first slice of pizza. A medley of expressions crossed his face while his jaws worked on the food.

Finally he swallowed the mouthful, and she leaned toward him. "So, how is it?"

"It tastes every bit as good as it smells."

"I told you you'd like it."

His answering smile warmed her. "So you did. But then I like everything you tell me. Everything you do. Everything you are."

She looked at him, her pizza forgotten. "Just wait until tomorrow," she said unsteadily. "You are going to love the boardwalk."

Early the next morning Corie awoke with a start, her mind instantly registering Granger's arm lying heavily across her waist. She lay still for a moment, enjoying the sweet intimacy of sharing her bed with the man she loved above everything else.

He lay still, his shoulders lifting evenly in his sleep, and after a while she slid out of bed, careful not to waken him. Drawing back the curtains, she looked out onto the tree-lined street, delighted to see the heavy clouds that had layered the sky the day before had disappeared, leaving behind a hazy blue sky.

Pleased at the prospect of good weather for their outing, Corie turned back to the bed. Granger lay watching her, his gray eyes narrowed against the sunlight. "Did I wake you?" she said quickly.

"I'm glad you did." He propped himself up on one elbow and blinked sleepily at her. "I wouldn't want to waste the vision of you wandering naked around the bedroom in front of my eyes."

She grinned at him, no longer self-conscious under his burning gaze. "It's getting to be a habit," she said, walking back to the bed.

"I like it."

Leaning across the pillow, she pressed a kiss to his mouth. Immediately he folded his arms around her, trapping her against the warm comfort of his body.

"We have to get up," Corie protested, trying to wriggle out of his grasp. "We have a long day ahead of us and I want to make the most of it."

"So do I." With a hand at the back of her head he pulled her mouth down to his. By the time he let her go she was breathless.

Looking down at him, she murmured, "I guess a few minutes won't make that much difference."

"That's what I wanted to hear." With a low growl he pulled her under the covers, and spent the next few minutes making her forget why she was in such a hurry to leave.

An hour or so later, Corie showed Granger how to fasten his seat belt, then switched on the ignition in her car, and did her best to reassure the apprehensive man seated next to her.

"I promise you, it's perfectly safe," she said, as she backed out onto the road. "No one will notice you in the car if you keep your head down, and I'll stop and get you a cap and sunglasses at the store, so no one will recognize you."

"I'm not so worried about someone seeing me," Granger said, holding on to the dashboard with both hands. "I'm more concerned about surviving the journey in this contraption."

She glanced at him, thinking he was joking. When she saw the bare bones of his knuckles sticking out from his clenched hands, she finished backing out, then brought the car to a halt. "I'm a good driver," she said, feeling a little put out by his lack of faith in her abilities.

"I've no doubt you are," Granger said, sitting back stiffly in his seat. "But this is my first time in one of these things. The speed is unbelievable. The fastest I've ever traveled is on the back of a horse, when I've been in full control of the animal."

"You've traveled a great deal faster than that," Corie said dryly. "Faster than anyone else in the world, in fact. I don't know of anyone else who has traveled through time."

He looked at her with a pained expression. "I was unconscious at the time. Right now I am fully awake, and just a little concerned about my safety."

Immediately she was contrite. "I'm sorry. You're right. Of course you're nervous. It must be like a first flight in space to you."

She waved a hand at the road ahead of her. "Look, everyone drives these things nowadays. It's quite safe, I promise you. It's no different really to riding in one of your carriages. I won't go any faster than we absolutely have to, if it will make you feel better."

"It will make me feel better," Granger said grimly.

She put the gear in Drive, and let off the brake. "You'll soon get used to it, I promise."

He nodded, in a tight-lipped way that told her he was unconvinced. Nervous herself now, she pulled out onto the road and set off at a snail's pace, conscious of Granger sitting tense and silent next to her.

They hadn't gone far before someone honked at them from behind. Granger shot up in his seat. "What was that?"

She was beginning to think she'd made a mistake bringing him out today. But he would have to survive the ride to Philadelphia, which promised to be far more hair-raising than this sleepy little town.

"It's just some impatient devil wanting me to go faster or let him pass," she said gently. "I'm sorry, Granger, but I really will have to speed up a little. We'll be at the store in a few minutes and you'll be able to relax for a while."

He sent her a look that was supposed to reassure her. "Please, don't let me hinder you. I am quite relaxed now. I'm even beginning to enjoy the experience."

Hoping he meant that, she carefully pressed down on the accelerator, and reached the magnificent speed of thirty miles per hour. Granger still seemed tense, but now he was looking around, his attention caught by what must seem very strange sights to him.

Answering his rapid-fire questions, Corie did her best to explain the various miracles of modern technology. She almost laughed at his bug-eyed expression when two young boys streaked down the sidewalk on skateboards, each of them executing a smart flip around at the curb in order to stop.

She was explaining the traffic lights system when three motorbikes passed them, the riders in black leather jackets and helmets leaning back in their seats, their feet encased in studded leather boots.

Right behind them a pickup truck, impatient at the delay, honked loudly, then cut in front of Corie to get around the bikes.

She slammed her foot on the brake, and Granger jerked forward with a muffled exclamation. "How in the hell do you all miss each other?" he muttered, righting himself.

"Mostly skill and paying attention," she said cheerfully, pulling around a delivery van double-parked in the street.

"I would say it's more likely divine providence." Granger closed his eyes as she pulled into the parking lot of the grocery store, narrowly missing a car backing out of the aisle.

"Believe me," Corie said, as she shut off the engine, "by the time we get home you'll be as comfortable with this as you are on your horse."

"I seriously doubt it." He looked so rattled she couldn't resist leaning over to give him a quick kiss.

"Hunch down on the seat," she said, "just in case anyone should be snooping around. I won't be more than a few minutes."

He nodded, looking quite relieved to be stationary for the time being.

Corie hurried into the store, uneasy at the thought of leaving Granger out there in full view of anyone passing by. Hopefully it was still too early for most people to be about. And it was unlikely that anyone from the lab would choose that particular moment to visit the grocery store. Even so, she couldn't dismiss the possibility of some chance coincidence.

Seeing the lengthy line at the checkout counter, her uneasiness intensified. She could only hope that Granger stayed out of sight until she got back.

The shoe department was at the far end of the store, and she hurried over there, anxious now to get her errand over with and get back to the car.

It would have been fun to bring Granger into the store, she thought, as she sorted through the rack of men's sneakers. He would have been fascinated by the variety of unfamiliar objects on display.

She found a pair of inexpensive shoes in the same size as those he'd 'borrowed.' After all, she thought, he wouldn't be needing them for long. She tried to ignore her little quiver of apprehension when she thought about the trip.

For this day, at least, she wanted to forget about the uncertain future. This day would belong to her and Granger, and nothing was going to spoil it for them. Not if she could help it. It would be all they had of this time together.

Carrying the shoes, she picked out a pair of sunglasses for him, then hurried over to the sports department for the baseball hat.

She found one with a Phillies emblem on the front, and as an afterthought, she chose a light Windcheater jacket from the rack. The maroon shirt he was wearing with his jeans might not be warm enough in the stiff breeze from the ocean.

Standing in line at the checkout counter, Corie tried to decide what would be best for her to wear when she joined Granger on his journey back through time. Nothing she had would exactly fit in with the clothes the women wore then.

Concentrating on the problem, she moved slowly forward. Perhaps she could persuade one of the photo booths to sell her an outfit. They had plenty of old-fashioned clothes for their customers to pose in while they took a picture of them.

Still deep in thought, Corie approached the checker. She laid her purchases on the counter, and rummaged in her purse for her credit card. She almost dropped the purse when she heard a voice behind her speak her name.

Twisting her head, she felt a jolt of dismay when she saw Helen Grant, Dr. Richards's secretary, grinning at her. Hastily handing over her card to the checker, Corie edged sideways to screen the counter. Helen knew Corie didn't have a man in her life. She didn't want to have to explain the baseball cap and sneakers.

Casually chatting with the older woman, Corie felt distinctly uncomfortable when she saw the secretary's inquisitive eyes peering past her shoulder. Raising her voice, she did her best to keep the other woman's attention on her.

"I hear you're leaving," Corie announced, fixing a bland smile on her face. "Are you retiring?"

Helen's eyes snapped back to Corie's face. "Leaving? Who told you that?"

At least the outrageous lie had grabbed her attention, Corie thought, praying that the checker would get a move on and ring up her purchases.

"I don't remember who told me." Corie pretended to think. "I think I heard about it in the lunchroom."

"Well, whoever told you that is lying." Helen's eyes narrowed. "Unless they know something I don't know. Who was it, do you remember?"

Corie shook her head. "Sorry. But I wouldn't worry. It's probably only a rumor."

"That's the trouble with that place. Too many rumors flying around." Helen lowered her voice. "Why, only the other day I heard that someone stole Professor Butler's clothes and made off with them. Can you imagine? If I was going to steal someone's clothes, I sure as hell wouldn't have chosen Professor Butler. Now if it had been Dr. Richards—"

"That'll be $48.30," the checker stated loudly.

Corie wanted very much to know where Helen had heard that particular rumor. By the time she'd finished with the checker, however, Helen had said goodbye and left. Maybe it was just as well, Corie thought as she hurried out of the store. She didn't want to arouse suspicion by asking too many questions.

The car was where Corie had left it, and the top of Granger's dark head could just be seen above the level of the window.

With a rush of relief, Corie sped across the parking lot and opened the car door.

Granger sat up immediately, his eyes wary on her face. "Is it all clear?"

She nodded, "All clear. But I'll feel better when you're wearing these." She dumped the sack in his lap then went around to her side of the car. After settling herself on the seat, she watched Granger take each article out of the sack and examine it.

He turned the cap over in his hands, looking at it from all angles. "So this is what the well-dressed man of today is wearing," he muttered. He gave her a questioning look. "Phillies?"

She nodded. "Baseball team. They play for Philadelphia."

"Philadelphia has its own baseball team?"

Corie nodded. "I think you'd better prepare yourself for a shock when we get there," she said slowly. "Philadelphia has gone through some changes since you last saw it."

He looked solemn for a moment. "I imagine it has." He pulled the baseball hat onto his head. "How does it look?"

"Not bad." Reaching up with both hands she gave it a tug and bent the peak a little. "There, that's better. You look like a Phillies fan now."

"I know about baseball, but I've never heard of the Phillies."

She shook her head at him in mock despair. "No pizza. No Phillies. You have been sadly deprived, Granger Deene."

"I most certainly have." He gave her a suggestive leer. "I'm just beginning to find out how much."

"Put the sunglasses on," she said primly. "You're distracting me."

He fitted the glasses on his nose. "I'm not surprised so many people wear these things. They certainly take the glare out of the sunlight. I like them." He turned his face for her inspection.

"Very nice," she said, grinning at him. "Now you really look the part. Try the shoes."

He did so, assuring her they were a lot more comfortable than the shoes he'd confiscated from the scientist. He seemed really pleased with the jacket, which was a light gray to match his eyes.

"I always keep one in the car myself," she told him. "Just in case."

"I really like this," he said, fingering the fabric. "What kind of material is this?"

"A blend of cotton and an invention you won't have heard of. It's a synthetic fabric called polyester," she said, as she started the engine. "And the jacket is shower proof."

"Shower proof?"

She glanced over at him before pulling away out of the parking space. "It means the fabric will repel water. At least drops of water. You'll probably get wet in a real downpour."

Seeing his look of amazement, she added, "You'll see. I just bought it to give you some extra warmth. It could be cool on the boardwalk."

She didn't know what made her look up into her rearview mirror. Maybe some sixth sense had warned her. For as she paused at the curb before pulling out onto the street, she saw Helen Grant standing just a few feet away, her eyes fixed with great interest on Granger's face.

Chapter 10

Corie tried to put the vision of Helen Grant out of her mind as she drove into Wildwood a short time later. Helen was a gossip, but Corie doubted if the secretary would talk to her boss about his assistant's private life. At least, she hoped Helen had more sense.

Cars jammed the streets as they drew closer to the boardwalk. Teenagers darted across in front of Corie, causing her to keep one foot hovering over the brake. Granger seemed to have relaxed after his initial uneasiness, and sat watching the chaos of people and vehicles with a look of disbelief on his face.

"We should find a parking spot soon," Corie said, scanning the side streets that led to the beach. "We can park anywhere along the boardwalk, and the tramcar will take us where we want to go."

"Tramcar?"

She flashed him a quick smile. "You'll see. Ah, there's a spot."

Quickly she pulled into the space before the red sports car behind her could beat her to it. "Okay," she said cheerfully, "we're here. Now let's go and have some fun."

Granger looked as if he wasn't too sure he wanted to have fun, but obediently, he took off his sunglasses and clambered out of the car.

The clamor of music and raised voices almost drowned out his words when he spoke. "They make a worse noise than a battlefield."

She pulled a face. "You'll get used to it. Are you warm enough?"

He nodded, his gaze on the throng milling back and forth at the top of the steps.

Deciding to leave the jackets behind, Corie led the way up the steps to the crowded boardwalk. When they reached the top, she paused, watching Granger's face as he took in the scene.

Ahead of them, the beach stretched down to the sea in a golden expanse of sand. On their left a pier reached out to the ocean, and on the very end of it a huge Ferris wheel slowly revolved, its garish painted sides gleaming in the sunlight.

Granger seemed transfixed, unable to tear his gaze away from the strange spectacle. Corie touched his arm and pointed across the beach to their right. Almost at the edge of the waves, another pier supported several large iron frames, from the top of which figures could be seen flinging themselves into midair, only to be jerked up again just when it seemed they would crash to earth.

"Bungee jumpers," Corie explained, as Granger's face blanched. "It's quite safe."

He looked down at her with a dazed expression that made her feel sorry for him. "It depends on what you consider safe," he said. "Frankly, I would rather face a line of enemy rifles than venture anywhere near those iron monsters."

"I've got to get that expression on your face." Corie opened her purse and took out her camera. "Stand over there and don't smile."

Granger gave the camera a suspicious look. "What are you doing?"

"I'm taking your picture," she explained. "At least, I will, if you stand still for a moment."

"That's a camera?"

She nodded, lifting it up for him to see.

He shook his head. "And you're going to tell me that the picture comes out of it already developed?"

"How'd you guess?" Seeing his expression, she laughed. "Not this one, no. But there are cameras like that. I just don't like the quality of the pictures. And it's expensive to make copies."

He stood with his back to the sea, staring at the camera as she snapped his picture, as if expecting something to jump out of it. He seemed almost disappointed when she lowered her hands.

"You want to try it?" she asked, handing him the camera.

He took it from her eagerly, and she explained how to focus and where to press the button.

The pier seemed to provide a good backdrop, and she positioned herself to be sure it would appear in the picture. Granger took a long time focusing, but finally announced he was ready.

Corie put everything into the smile she gave him. They wouldn't have too many pictures of each other, and she wanted to keep the memories of this special time always fresh in her mind.

"I have been fascinated by the idea of photography ever since I heard about it," Granger remarked, as he handed the camera back to her. "It's a fairly new concept in my time."

"I'll get these developed at a one-hour shop, so you won't have to wait to see the results of your handiwork." Tucking her hand in his elbow, she added, "Now, come on. Put your sunglasses back on and let's go. In the words of a famous singer, 'You ain't seen nothing yet.'"

She led him along the boardwalk, enjoying the experience in a way she never had before. Seeing it through his eyes was like seeing it for the first time, and his reaction to everything was a joy to watch.

Wearing the baseball cap, his eyes hidden behind his sunglasses, he looked far less formidable. He seemed to be enjoying himself, strolling along with her hand tucked in his arm, making her laugh with his vivid comments that brought the volatile scenes to life.

She took him along the pier, watching his horrified expression as the cars hurtled around the steep bends and sheer drops of the roller coaster.

After watching the cars twist upside down, leaving the riders dangling for the space of a second or two, he turned to Corie. "And they call this fun?"

"They most certainly do." She winced as the ear-splitting shrieks drowned out her voice. Tugging his arm, she dragged him away from the roller coaster to a quieter part of the pier.

Catching sight of a sign posted above a huge swimming pool, she paused. "This is more our speed," she said, pointing at the sign.

Granger peered at it. "Rapid Waters," he read out. "What's that?"

"It's very relaxing. You'll enjoy it." She grabbed his hand and pulled him toward the ticket booth.

Granger shot an apprehensive glance behind him at the roller coaster. "Wait a minute. I'm not going to be flung into the sea, am I?"

Corie laughed. "I don't like being thrown around either. I promise you, this is very calm and peaceful."

"And safe," Granger said dryly.

"And safe."

"I wonder why that doesn't reassure me."

Ignoring his comment, she pulled him down the stairs and past the swimming pool to where two young men in wet suits stood chest deep in swirling water.

They were helping people into inflated dinghies, handing them paddles, then pushing them out into the water where the current took the craft beneath a low bridge and out of sight.

"There," Corie said, pausing at the end of the line of chattering teens. "That's all it is. The current takes the boat along a canal that twists and turns around the pier and ends up back here. You even have paddles to guide it if you want."

"If I remember," Granger said, taking off his sunglasses to look at her, "rapids are where the river tumbles down the rocks at great speed, smashing anything that gets caught up in it."

"That's just the name they give this ride," Corie assured him. "I promise you, no rapids."

"No rapids." He gave her a long look, then smiled. "I trust you."

He squeezed her fingers, still caught in his grasp, and she wondered why the simple gesture could make her feel so warm and weak inside. Soon, she promised herself, she would tell him about her decision to return with him. When the time was right.

Granger appeared to enjoy the boat ride, and allowed Corie to take another picture of him struggling with the paddle. Though he complained afterward about getting his seat wet.

Corie laughed as he pulled the damp fabric away from his skin. "Too bad we don't have time to go to a water park," she told him. "That's where you really get wet."

She took him to see the log flume, and was relieved when he declined to go on the ride, saying he was quite wet enough. She was intrigued when he paused at a shooting gallery, where several people were trying to win an enormous stuffed bear.

Watching them aim water pistols into the mouths of plastic clowns, he seemed fascinated by the model planes that were driven up the board, until one reached the top accompanied by a red light and a loud clanging of a bell.

"Here," Corie said, laying a bill on the counter, "you try it. You should be an expert with a gun."

"I've never seen a gun that looks like that," Granger said, but after a moment's hesitation, he swung a leg over the stool and sat down.

Sandwiched between a large woman who seemed intent on nudging him out of the way and a gangly teenager whose jaws worked earnestly on a wad of chewing gum, Granger concentrated on his aim and waited for the starter's signal. Several minutes later Corie held three miniature versions of the large bear.

"Enough," she said, when Granger looked as if he would sit there all day. "Give someone else a chance."

He looked disappointed, but climbed out of his seat. "I wanted the big bear," he said, as they walked away.

"I don't think we'd get it in the car," she said, tucking the bears under her arm. "Besides, I like small bears."

He seemed disturbed by something, and thinking he might have resented her dragging him away from something he was enjoying, Corie said tentatively, "We could go back if you really want the bear."

He smiled down at her, with a quick shake of his head. "I wanted it for you. I feel very uncomfortable though, watching you spend your money when I don't have any to pay you back."

She stopped, standing in front of him so she could look up into his face. "Granger, I don't want to hear another word. You have saved me a fortune by working on my house, and you have more than earned this day out. I'm the one who owes you a salary for all that work."

He lifted his hand and drew his finger down her cheek. "I'm not going to need money if I can get back. I can't spend your money back there."

And neither could she, Corie thought, with a shiver of apprehension. But that was something she'd worry about later. "Then please stop worrying about spending it now," she said firmly. "Speaking of which, let's find something to eat. I'm starving."

By the end of the day, they'd had their fill. Granger had enjoyed his first cheese steak, his first frozen banana, and probably his last foot-long hot dog, judging by his face when he ate it. The candy floss Corie bought for him intrigued him, and he'd declared it the best treat of the day.

Arriving back at the house, he sank down on the couch with a satisfied sigh. "That was, without a doubt, the most fascinating, enjoyable day of my life."

Corie laughed down at him as he yawned. "You'll probably sleep like a baby tonight. No bad dreams."

He looked up at her suddenly serious. "I haven't had any dreams since I've been sharing your bed."

"I don't think they were dreams." She sat down next to him and leaned into him as he put his arm around her. "I think it was your memory struggling to repair itself after those heathens had done their best to destroy it."

He was silent for a moment, then said quietly, "Corie, I'm very concerned for your safety. After I leave, I mean. I'm afraid they might harm you in some way."

She tried to sound unconcerned when she answered him. "The scientists? No, I don't think so. There would be too many questions asked. The worst thing they could do is fire me."

"But then you would be without work, or money to finish the house. How would you live?"

Now was the time, she decided. There wasn't going to be a better time. She took in a deep breath, then said casually, "I won't need a job. Or the house."

She felt him tense at her side. "What do you mean?"

"I mean I'm coming with you."

The pause seemed to go on forever. Then he sat up, and turned her to face him. "You can't do that, Corie."

She stared into his eyes, striving to read his mind. Hoping he meant those words literally, she said quickly, "I don't know for sure, but it should work. That's if it works at all. But if we both stand inside the rays of the beam, we should either be zapped back to the past together, or at the very least we'll both end up in the same place, wherever or whenever it is."

He didn't answer her, but she could see the struggle going on in his eyes. Something told her she didn't want to know what it was he was trying to tell her.

"Of course," she went on desperately, "it might not work at all, and neither of us will go anywhere."

"Corie..." He stopped, then started again. "It's one thing to come here from there. Quite another to reverse the situation. I look around here—" he waved a hand around the room "—and I see nothing but improvement in the way you live, the way you eat, everything about your life."

He got up abruptly from the couch and crossed over to the fireplace. It seemed to be his favorite place when he needed to think. Once more he stood there, his arm on the mantelpiece, staring down into the empty grate.

Corie wondered if he imagined the flames of a fire there, and why that particular image seemed to bring him comfort. He must have stared into a lot of fires in his life, both on the battlefield and off it.

"If you went back with me," he said, after another long pause, "life would be very different, in every way imaginable. You would not be able to do the work you do now. In fact, it would be extremely difficult for you to work at all. You would have to wear clothes that hamper your movement, cook food on wood stoves, travel miles in a horse-drawn vehicle to shop for food."

"I know," Corie said quietly. "I've considered all that."

"There are no machines, no cars, no television. The only music you will hear is what you make yourself, unless you know someone else who can play a musical instrument. Your entertainment will be little more than reading, or the occasional barn dance or county fair. Certainly nothing remotely like the sights we've seen today."

Corie got up and went over to him. Placing her hand on his bowed shoulder, she said carefully, "Granger, I do know what it was like then. I've studied the period. I've seen pictures, I know what to expect. But what I'll be doing is no more than the pioneers did then, when they left their comfortable homes behind and traveled for long, hard months in wagon trains to begin a new life."

He didn't answer and she felt a knot of depression forming under her ribs. Afraid she was losing the argument, she added, "They faced untold hardships when they reached their destinations, if they ever reached them. But they believed in what they were doing, and they were willing to make sacrifices. I believe in what I want to do. I want to go with you. I have nothing here to keep me."

"Yes, you do." His harsh voice made her jump. He turned to look at her, and his eyes were as cool as a frosty morning. "You have a life, a job you enjoy, a house you love, a future to look forward to. I can't give you any of those things."

Her pride kicked in and she lifted her chin. "I'm not asking you to. I am independent, I can take care of myself."

"The battlefield is no place for a woman. That's where you'd end up if we landed back at the same place."

She stared at him, wondering how she could make him see that nothing mattered to her except being with him. That as long as they were together, they could work out the problems somehow. He was just trying to protect her, she told herself. He was afraid for her.

For a long time he met her gaze, then his face softened. "Corie," he said gently. "You must try to understand. I am a military man. It isn't just a job to me, it's a way of life. It's what I am. It would be hard enough for you to adjust to that life even if I was with you all the time. But you would be alone, and unprepared for the hardships you would face. I can't let you go."

He was right. Deep down she knew he was right. But part of her didn't want him to be practical. Part of her wanted him to beg her to go with him, wanted him to tell her he couldn't live without her, as surely as she knew she could never be happy without him.

But then he had never told her he loved her. Neither of them had talked about love. Perhaps the distance between them was much more than a matter of time. At least in his eyes.

Swallowing past the lump in her throat, she managed to keep her voice steady as she answered him. "It's all right, Granger, I understand. And you are right. It would be very stupid of me to leave all this. It really is a pretty good life."

Turning away from him, she blinked back a threatening tear. "Don't worry about me getting into trouble. If they find out what I did and tackle me about it, I'll just pretend I have no idea what they're talking about. They can't prove I had anything to do with it."

He moved swiftly, coming up behind her to pull her into his arms. His kiss was long and sweet, and it seemed as if things were good between them again. But she was aware now of an underlying tension that hadn't been there before, and she knew he felt it, too.

Lying in his arms that night, long after he'd fallen asleep, she felt the full force of the pain that would be with her as long as she lived. These precious hours were all she would ever have of him. And the memories. The bittersweet memories that would haunt her throughout this life and beyond.

They worked together on the decorating the next day, not wanting to be out of each other's sight, yet needing the work to keep their minds off the fast approaching moment they would have to part.

On Monday morning, Corie left the house with an aching heart, knowing she still had two long days to get through at the lab before leaving for Gettysburg on the Wednesday morning.

She planned to call in sick that morning, and take off the rest of the week. She would need the long weekend. She would have to get herself together enough to go back to work the following Monday, knowing that Granger would not be there waiting for her when she got home that night.

That's if she still had a job. Though she couldn't help thinking that Granger's fears were groundless. No one knew at this point that she had any idea Granger Deene existed.

The memory of Helen Grant standing in the parking lot bothered her for no more than a moment. If Helen asked questions, she'd come up with some answers.

After dropping off the film at the camera store, she walked briskly to the lab, determined to put her worries behind her, at least for the day.

It was halfway through the morning when she remembered Granger's clothes. It didn't seem likely that they would be there at her lab, more than likely they had been kept at the headquarters in Philadelphia.

Still, she had promised to try to find them, and she would at least make the attempt, even though Granger didn't want her taking risks. It would be the last thing she could do for him, always supposing her theory about Specturne worked.

She tried not to think about the selfish part of her that wanted the plan to fail. Granger was right, history couldn't be changed. He had to go back. What really hurt was the niggling suspicion that even it if hadn't been so imperative for him to return, he would have made the same choice.

As he kept telling her, he was an army man, and his duty and his life belonged to the cavalry. That was why no woman had ever held him, nor ever would.

Impatient with herself, Corie left her desk and walked down to the lunchroom. Maybe coffee and a doughnut would help her banish her depressing thoughts, she told herself, as she entered the quiet room.

Two men sat at a table in the corner, engaged in earnest discussion. Corie's pulse jumped when she recognized Dr. Richards and Dr. Spencer. Their voices were lowered, and they were so engrossed in their conversation they didn't see Corie walk into the room.

Corie eyed the steaming cups of coffee on the table between them. It looked as if they had just sat down. That might give her enough time to check out their offices. If the clothes were anywhere, they would most likely be hanging in the personal closet in one of the offices.

Silently, Corie turned and crept out of the room. Speeding down the hallway, she prayed no one would see her. She didn't want to have to explain why she was snooping around the chief scientist's office without his knowledge.

Just in case Helen should be in there, Corie tapped on the door of Richards's office. Receiving no answer, she opened the door and peeked in. The room was empty.

Stepping inside, she closed the door behind her, then darted across to the closet in the corner of the room. Grasping the handle, she tried to turn it, letting out a grunt of frustration when she realized it was locked.

If Richards hadn't taken the key with him, it would most likely be in his desk drawer, she decided, crossing the room again. The drawer slid open silently, revealing its contents. A yellow pad, several pens, rubber bands, a worn eraser, paper clips, staples and two keys.

Corie snatched them both up and darted across the floor again. The first key was too large for the lock, and it took her several precious seconds to exchange the keys and fit the second one. It slid inside the lock and turned.

Holding her breath, she eased the door open. A raincoat hung in the closet, next to a propped up umbrella. That was all.

Her hopes dashed, Corie cursed under her breath. She would have to look in Spencer's office. She closed the door hurriedly, and locked it before returning the key to the drawer. She was halfway across the room when she heard the voices outside.

"I'll see you tonight, then," Spencer's gruff voice said from the other side of the door.

"Midnight, no later," Richards answered.

Corie sent a wild glance around the room, trying frantically to think of a good excuse for being in the office. She could see no way to avoid being seen. Her only chance was to bluff her way out. And Dr. Boyd Richards did not fool easily.

Swallowing hard, she stood by the desk and tried her damnedest not to look guilty as the door opened and Richards's gaunt figure stalked into the room.

His start of surprise at seeing her was comical, and Corie felt a crazy urge to laugh. Suppressing the nervous impulse, she said brightly, "Oh, there you are, Dr. Richards. I got a message to come to your office, but you weren't here, so I thought I'd wait."

"A message?" His eyes narrowed as he stared at her. "Who gave you the message?"

"I don't really know. It came up on my computer." She stared up at him with what she hoped was an innocent expression. "You mean you didn't send me a message?"

"I most certainly did not."

Edging past him toward the door, Corie shrugged. "Either someone's playing games, or the message was sent to the wrong person. That's the problem with computers, it's so easy to key in the wrong code."

She flashed him a quick smile, her heart skipping when he continued to stare at her with a suspicious frown. "Well, that was a complete waste of my time. Just when I have loads of work to get through. I'm sorry to have bothered you, Dr. Richards. I'll get back to my desk now."

Before he could answer, she slipped out of the room and flew down the hallway to her office. Once inside she flopped down on her chair, holding a hand over her pounding heart. That was close. Too close.

It might be better to forget about finding Granger's clothes. In any case, it would be difficult carrying them out of the building, even if she did manage to find them. Granger would just have to go in modern clothes. Hopefully she could find an outfit in a thrift store that would work. From what he had told her, the jeans and flannel shirt he'd been wearing as a disguise should be easy to duplicate.

The ache spread quickly, so intense she wrapped her arms around her body in an attempt to ease it. Someday, she told herself, all this would seem like a dream. Someday it would stop hurting.

At least, for now, she had the comfort of knowing she still had some time with him. A few more precious hours into which she would have to cram a lifetime of loving. The thought did little to cheer her.

The hours seemed to creep by that afternoon, and more than once she found herself staring aimlessly at the clock, instead of concentrating on her work. Somehow the fascination had gone out of it, and she wondered if she would ever feel the same about her job.

Every time she saw a mention of Specturne in the future, or any other wayward star for that matter, she would think of Granger, and wonder how he was doing.

There was another possibility that she hadn't allowed herself to think about as yet. But she had to face it sooner or later.

The Battle of Gettysburg was the bloodiest and most costly battle of the Civil War. It was entirely possible that Granger might not survive the fighting. Or even if he did, he might not survive the war.

And she would never know. That made it worse, the not knowing. If she knew for certain he was dead, she could mourn for him, and then close her mind forever to the chance of ever seeing him again.

But not knowing what had happened to him, whether he had lived or died, without the comfort of knowing he was reasonably happy, safe and well, that was going to be the hardest part to bear.

But, she told herself grimly, as she cleared her desk for the day, bear it she must. Corie had no choice but to go on without him. And she would not spoil her last few hours with him moping over what might have been.

Granger was eagerly waiting for her when she got back to the house later. No sooner was she inside the door, with it firmly closed behind her, than he pulled her into his arms and kissed her hungrily, his body already eager for her.

Corie closed her mind to the dismal thoughts that had plagued her all day, and clung to him with a fervor that matched his own.

"God, how I missed you today," he whispered in her hair, as he led her down the hallway with his arm around her. "I managed to get a great deal of work done, though. It was the only way I could keep my mind from dwelling on you."

"I'm glad someone did," Corie said, laughing up at him. "I didn't get a stick of work done. I just couldn't concentrate."

He paused in the doorway to the living room, his hands on her shoulders. Looking down at her with a grave expression, he asked quietly, "Are you all right?"

She nodded, fighting back the unexpected tears that threatened. "Of course I am. And I'm hungry. I'll feel a good deal better when we've eaten."

"Can we order in some pizza?"

She burst out laughing. "Oh, Granger, how I'm corrupting you. What kind of food are you used to eating?"

He shrugged, following her into the living room. "Mostly chicken or beef stews, when I'm in town. We don't get much meat on the battlefield . . . strips of dried beef, the occasional slice of salted ham . . . lots of beans. Never in my life have I eaten the kind of food I've enjoyed here."

Corie shook her head. "No wonder you like my cooking. Anything would taste good after that diet."

"No, not anything." He stood in front of her, his finger tracing down her cheek. "No one has ever prepared a meal for me with such loving care as you do, my sweet Corie."

"Well, I can't be doing that great a job, since you prefer to order in pizza than eat my lovingly prepared dinner."

He bent his head and left a lingering kiss on her mouth. "I was simply trying to save you work. You look tired."

She smiled up at him, warmed by his concern. "I'll make a deal. We order pizza tonight, and tomorrow, our last night here in this house, I'll cook you a dinner that will knock your socks off."

His eyes lit up. "That, sweet lady, is a deal. Now come with me, I want to show you what I've accomplished today."

He led her upstairs, then made her close her eyes while he led her into the bedroom. "All right, you can look now," he told her, after turning her to face in the right direction.

She opened her eyes, crying out when she saw the finished room. It looked far better than she had ever envisioned. Tiny yellow roses tumbled down the walls in even stripes, while pale green ferns twisted lovingly between them. A golden frieze bordered the walls below the pale green ceiling.

The same gold shade gleamed on the woodwork of the window frame and the door, spreading a feeling of cozy warmth throughout the room. The entire effect was faintly Victorian, yet far brighter than the somber shades so beloved by homeowners of a hundred years ago.

"It's beautiful," Corie said, no longer able to hide the tears. "You have done an incredible job. This will be my favorite room." Her heart ached at the thought of entering that room through the long years ahead, with the constant evidence of his touch everywhere she looked.

"I wanted to give back to you in some small way everything you have given to me." Granger looked around the room with pride on his face. "I wanted to put the same loving care into this as you have put into everything. I wanted to leave a small part of me behind, so that you will never forget me."

She was crying now, helplessly, with the ragged sobs of a wounded child. "How can I ever forget you, Granger? You have given me more joy these past few days than I have known in a lifetime. I'll never forget you. Or stop thinking about you."

He gathered her into his arms and held her close, his hand clasping the back of her head. "I am sorry, Corie. I wish with all my heart that things could be different. I wish I could make you understand why I have to go back . . . why I cannot turn my back on my duty to my country."

"I do understand," Corie whispered, trying her best to control her ridiculous outburst. "I just have trouble dealing with it, that's all." She sniffed, and drew back, searching in her pocket for a tissue. "I'm being childish, I know. I'm better now. Just ignore this, okay?"

With a sigh, he placed his warm palms on either side of her tear-stained face and tilted her chin up. "Perhaps one day we shall meet again, Corie. Maybe not in this world, but in the world hereafter. Somewhere inside the gates of heaven, if God is kind to us, we will once more hold each other as we are now. Until then, my sweet Corie, promise me you will remember me, as I shall remember you."

She managed to smile at him through her tears. "Always, Granger. Always." How she longed to tell him she loved him. But that would only deepen his remorse and she could not do that to him. He couldn't help the kind of man he was. And she could feel nothing but pride for a man who cared so deeply for his country, who was so completely committed to the cause, that he was incapable of giving anything more.

Dashing away the spilled tears with the back of her hand, she said with a determined smile, "Now, how about that pizza?"

Granger caught a stray tear with his thumb, gently brushing it from her face. "That sounds like a good idea."

Pulling away from him, she crossed the room to the phone. "I could always order you a cheese steak if you prefer, seeing as how you devoured that one yesterday...." She paused in the middle of the room. "The pictures!"

Granger gave her a questioning look.

"I forgot to pick up the pictures." Corie glanced at the clock. "I'll order the pizza, if that's what you want, then I'll go and pick up the photos. I should be back by the time the pizza gets here."

Granger looked worried. "What if you're not?"

"Don't worry. I'll give you the money and you can just hand it to him when he gives you the pizza." She picked up the phone and looked at him. "Pizza or cheese steak?"

"Pizza." He moved closer to her and put his arm around her. "The kind we had the other night."

Turning her face up for his kiss, she closed her eyes briefly with the bittersweet pain. "Supreme it is."

She gave the order, then replaced the receiver, saying, "I'll just run down and get the pictures. I won't be more than a few minutes."

She picked up her purse and pulled some bills from her wallet. "Here, just give him this if he gets here before I get back."

Granger took the bills. "I hope it doesn't get cold before you can eat it."

"It won't." She paused in the doorway and looked back at him. "Just don't start eating until I get back. I want at least one slice of it." Laughing at his offended expression, she let herself out of the front door.

The camera store was still open when she reached it. She hurried inside and handed the somber young man behind the counter her receipt. Excited now to see the results, she could hardly wait until the fat packet was in her hands.

Returning to the car, she decided to hold on to her patience until she got back to the house. She and Granger should see the pictures together. She couldn't wait to see his face when he saw the very first photo of himself.

The pizza still hadn't arrived when she got back, and she sat down on the couch with Granger beside her, full of excited anticipation.

Drawing the first picture from the envelope, she studied it quickly, delighted to see the intrigued look on Granger's face as he gazed at the camera.

"Here," she said, handing it to him. "Now you have to agree, you look just like a Phillies fan."

His astonished expression was everything she could have wished for. He stared at the picture for so long, she couldn't help teasing him.

"For heaven's sake, Granger, you're not that fascinating."

He looked up, his smile spreading over his face. "This is unbelievable. Look how clear it is. You can even see the foam on the waves as they break. It looks so real."

"It is real." She handed him the next picture, looking at it over his shoulder as he held it. "There, you see? You can see everything that was on the pier behind me."

Granger shook his head. "Beautiful," he murmured.

She wished she knew if he meant her or the pier. "It is a pretty good picture of me," she said smugly. "You did a good job. Usually I don't—"

She broke off, leaning closer to get a better look. With a muffled exclamation, she took the picture from his hand and peered even closer. She hadn't been mistaken.

Her blood ran cold as she stared at the figure half-hidden in the background behind a group of young girls. It was Helen Grant, and she was staring straight at the camera...and Granger.

Chapter 11

Corie's mind raced with possibilities. It was too much of a coincidence to expect to see Helen Grant in both places. For her to be in that precise spot as they were, at the same time, Helen would have had to follow the car. Which meant that Dr. Richards's secretary had more than a passing interest in Corie's passenger.

Helen must have seen the photo of him that Dr. Richards had taken. Corie inwardly cursed herself. Why hadn't she thought about that before? Of course the scientist would have shown his secretary the picture, probably giving her the same story of wanting to surprise his friend.

Granger must have sensed Corie's distress. He leaned over to look at the picture again. "Is something wrong?"

"Yes," Corie said unsteadily. "Something is very wrong." She pointed with a shaking finger at the blurry figure. "That woman there, with the red hair. She is Dr. Richards's secretary."

Granger drew in a sharp breath. "You're sure?"

"I'm sure." She looked up at him. "I think she recognized you."

"It could just be coincidence. There were a lot of people there."

"I don't think so." Corie looked at him unhappily. "I saw her earlier, Saturday morning, when we were at the store. She saw me at the checkout and could have seen the men's sneakers and baseball cap."

Granger pursed his lips. "You think she followed us." It was more a statement than a question.

"Yes, I do. I also think it's possible she has told Dr. Richards—" She paused, suddenly remembering something. *I'll see you tonight.* And the reply. *Midnight, no later.*

"What is it?" Granger asked sharply.

Corie didn't answer, her mind grappling with the implications of that terse exchange. Vaguely, she heard Granger repeat his question.

"Corie, what is it?"

"We have to leave here tonight," she said slowly.

"Tonight? But I thought—"

Quickly, she told him what she'd overheard that morning. "I think they are planning on coming here tonight," she finished, surging to her feet. "We can't wait around for them, Granger. We have to head for Philadelphia tonight."

The expression in his eyes mirrored her own despair. He stood, reaching for her, and she went into his arms, burying her face against the soft fabric of his shirt.

They stood like that for several moments, just holding, comforting, each taking strength from the other. Then the doorbell rang, jangling in the silence like a clarion of doom.

With a gasp, Corie pulled away from Granger, her heart pounding.

"Pizza," Granger said softly. "I'll get it."

He went out into the hallway, and Corie called after him. "Granger, be careful. Look through the peephole first."

Too late, she realized he had no idea what the peephole was. Holding her breath, she heard the door open, then Granger's deep voice thanking someone for the pizza.

She let out her breath, her mind once more racing with the details crowding her mind. They had until midnight. That gave them about five hours. She would have to pack a few things and get some cash.

There was no point in calling in sick at the lab, now that the scientists knew she was helping Granger. She would simply have to deal with that when she got back. Always supposing they didn't catch up with her before then.

Granger came back into the living room, carrying the pizza. His face looked set, and she could see the signs of strain. She felt a rush of concern for him as she took the pizza from him. She loved him, and although she had told him she understood, deep down she wished he had loved her enough to stay. But right now he must be going through hell, wondering what was going to happen to him.

She put the pizza down on the coffee table and held out her arms. "Try not to worry," she said softly. "I'm sure everything will work out just fine."

"What about you?"

His voice was muffled in her hair and she closed her eyes against the pain. "I'll be fine," she lied. "After all, what can they do to me? Have me arrested for helping a runaway captive, whom they were holding illegally, escape to the year 1863? Who in the world would believe them?"

He raised his head, saying in a resigned tone, "I suppose when you put it that way..."

She looked up at him, forcing a smile. "Come on, let's eat the pizza. Then we'll take off for Philadelphia. You're gonna love what they've done to it."

Granger sat in the passenger seat of the car, wishing he could see the scenery flashing by the window. All he could see were the yellow beams of headlights eating up the road, and the shadowy line of trees against the night sky.

The woman at his side sat silent, no doubt working out the last minute details of his attempted return to his own time. He couldn't help wondering what would happen to him if the experiment failed, leaving him stranded at the end of the twentieth century.

He was surprised to realize that he wouldn't be devastated by the prospect. He would have done everything in his power to return, to obey the creed he had sworn to follow so long ago. If he was prevented by Providence from following his duty, he could live this new life with a clear conscience.

The thought jolted him, giving him an entirely new perspective on his life. What had happened to his fierce resolve, his intense conviction that he belonged to the military and the causes for which he risked his life?

But then he had to go back. He had to be in Ewell's camp to spread the rumors. The entire course of the war, and ultimately the future of the Union, might well have depended on him.

But what if it hadn't? What if, as Corie had suggested, Ewell was simply too tired, too sick to launch the attack earlier? The general had been given a choice. Would he really have based such an important decision on mere rumors?

If only he knew for sure, Granger thought desperately. If only he knew. But then Corie had said that no one knew why Ewell had delayed the attack. The only way he could know for sure was to go back and carry out the orders he'd been given.

Confused by his chaotic thoughts, he tried to analyze why he was asking these questions now, when it was almost time for him to make the attempt.

"There," Corie said suddenly, shattering his thoughts, "you can see the lights of the city. Over there on the left."

Eagerly he followed the direction of her hand. They had reached the top of a rise, and in the distance he could see what looked like a thousand stars all bunched together in a cloud of brilliant light.

"I've never seen Philadelphia look like that," he said, his voice hushed in awe.

Corie laughed. "Wait until we get closer. You'll really be amazed."

He saw her glance up at the little mirror on the window, as she had so many times during the trip. "Is everything all right?" he asked quietly.

She nodded. "So far. They are not expecting us to leave before tomorrow. What worries me is that they know as well as we do exactly where to look for you, if they guess that I'm trying to get you back."

"Will they try to stop me?"

She shrugged, and he knew the effort it cost her to sound unconcerned. "Who knows? If they think they are losing their guinea pig, a real live person who had actually traveled through time, they might try to stop you. After all, no one has ever done it before, at least not to my knowledge."

"They want to experiment on me?"

"I can't imagine why else they were holding you, drugging you so that you wouldn't remember who you were. It's hard for me to believe they would do such a thing. They're scientists. They're supposed to be committed to preserving life, not destroying it."

She shivered, and he was about to change the subject when something on the horizon silenced him. Staring him straight in the face was the most awesome sight he had yet seen on his strange journey through time.

The lights on the boardwalk had fascinated him beyond belief. But even they paled into insignificance as he watched the skyline of Philadelphia draw closer. It was impossible to equate the town that he knew with this monstrous, sprawling mountain of structures such as he'd never seen before.

The lights dazzled him. They seemed to shine everywhere. Twinkling bands of gold outlined windows, walls and roofs, reflecting on the pointed spire of an impressive-looking building that was almost dwarfed by the towering monsters behind it.

Granger blinked, leaning forward in disbelief. He *recognized* the building. It was Christ Church, no longer dominating the skyline in solitary splendor as he'd last seen it, but now battling for space among the mass of stone and iron.

His problems forgotten now, he could only stare in wonder as the car swept across a wide bridge, over what had to be the Delaware river, changed beyond recognition. Everywhere he looked there were new sights to marvel at, new wonders to try to grasp before the next one took his breath away.

"This is the Ben Franklin Bridge," Corie said, beside him. "That's a name you should recognize."

"Tell me," Granger said, his voice hoarse with emotion, "is Independence Hall still standing?"

"Yes," she said softly. "It is still standing. I'll take you there tomorrow. Thousands of people visit the building every year. It is just as revered now, if not, more so than it was all those years ago."

"I'm glad," Granger murmured. "I'm so very glad."

He sat back, still unable to take in the myriad of images that flashed before his eyes. When Corie brought the car to a stop in front of a brightly lit building, he could only stare helplessly at the splendor of the entrance and beyond.

"We might as well do it up in style," Corie said, smiling at his expression. "I'll take you sightseeing tomorrow. We'll leave early Wednesday for Gettysburg. We'll have to be on the battlefield before 3:20 on Thursday morning."

Granger couldn't answer. He was too busy watching a stretch limousine pull away from the curb.

Corie slept little that night, her mind busy with 101 questions that didn't seem to have answers. What would she do with Granger if her theory didn't hold up? She couldn't just set him adrift. He couldn't function on his own. Yet he wouldn't let her support him indefinitely. She was sure of that.

As it was, he was only accepting her help in return for the work he'd done on the house.

She ignored the small voice that suggested they could run the bed and breakfast inn together. It wouldn't work, she told herself firmly as she turned restlessly onto her side. He cared for her a great deal, she knew that. But it was more gratitude than anything. And that was a far cry from the way she felt about him.

She couldn't see him clearly in the darkness, the room wasn't as well lit as her bedroom in Cape May. But she could hear the steady rhythm of his breathing, feel the comforting warmth of his body, and breathe the clean, musky fragrance of his skin.

Soon, he would be gone, leaving only the memories of his deep chuckle, the odd way he lifted his eyebrows when surprised and the soft graze of his fingers down her cheek.

Carefully she rested her arm across his chest in a vain attempt to ease the ache of loss. She would carve the sensations into her mind, she told herself, and in the lonely darkness of the night, when sleep was impossible and the wakeful hours unbearable, she would hold on to the memories, finding some small comfort in their presence.

When she awoke in the morning, her arm still lay across Granger's broad chest, now clasped in the warmth of his fingers. She opened her eyes to find him watching her.

Smiling, he drew his finger down her cheek. "Good morning, sweet lady."

She answered him with a firm kiss, then with a swift movement threw the covers aside. "Come on, we have a long day ahead of us and I want to show you everything. When you get back you'll be amazing everyone with your prophecies."

"When I get back I'm not going to mention anything about the things I've seen," Granger said, climbing out of the bed. "I don't want to be burned at the stake for witchcraft."

"Did they still do that in 1863?" Corie asked, astonished at the thought.

"I don't know." Granger crossed to the window and drew back the drapes. "But I'm damned if I'm going to find out." He leaned forward and looked out. "Great heavens!"

"What is it?" Nerves jumping, Corie sped across the carpeted floor to join him. She was afraid to look out, half expecting to see the entire Philadelphia police force lined up in their cars outside.

Peering through the window, she scanned the street below. Everything seemed normal, the usual cars, pickups and buses all jostling for space, with cabs flying in and out like bees among the flowers.

"I can't see anything," she said, wondering what it was that had upset Granger. He looked uneasy as he stared down at the traffic.

"I didn't realize we were so high up," he said at last.

"Sorry," Corie said, sympathizing with him. She had no head for heights herself. "We're on the 24th floor. If I'd known it upset you, I'd have tried for something lower."

"It doesn't upset me. I just wasn't expecting it. I'm wondering how we got up here."

"Remember the elevator? That brought us up here."

Granger looked puzzled. "It only seemed to move a few feet."

"An illusion of speed." Corie picked up her night bag and headed for the bathroom. "I'm going to take a shower. If you want to join me, I suggest you make it quick. There's a lot to see in one day."

It was over an hour later before they finally left the hotel. Corie had made a tentative plan while lying awake the night before. The first stop was Independence Hall, then the Liberty Bell, also a thrift store for his clothes.

Throughout that long day, she was never sure who was the most fascinated, Granger with his avid interest in the modernization of the city, or she with his knowledge of the history, including details she had never heard before.

Granger's face when he saw Elfreth's Alley, the oldest, continuously inhabited street in the country, was a delight to watch. The quaint row of houses and cobblestones, preserved and maintained exactly as it had been since 1690, brought a shout of recognition from him.

"I know this place," he said, staring about him in wonder. "It looks almost the same as when I last saw it."

His revered silence as they entered the Legislative Room in Independence Hall, where the forefathers had signed the Declaration, reduced her to tears.

By the time they returned to the hotel, exhausted and emotionally spent, Corie was more than ready for the quiet dinner she'd planned.

Ordering room service was another new experience for Granger, and one he apparently enjoyed. They shared a bottle of champagne, chilled in a pewter bucket, and devoured the lobster and steak, while Corie tried very hard to keep the conversation light.

Granger had fiddled with the radio, finally finding a channel of mellow music. The candlelight threw soft shadows across the table, playing over his harsh features as he looked at her, his raised glass in his hand.

"To us," he said softly.

"To us." Her smile faltered, just a little, but he caught the change of expression. Stretching out his hand, he laid his palm over her fingers. "I will never forget this time with you, Corie."

"Neither will I." She sought vainly for something else to add.

"I wish things could have been different," Granger said, his eyes full of compassion. "I didn't want to hurt you."

"I know." This time she managed the smile. "I wouldn't have missed these days for anything. It's worth a little sadness."

"I'll miss you."

"I'll miss you, too." She caught her bottom lip in her teeth, then added brightly, "But I'll have plenty to keep me busy. If I lose my job I'll be able to work on the house full-time. Who knows, I might even be able to open before the end of season. Then there's always the Christmas season. Cape May has lots of visitors then. Did you know—"

"Corie."

She gazed at him, unable to control the ache of misery that threatened to overwhelm her. "Did you know," she went on determinedly, "that at Christmastime everyone dresses up in Victorian costume—" she broke off with a forced laugh. "You'd be right...at...home...."

The last words ended on a sob, and she snapped her mouth shut, furious at her own weakness.

Swiftly, Granger shoved his chair back and rose to his feet, his hands reaching for her.

She closed her eyes as his arms folded around her, seeking desperately the comfort he could always give her. Tonight, however, even that eluded her. She wanted to hang on to him, to hold him and never let him go—to keep him there, in her world, in her time.

"Corie," Granger whispered, his hand stroking her hair. "I have to go back, you do know that, don't you?"

She nodded, her throat too tight for her to speak.

"Always remember, my sweet Corie, that you will always hold a special place in my heart. Wherever I go, you will be with me, in my mind and in my soul."

She squeezed her eyes tighter, willing herself not to cry.

"I will take you with me, wherever I go," Granger said softly. "I will think of you in the morning sun, and hear your voice in the wind, whispering to me. In the still shadows of the night, I will close my eyes and in my mind I will hold you, as I have done so many unforgettable nights."

She felt his fingers lift her chin, and opened her eyes. The look on his face almost destroyed her. Now the tears fell, unheeded, as he lowered his mouth to hers.

"Don't cry, my sweet lady," he said gently, when he finally lifted his head. "If this is to be our last night together, let it be one to remember. Let us fill it with love, and laughter."

Placing his hands on either side of her face, he brushed away the tears with his thumbs. "You are a very brave lady. Let us both be brave tonight, and forget about tomorrow."

She nodded, summoning a smile. "I'll try."

Holding her hand, he pulled her over to the bed. He undressed her slowly, savoring each moment as if he wanted to commit it all to memory.

Before he was finished the fire consumed her, and she became impatient to lie by his side, caressed by his naked flesh. Expert now at pleasing her, his hands and lips worked their magic, tormenting with a fiery pleasure that quickly built inside her.

Even so, she wasn't ready for the swift movement of his mouth down her belly and for a moment she tensed, her body going rigid.

He lifted his head and whispered urgently, "Please?"

She shook her head, her fingers gripping his shoulders. "I don't know . . . I never . . ."

"Neither have I. But I want to . . . tonight . . . with you."

She relaxed her fingers, and made her body succumb to his touch. His mouth moved lower, and the tiny shiver of shock lasted no more than a second. Then she closed her eyes as the onslaught of pleasure shook her body.

She heard herself whispering, "Oh, Granger," as she curled her fingers into his soft hair. Meeting each wave of rocketing sensation was like crashing through the sound barrier. She was beyond thought now, striving only for the release from the pleasure that was almost pain.

With a final shudder, she cried out as the heady torment exploded into a torrent of relief, leaving her floating in a warm, contented haze.

She wasn't allowed to rest there for long. With a swift movement Granger moved up her body, and now she could see the same raw hunger in his eyes that had ravaged her body a few moments ago.

"I hope I pleased you."

She lifted a finger and laid it across his lips. "I never knew it could be like this. No man has ever made me feel like this."

His smile flashed across his face. "I'm so very glad."

"Now it's my turn." She twisted onto her side, and pushed him down on his back. "I want to give to you as much as you have given me."

The answering fire in his eyes thrilled her as much as his touch had done. She gave herself up to the joy of exploring his body with her lips, each soft moan of appreciation from him firing her blood again, until her own passion seized her once more.

His voice sounded ragged when she slid up over his body again. "Oh, Corie, what are you doing to me?"

"Pleasing you, I hope." She propped herself up on her hands, looking down into his face. His skin looked flushed, his eyes clouded with his passion. She had created that look on his face. She alone.

With a surge of triumph she lowered her mouth to his, and felt his arms clamp around her back, holding her in a grip that flattened her breasts against his chest.

Now she wanted him. Right now. Her entire body clamored to feel him inside of her. She settled slowly down on him, then with a groan he thrust upward to meet her.

The pressure built swiftly as she fought with him toward the crest of relief. Muttered words she couldn't understand mingled with her cries as he strived and strained, his body arching again and again. With a strength that shook her, he flipped her over onto her back.

Once more they dueled, their bodies finding the primitive rhythm that would send them through the barrier together. One final thrust, one mutual, ultimate effort and the rush began, soaring into the unknown before allowing them to drift slowly back to reality.

The morning came too soon. Granger watched the room gradually lighten, the shadows slowly acquiring hard edges of furniture and walls. His stomach churned as he thought about the day ahead.

Corie had explained the schedule to him. They would arrive in Gettysburg around midday. They would book into a hotel, then go out to the battlefield, where Corie would juggle with her figures and her compass to locate exactly the spot where the star's beam was scheduled to hit.

If her calculations were correct, she'd told him, she would be within twenty-five yards of the area. Since the beam had a radius of five feet and would be easily visible, he should have time to reach it, even if they were on the outer edge of the target area.

Five seconds. That's all he would have. No time for goodbyes, no last kiss, no last whispered words of love.

The word jolted through his mind, freezing his body. Great heavens, why hadn't he realized it before? He loved her. Beyond reason, beyond understanding, he loved her.

Staring at the ceiling, he felt as if a hand squeezed his heart. Now he knew why he hadn't been devastated at the thought of staying in this strange new world.

The question was, what in the hell was he going to do about it? He knew what he wanted to do. He also knew what he had to do. He had to go back. He had no choice.

He turned his head, carefully so as not to waken the sleeping woman lying nestled at his side. Her face was turned toward him, her lashes fluttering slightly on her cheeks. Her hair was mussed, the color of corn not quite ripe.

His heart turned over as he gazed at her. How in the world would he live without her? The sobering thought that followed suddenly held more meaning than it ever had before. Maybe he wouldn't live. He was going back to a war. There was no telling what would happen to him.

How could he tell her he loved her, only to leave her? He couldn't of course. Did she love him? He didn't know. Didn't want to know. It would be hard enough to leave her, without carrying the knowledge with him of what might have been.

He thought about what she had told him. *This is probably your only chance to leave here and return to the right place and time... there will be no coming back.*

But she didn't know that for sure. She'd said so. It was all guesswork—supposition. *What if she was wrong?* What if he could come back, the next time the beam hit the earth? It was worth a try.

He was amazed how that one tiny spark of hope lifted his spirits. Lifting his hand, he touched her cheek, feeling his body grow warm as she opened her eyes and smiled sleepily at him.

A second later, her eyes clouded, and he knew she had remembered this was to be their last day. How he longed to tell her he loved her. But he could not. Not until he could know that he would never have to leave her again. If that was at all possible.

"Would you do me a favor?" he asked quietly.

"What is it?"

His heart ached as he watched the pain in her eyes. "Show me how you calculate the spot where the beam will land."

She nodded. "Of course. It's a bit complicated."

"Do you think I could do it?"

She frowned, her face wary. "I don't know. I suppose so, with the right figures in front of you. I'd have to show you how to use the instruments—" She broke off. "Wait a minute. You're not proposing to go to Gettysburg without me, are you? Because if you are—"

He laid a finger over her lips. "No, I'm not going to Gettysburg alone. I just want to learn how to find the spot of the beam's target area, that's all."

Her face still wore an apprehensive expression. "I don't understand. Why?"

He didn't want to tell her, in case it couldn't be done. But he needed her help. Besides, if he could offer her a tiny ray of hope, too, then maybe it would make things easier for her.

"Tell me," he said quietly, "where the star is expected to hit on its next trip around. You said you'd calculated the area."

"Yes, I have. Richards wanted to know. But I told you, we don't think it will follow the same orbit."

"I know. But there is a chance?"

"A very slim one."

"But a chance, nevertheless."

She stared at him, her head propped on her hand, and his heart bounded at the hope that shone in her eyes. "You mean—"

"I mean, sweet lady, that if things don't work out for me back there, I might just make the attempt to come back here again."

He'd deliberately made his voice light. He couldn't admit his love for her. Not now. Not yet. He saw the glow in her eyes dim, just a little.

"Aha," she said, smiling at him, "so you've become addicted to the advances made in the last century. Don't want to give up the luxury and conveniences, right?"

She'd forced a lightness to her voice, too, though he'd heard the underlying pain. "Something like that. Tell me where the star is expected to hit next."

"Just east of a tiny town called Del Muerto." She watched him intently. "It's on the border of Arizona and New Mexico."

"Arizona? Yes, I've heard talk of the territory being established some time this year. I know where it is."

"If Specturne returns on the same orbit, the beam should contact Earth on January 2, of next year."

"That will be 1864 my time."

"Granger, there's something you should know."

He could see by her face it wasn't good news. "What?"

"We have no idea if the transformation from the past is the same time period then. We only know it is the same one at this end."

He nodded. "I understand."

"The chance is very slim, Granger."

"There is no guarantee that I could be at the right spot at the right time, either. But it can't hurt to know the details, can it?"

She managed a smile. "No, it can't hurt. When I take the measurements this afternoon, I'll show you how to do it. I'll give you the instruments you'll need to take back with you. And the set of figures. After that, it will be up to the vagaries of nature."

"That's all I can ask." He touched her lips with his. "Now, come here while I show you some vagaries of my own."

An hour later they were on their way to Gettysburg. Corie's hands were clenched on the wheel as she concentrated on the road, while Granger sat silently at her side, his gaze on the unfolding scenery.

Some of the rolling fields and thickly wooded hills must have seemed familiar to him, because every now and then he would sit up and look around, as if expecting to see someone he knew come charging out of the trees.

As they drove through the tiny town of Gettysburg, he became very excited. "It's hardly changed at all," he said, as they passed through the Town Square. "I remember these buildings well. I was here just a week or so ago."

Corie glanced at him, finding it hard to believe he was actually fighting in the Civil War just a few short days ago.

He seemed preoccupied now, leaning forward in his seat, his gaze intent on the road ahead. "You did say we won this battle?" he said, his voice low.

"Yes, the Union won at Gettysburg."

"Our first real victory."

"Yes, it was." She glanced at him again, struck by the tension in his face. Already he was back in the war, she thought sadly. Already she had lost him.

"We'll check into a motel first," she said, her foot on the brake as she approached one. "Let's just hope they have room for us. It's close to the Fourth, they'll be getting ready in town for the reenactment."

"Reenactment?"

"Of the battle. They usually play out the whole three days, though not on the battlefield itself. It's usually held a couple of miles away from here. Though they did use the battlefield once to film a movie—" She broke off when she caught sight of his expression.

"Three days? The battle lasted three whole days?"

She nodded, sick at heart when she realized he couldn't know it all.

"How many men died?"

"Granger—"

"How many?"

"I believe there were more than seven thousand men who actually died in the battle." How she hated to tell him that.

"Oh, my God." Granger closed his eyes, shading them with his hand, his thumb and forefinger pressed into his forehead.

And he could be one of them.

Somehow she knew that thought had entered both their minds at the same time. Fortunately, at that moment she reached the lobby of the motel. The next few minutes were taken up with the details of checking in and then locating their room.

Less than thirty minutes later, she was heading the car into the battlefield itself. Granger was on the edge of his seat, exclaiming at the sight of the monuments to the different generals and commanders, and the rows of cannons lined at intervals along the roadside.

"It is the strangest feeling," he whispered, as they passed by the site at Cemetery Hill. "It's as if I never left. As if time has stood still. If it weren't for the cars on the road, I would swear I was looking at the battlefield in 1863."

"If all goes well," Corie said unsteadily, "tomorrow morning, you will be."

She pulled the car into a shaded area underneath an oak tree. She had kept a sharp lookout all the way into the battlefield, but had seen no sign of Dr. Richards, or his partner, Ivan Spencer.

Still seated in the car, she laid out her list of figures on her lap, and showed Granger how to calculate from the figures exactly the spot where the beam was supposed to land. Using the compass and the direction finder, she showed him how she drew the cross line on the map, which gave her the exact point of impact.

"All we have to do now," she told him, "is find this spot in the actual field."

They had to drive another mile or two along the road that wound through the trees before they were close enough to walk. The directions taken from the compass led them across a field, and down a steep incline to a valley between the hills.

"This is it," Granger said, his voice hoarse with excitement. "I recognize it. I was riding along this trail when I was suddenly blinded by the light. I didn't see a beam though, just a flash, like a bolt of lightning."

"That's because you were a direct hit," Corie said, studying the compass. "Can you remember exactly the spot where you fell?"

Granger shook his head. "It was somewhere along here, I think," he said, gesturing with his hand.

"It doesn't matter. I have it pinpointed." Her eyes on the small instrument in her hand, she walked along the trail for several yards.

The moist heat of the afternoon seemed to saturate her clothes. She could feel the perspiration forming on her forehead, and her arms burned under the fierce sun.

Flies, gnats and a host of other insects buzzed all around her, bumping into her face and stinging her arms. Far from the tourists now, the wooded slopes hummed and rustled with the tiny creatures that lived there.

There was no breeze to freshen the air, and the musty smell of burned grass and decaying wood seemed almost overpowering. Corie could just imagine what it must have been like there 130 years ago.

"This should be the place," she said at last, pausing by a large rock that radiated intense heat. "Or as near as we are going to get. Now all we have to do is remember how to get back here in the dark. I just hope we get a clear sky."

She glanced up, thankful to see only a few wispy clouds marring the sky.

"Will the beam get through if it's cloudy?" Granger asked, following her gaze.

"That beam will get through solid wood. It's pretty powerful." She led the way back to the car, anxious to get back to the welcome relief of air-conditioning.

Granger said little on the way back to the motel, and she could imagine the turmoil his thoughts had to be in.

"We'll have dinner early," she said, as they reached the parking lot of the motel. "Then as soon as it gets dark we'll go back to the battlefield and wait. We—" She broke off, her foot slamming down on the brake.

Granger was jerked forward, and he planted his palms on the dashboard in front of him. "What—"

"Those two men," Corie said urgently. "Coming out of the motel office. Do you recognize them?"

Granger looked, then swore softly. "Yes," he said grimly. "Those are two of the doctors who held me prisoner."

"They're not doctors," Corie said, throwing the gear into reverse. "At least, not in the way you mean. That's Dr. Richards, head scientist at the lab, and his partner, Dr. Spencer. And apparently they have tracked us down."

Chapter 12

The moon rode high in the sky when Corie returned to the
road that led through the battlefield. After leaving the motel parking lot earlier that afternoon, she'd taken the road
back to town, and had stayed out of sight until the sun had
finally set behind the hills.

Granger seemed to enjoy the hamburgers they'd eaten for
dinner, though Corie would have much preferred one of the
nice restaurants in the area. Afraid to take the chance on
running into the scientists, she had introduced Granger instead to the joys of a drive-in fast-food restaurant.

He'd been fascinated by the concept, and wondered aloud
how she managed to keep her figure if she did everything in
the car instead of walking.

Now they were both silent as she slowed the car to a crawl,
then drove it carefully off the road and into the shelter of the
trees. She switched off the engine, and the silence settled
around them.

"They haven't followed us yet," Granger said, his voice hushed.

"They don't need to. They know where to look."

Warily, Corie opened the door and looked out. "We will have to walk in from here. Officially the park is closed, but no one will expect us to be walking around at this time of night."

"You will have to walk back alone."

She glanced back at him. "No, I don't think so. I'm quite sure the good doctors Richards and Spencer will accompany me back."

"It will be dangerous for you."

She shook her head. "No, I really don't think they will hurt me. I am just worried that they will try to stop you from reaching the beam."

"They won't stop me."

He'd sounded so confident, so sure of himself. She hoped he was right. She tried not to imagine the two scientists holding a gun on him. Though she couldn't imagine them actually shooting him. No matter how desperate they were.

The clicking of hundreds of crickets seemed deafening as she climbed out of the car. They were everywhere—in the grass, in the trees, she could even hear one on the warm hood of the car.

"Come on," she whispered, as Granger joined her in the darkness, "we don't have much time. I deliberately left late so we wouldn't be out in the open for too long."

Lightning bugs danced all around them as Corie led Granger through the trees, the momentary gleams of light swooping in and out of the long grass. The moon bathed the fields with silver shadows, and reflected in Granger's eyes when he looked down at her.

She remembered the first time she'd seen that strange silver gleam in his eyes. The memory brought the first bittersweet ache of nostalgia that she knew would return to wound her again and again throughout the years ahead.

She tried not to listen to the faint flicker of hope that refused to die. The chances were too slim, she told herself. Too many things could happen to prevent his return. It would be better to let go, and try not to look back.

"They will probably be waiting for us when we get there," Granger said softly, as they reached the rise that led down to the narrow trail.

"Probably." She checked the compass in her hand to make sure. "But in the dark we will be hard to see in the cover of the trees. It's a large area. Unless they are very lucky, or we are very careless, they won't have time to find us before the beam hits."

"How long do we have?"

She looked at her watch. "Ten minutes at the most. By the time we get down there we should have no more than a couple of minutes to wait."

"Corie—"

Afraid that anything he said to her would reduce her to tears, Corie thrust the compass into his hands. "Here, you'll need this, just in case."

He took it from her, his face etched in hard lines in the moonlight.

"You've got everything else I gave you?"

He nodded, patting the pockets of his jacket. "I have it all."

She had chosen his outfit carefully, down to the button-fly jeans and boots. He looked the part at least. "Then let's go."

"Corie, wait a minute." His hands gripped her shoulders, and she welcomed the gentle pain. This would be the last time he touched her. She wanted to remember how it felt.

For a long moment he looked deep into her eyes, burning the memory of his silver gaze right into her soul. "I am sorry, my sweet Corie. You have given me so much. I wish I could have given you more."

She made herself smile. "You have given me more than you know."

"I have no words to thank you for everything you have done for me. I will not forget you, Corie." He pulled her to him, and covered her mouth with his in one last, demanding kiss that left her fighting for control of her emotions.

He let her go, and without a word, she turned and plunged down the slope, her throat aching with the effort to hold back the tears. She heard his light footsteps behind her, and all she could do was pray that it would soon be over.

They reached the end of the trail, and she began to run, with Granger pounding behind her.

It happened all at once. A muffled shout from somewhere on her right, then another. As if in answer, from out of nowhere, the blinding glare silently descended from the sky, slanting through the darkness in a steady stream of pulsating light.

Like a giant white-hot stage light it struck the earth, vapors rising from the perfect circle of its gleaming circumference no more than twenty yards in front of her.

Again the shouts, closer now. Corie halted, gasping for breath as Granger paused, panting at her side. "Don't stop," she screamed at him, her voice echoing eerily from the empty hills. "Run, Granger, run into the beam! Now!"

He gave her one, last desperate look, then leapt forward. From behind her Corie could hear the pounding of feet, then a tall figure dashed past her. In the same instant Granger reached the beam. He stood for a second, ablaze in the dazzling light, his face turned toward her.

Lifting his hand, his voice carried clearly across the space between them. "I will not forget."

Abruptly the light shut off, leaving only a black darkness behind.

For a second or two Corie could see nothing but tiny stars dancing in front of her eyes. She blinked, trying frantically to see the trail ahead. Still dazed by the afterglow, she saw a figure walking slowly back toward her.

Her heart soared as she stared at the moving shadow. It hadn't worked. He was still there. She blinked again, and this time her vision cleared.

"He's gone," Dr. Boyd Richards said.

Corie closed her eyes and sank to the ground.

She sat in the car, shivering in spite of the muggy heat of the dark, humid night. She couldn't forget the sight of that empty trail, a fine wisp of steam still rising from the spot where Granger had last stood.

"Will you be all right to drive?" Dr. Richards said, peering at her through the open door.

She nodded. "I'll be fine."

"We'll discuss all this back at the motel later on this morning then. Say 11:00. Room 220."

Again she nodded, weary beyond belief. "I'll be there." What did it matter what happened to her now? Nothing mattered. The only man she had ever truly loved was gone, and life was nothing but a cold, empty sea of pain waiting to swallow her up.

She hardly remembered getting back to the car. With Dr. Richards supporting her on one side, Spencer on the other, somehow she had stumbled back through the endless trees. Now, at last, she was alone.

Ahead of her she saw the low beam of headlights cutting through the darkness. At least the scientists trusted her to be there in the morning. Maybe she wouldn't lose her job after all. Not that it mattered. Nothing mattered anymore.

Somehow she found her way back to the motel. She slept in fits and starts, finally waking up from a doze shortly before ten.

After a shower and hot coffee she began to feel a little better, and prepared herself to face the music. She wasn't going to let them fire her without a fight, she told herself as she located Richards's room. She had only done what was right.

The scientists answered her light tap by opening the door, and she stepped inside the room. Spencer sat in a chair across from the bed. He stood up as she entered, looking very ill at ease. Even Richards looked sheepish as he pulled another chair forward and indicated she should sit.

"I assume that Granger Deene has been with you since he left his room," Richards said, when she was seated.

"You mean escaped from his prison."

He met her accusing stare without flinching. "We kept him confined for his own good. We were afraid he would get into serious trouble if he was allowed to wander around without supervision."

"And what about the drug you pumped into him? That's an illegal drug, still in its experimental stage. You could have destroyed his mind altogether."

Spencer made a small sound in his throat and Richards appeared to be shocked by her statement. "I assure you, Corie, that the drug was perfectly safe. We had all the findings on it and there was nothing in there to suggest the drug is dangerous."

"The data referred to animals." She was shaking so hard she could barely speak. "Any moron knows that a human's brain can hardly compare to an animal's."

"It has been tested on monkeys," Spencer said nervously. "It didn't do them any harm."

"I just don't understand why it was necessary to block out his memory at all," Corie persisted. "He might never have recovered it."

"Then he would have been able to function in this time, eventually." Richards sat down heavily on the edge of the bed. "That's what we were hoping for, Corie. We were afraid that if he knew what had happened to him, it would unbalance his mind. I admit, it was an experiment, but we had the best of intentions."

She glared at him. "How can you say that? Didn't it occur to you that it might just be better to help him get back to where he really belonged? Wouldn't that be a thousand times better than having to spend the rest of his life here, constantly drugged and unable to remember anything about his life before this happened?"

Richards's face changed, and his expression scared her. "I'm sorry, Corie," he said quietly. "I realize this man has come to mean something to you, and I admire your courage and determination in trying to do the right thing for him. The reason we didn't consider sending him back was because we knew it was likely to fail."

She lifted her chin, determined not to let him see her apprehension. "Well, it didn't fail. You saw it. He entered the beam and vanished with it. By now he is most likely back in his own time, getting on with his life."

Richards and Spencer exchanged looks. Thoroughly alarmed now, Corie rose to her feet. "What is it? What aren't you telling me?"

"From the information we've been able to gather," Richards said slowly, "it seems extremely unlikely that Deene could survive the return trip. It was a miracle he survived the first transformation. I'm afraid that this attempt to return will almost certainly end in his death."

Her mouth suddenly dry, she could only stare into his bland, unemotional face. "I don't believe it," she said flatly.

Richards shrugged. "It happens to be the truth. Anyway, it's over and done with now. I suggest we all forget about this strange little episode, and put it behind us. Happily the media didn't get a hint of it or it would have been all over the tabloids."

Her heart was pounding so hard it hurt. He was wrong. He had to be wrong. She wouldn't, couldn't believe she had sent Granger to his death.

Richards got to his feet, and patted her shoulder. "Why don't you take the rest of the week off, Corie? You've been through quite a trauma. Come back next Monday, and we'll go on from there as if nothing had happened."

She nodded, no longer able to speak. As if in a trance, she walked to the door and opened it. She heard both men say goodbye to her, but she couldn't answer. She was beyond thought. All she wanted was to be alone. For the rest of her life.

The door closed behind her and Spencer asked nervously, "Do you think she believed you?"

"The excuses I gave her were feasible." Richards walked to the window and pulled aside the drapes to watch her leave. "I didn't want her going above my head to complain about our treatment of Deene."

"Is he really going to die? You told me that it was only a possibility."

"How do I know what will happen to him? I can only make guesses. But as long as Corie Trenton thinks she is responsible for Deene's death, she won't make any noises about what happened. It's just too bad we lost him before we had a chance to do the experiments."

"Do you think it will happen again? When Specturne hits Earth again, do you think it might bring someone else back with it?"

Richards dropped the curtain. "Who knows? I would imagine there's a million to one chance of anyone standing directly inside the beam when it hits. Then again, the star might never return. Frankly, if it's going to cause this much trouble, I'd just as soon wash my hands of Specturne. We have plenty to work on without it, our studies will just take us a little longer, that's all.''

''At least we know that Deene won't be back.''

''That's for sure. Let's just be thankful that he won't remember anything about what happened to him here. If he does get back in one piece, it will seem to him as if he never left. There will be nothing in his memory to remind him of this place.''

''Or Corie Trenton,'' Spencer said thoughtfully.

She stayed in Gettysburg until after July the Fourth. She didn't go to the reenactment. She couldn't face that. She spent the time instead wandering around the battlefield with the manual someone at the tourist center had given her.

As each day dawned, she made her way to the focal point of the battle on the corresponding day in 1863. She made herself believe that he had returned safely and was where he was supposed to be. History couldn't be changed. Granger Deene had fought in the Battle of Gettysburg, and that was where he would be.

And if he was there, maybe somehow he would feel her presence and know she was thinking about him.

As she stood and gazed on the now silent fields and slopes of that momentous battle, in her mind she heard the pounding of the cannons, the cries and shouts of men engaged in deadly warfare.

She saw the bright flash of gunpowder, and the grimy uniforms moving through the clouds of gray smoke. She smelled the scorched grass, felt the thunder of hooves vibrating across the hard ground.

Little Round Top, Devil's Den, The Peach Orchard, all became more than names in a history book. They were real places, where real men had fought and died.

On the third and last day of the battle, she stood on Cemetery Ridge at the site of Pickett's charge. The oppressive heat closed around her, without the faintest movement of a breeze to stir the long grass of the open fields. Here, on this ridge, thousands of men had died in untold agony. Had Granger been among them? Or had he even survived until that day? She would never know.

Turning away, Corie faced the truth. She was never going to see him again. The faint hope she had struggled to hold on to flickered weakly, and died. Granger was gone, taking with him her heart.

He lay on his cot, staring into the darkness, as he did so often nowadays. Something had happened to him since Gettysburg—something strange and impossible to understand. At first he'd thought it was the aftermath of that terrible battle.

He'd recovered, slowly, from the wounds he'd suffered, leaving only the healing scars to show for the agony. They had told him he might never walk again, but something inside him hadn't let him believe their dismal conclusions.

It had taken him eight long weeks to prove them wrong. And another four to convince his commanders that he could ride as well as ever, in spite of his noticeable limp.

But there was something more. Something he couldn't define at first. He'd had dreams...strange, outlandish dreams, visions that were beyond his understanding, beyond even his own imagination. Alien structures and miraculous machines, carriages that moved without horses, boxes with moving pictures and an instrument that could talk in his ear.

Then there was the ache, somewhere under his ribs, that could not be explained by any of the doctor's examinations. It was as if he mourned for someone, yet he had no one to cause such mental anguish.

Gradually, as the painful weeks passed, and his mind could dwell on subjects more pleasant than his injuries, more was added to the visions that tricked his mind.

A fragrance, elusive yet somehow familiar, the flash of a smile, a soft voice calling his name in the quiet hours before dawn. A woman.

Yet he had known no such woman. Certainly none who had the power to torment his weakened body so. He could not chase the images from his mind, however, no matter how hard he tried.

It was as if she were with him, in spirit at least. All through the agonizing days of forcing his legs to function again, he'd felt her presence like a living, breathing thing.

It wasn't until he had finally been released from the hospital and reported back to his command, that the possessions taken from him when they'd carried him from the battlefield were returned to him.

Inside his unopened saddlebag he'd found some very strange objects. The compass he recognized as such immediately, though it was unlike any compass he'd ever seen. The other instrument was completely foreign to him. He also found a list of numbers, scribbled on an unusually fine piece of paper, with an ink that did not smudge when wet.

But the most astounding item was the likeness of a woman, dressed in men's clothing, printed on a thick, shiny paper such as he'd never seen before. Peculiar structures, similar to the ones in his dreams, towered behind her, and he could not understand the purpose of them. But it was the woman who held his attention.

He'd known immediately that it was the woman in his visions.

The only thing he could think of was that he'd found the objects when he'd fallen from his horse, that first day of the Gettysburg battle as he was heading for Ewell's camp.

He vaguely remembered stuffing something inside his saddlebag, but he had been dazed by the fall, and couldn't remember where he'd discovered them. Or where he'd found the odd clothes he wore.

He'd thought that the picture of the woman was the reason for his visions, but he knew now that it was more than that. Somehow, somewhere, he had known her. He had held her soft, smooth body in his arms and he had loved her.

Now he had a burning desire to find her. A desire that far surpassed his need to continue his service in the army. He had been offered an honorable discharge, and had refused. After that he'd received orders to report to Chattanooga, and had arrived in Tennessee just last month.

But now he knew, that given the opportunity, he would gladly give up his commission to follow the woman of his dreams.

Turning on his side, Granger saw through the dusty window pane the first flush of dawn lighten the sky. He knew no way of finding her. Yet something nagged in his mind, something that couldn't be denied.

He'd heard talk of Colonel Carson fighting the Navajo on the borders of New Mexico and the new territory of Arizona. Someone had mentioned a town called Del Muerto. Somehow it had struck a chord in his mind, so strong he couldn't rid himself of the name.

He knew, though how he knew he could not imagine, that he would find the woman there. He had asked for a transfer. Yesterday it had been granted.

Today he was to leave on the long journey west, to a town he'd never heard of before, to find a woman he didn't know. A woman who so possessed his mind, a woman for whom his love was so powerful, he was willing to give up all he had known—his career, everything he had, even risk his very life—in order to be with her.

As he lay there watching what would most likely be the last dawn he would see from an eastern town, he was filled with a sense of excitement, and a longing that was painful to bear. If he rode hard he would be in Del Muerto before the end of the year. Somehow he would find her and hold her again. If it took him until the end of his days.

Corie looked down from the tiny window of the jet and wondered why she was opening herself up to inevitable pain. As the weeks had crawled by she'd done her best to forget that Granger Deene had ever existed.

Sometimes she had almost convinced herself that it had all been a dream, until some sign of his presence had brought back the empty ache of loss.

Finally unable to bear the memories, she had sold the house and furniture at a profit that had astounded her. Deciding that a complete change was in order, she had put her few belongings in storage and planned a long vacation exploring the west coast. After that she would make a decision as to where she wanted to live.

Arizona had not been on her itinerary. Before she left the lab, Dr. Richards had informed her that Specturne, as expected, had veered off its orbit, and was no longer in the galaxy. They were therefore scrapping all the information on the star and closing the file.

Corie had flown to Los Angeles for Christmas, and planned to be in San Francisco to see in the New Year. At the last moment, she had changed her flight to Albuquerque. From there it would take her about five hours to drive to the tiny town of Del Muerto.

She knew he wouldn't be there. At least not in her time. But if he remembered, if he had really cared, he might be there in his time. And perhaps, for one fleeting moment, they might be in the same spot at the same time.

It was foolish, she knew, but if it was possible to reach across time and feel each other's presence for one last time, it would have been worth the effort. If he was there. If he had survived the trip back, if he had survived the battle, if he had survived the war, if he still remembered her, if he still wanted to return . . . So many damn ifs.

Catching her reflection in the window, Corie pulled a face at herself. She was crazy. But she had to do this. She had to put a final end to it. She had to say goodbye. There hadn't been time during those last few moments in Gettysburg. Now, at last, she could play the final inning. It was over.

It was cold in the mountains of Arizona. He'd resigned his commission two days ago, and he still didn't know why. He'd found the town, no more than a watering hole, one of many scattered about at the foothills of the Canyon de Chelly.

There were no women who vaguely resembled the woman in the picture. In fact, there were few women at all. He had no idea why he'd come to this godforsaken hole. He only knew that something, someone had driven him there, and soon it would be resolved.

He spent the eve of the New Year huddled in front of a blazing fire in an abandoned log cabin. By the light of a broken oil lamp, he studied the picture again. Then he unfolded the rumpled and creased sheet of paper that he'd carried with him all these weeks.

The figures danced in front of his eyes, and he could make neither head nor tail of their significance. He turned the compass over and over in his palm, his instincts telling him that he needed the instrument, but he could not understand why.

Finally, in seething frustration he stood, crumpling the paper up into a tight ball. He raised his hand, prepared to send the irritating mess straight into the flames so that he would not be bothered by it again, but some strange force inside him would not let him do it.

Instead, he shoved it back into his pocket and limped to the window, where the night sky glowed with a thousand twinkling stars. As he watched, a falling star left a white-hot trail across the dark velvet of the sky. Staring at the streak of light, something clicked in his brain.

A beam of light. An enormous beam of light that fell from the sky and lit up the ground like the glow from a hundred moons. Where had he seen such a beam? Somewhere, sometime, he had stood in the heart of it and felt the strange pulsating energy of it.

He frowned, turning back to the fire. That day in Gettysburg, when he had fallen from his horse. He remembered a flash of light, an odd feeling of being swept away as if borne by a fierce wind far more powerful than anything he'd witnessed before. Then he'd awoke, lying on the ground with his horse pawing impatiently nearby.

Slowly, he unfolded the piece of paper again and stared at it. Somewhere in between the time he'd fallen and the time he'd awakened, he'd found the strange objects. The figures, the compass, the other instrument and the picture.

From somewhere outside he heard the faint, distant sound of a church bell welcoming in the New Year. It was like a signal, triggering his thoughts, so that they tumbled ever faster, so fast he could hardly keep up.

The figures would lead him to the beam of light. And the light would lead him to the woman. How he knew that he couldn't imagine, but he was sure. Moving closer to the fire, he peered at the figures again.

With a feeling of rising excitement, he could make sense of them. The figures at the top represented a date—one, two, sixty-four. January 2, 1864. The day after tomorrow.

He studied the rest of the figures. There was the time—2:38 a.m. He would have to be there tomorrow night. He limped over to the sack of straw that served as his bed, and opened the saddlebag. He found the compass and the other instrument and drew them out, as well as the picture that had brought him to this desolate spot.

He knew now what he had to do. Tomorrow night, he would find the spot where the beam of light would shine. And he would step inside. After that, he could not imagine what would happen. He only knew he would find her. And now he knew her name.

Staring into the flames, he whispered it. "My sweet Corie. Tomorrow night I will come to you. I did not forget."

Corie shivered in the night wind that brought the chill of snow from the mountains. According to the calculations she had given Granger, he should arrive in that spot within the next fifteen minutes. That's if he was still alive, and still remembered.

How would he feel, she wondered, when the expected beam of light didn't materialize? She had impressed upon him that the chances were slim, that it would be a miracle if Specturne returned. If he cared enough to be there, to give up his life in his time to try to come back to her, then he would be shattered when the star failed to return.

How long would he wait? What would he do with his life after that? Would he feel as desolate and as lost as she did without him?

She directed the beam from her flashlight onto her watch. Ten minutes to go. She shivered, hugging her arms about her for comfort. She could see the lights of the small town of Del Muerto from where she stood on a piece of high ground.

Small trees and shrubs covered the dry earth, and a tiny trickle of water dripped aimlessly from a slab of high rock.

Above the ridge of mountains the sky looked clear, brilliant with the myriad of stars that can only be seen from the desert. Her heart ached as she stared up at the still universe.

"Damn you, Specturne," she whispered, her voice carrying across the empty ground. "Why couldn't you have stayed in orbit just one more time?"

It was time. He had watched the hands of the battered pocket watch crawl past the hour, and now he had maybe ten minutes before the beam would come.

He hoped he was in the right spot. He hoped the voice inside his head had not been his imagination finally scrambling his brain. He still didn't understand what he had done. He only knew it was right.

He stood on a rise outside of town, the wind chilling him as it whisked briskly around him. The trees were sparse, and afforded no cover. He could see quite clearly the dark slopes of the mountains rising above the canyon. From somewhere behind him he could hear water trickling down a rock.

He tensed, his nerves quivering. He had heard something else. The soft fall of unshod hooves on the dry ground.

Navajo.

Softly, he cursed. A hunting party returning late. They did not usually attack at night. If he was quiet, perhaps they would pass him by.

He moved to stand behind a spindly tree, knowing it would not conceal him in the bright light from the moon. His foot kicked a loose rock, sending it tumbling. The sound seemed to echo like thunder.

His hand went to his belt, where he kept his knife. It was the only weapon he had brought with him. How he wished he had his saber, or better yet, his revolver. It was too late to wish for such things now.

His mouth went dry when he saw the shifting shadows. There were seven of them, side by side, their horses slowly stepping in a line toward him. They had seen him. And they were not going to pass him by. He could smell them, they were so close.

Even without the limp, he could not have outrun them on foot. He cursed himself for giving away his horse. With it, he might have had a chance. Gripping the knife in his hand, he braced himself.

He would not turn his back for them to sink an arrow into his unprotected flesh. He would die facing them, fighting for his life.

Their war cry rang out in the night, chilling his blood. The ominous yells bounced off the rocks to sound like a hundred war cries. They were coming at him, hatchets raised, their eyes gleaming in the moonlight with the thrill of the kill.

He closed his eyes briefly, implanting the image of his woman on his mind. Slowly, he raised his hand.

Forty yards, thirty...

It came from nowhere. A giant beam so bright he had to close his eyes. It fell straight to earth, a few yards in front of him, spreading a wide circle of dazzling light, throbbing with energy.

Mist swirled inside the blazing column, and beyond it he could hear the terrified whinnies of the horses, and the harsh shouts of the Indians as they fought to control their crazed animals.

For one second...two...three...he stood, dazed by the spectacle. Then he heard a voice above the others. His woman. Corie.

"Run, Granger," she screamed. "Run into the beam. Now!"

Frantically he leapt forward. His weakened leg gave way and he fell, leaving him just short of the circle. With a supreme effort he rolled, over and over, and felt the warmth of the light engulf him. The wind came, sweeping him up in a wild torrent of speed, and he knew no more.

Corie was cold. So very cold. Shivering in the pale shadows of the moonlight, she looked at her watch once more. Only another minute or two and she would go, leaving her memories in this lonely place forever.

Once more she looked up at the sky, and her heart leapt. Staring in disbelief, she saw the star, brighter than any star she'd ever seen. She watched it grow, so fast she barely had time to draw breath before the beam screamed to earth, bathing the ground in front of her with its magnificent light.

She thought she saw something in the midst of it, shrouded by the swirling mist, but she couldn't be sure. Dazzled by the light, she could only stand there, her hand shading her eyes.

Then the light vanished, and she blinked. And blinked again. There in front of her, lay the huddled shape of a man.

She felt as if she would choke from the rush of hope and excitement. Not daring to believe it yet, she walked slowly forward.

He lay on his side in a pool of light from the moon, his face hidden from her. One wide shoulder hunched under his ear, pushing the collar of his jacket over his cheek. His legs were drawn up almost to his chin, and one arm seemed to reach out in mute appeal.

She reached out and took hold of his shoulder. Gently, she rolled him onto his back. The sight of his face, so dearly engraved on her mind, brought the tears to her eyes. She leaned over him, peering at him anxiously. For a moment a terrible fear held her frozen. Was he alive?

Then, without warning, his eyes opened, staring at her with the odd silver gleam she remembered so well. He gazed at her for a long moment, then said softly, "There is a God, after all."

The tears chased down her cheeks. "You came back," she said, as his arms closed around her. "You came back to me."

His hand stroked her hair, and he pressed his lips to her forehead. "I couldn't forget," he whispered. Then his mouth found hers, and the world slipped away.

The plane shuddered, howling defiance to gravity as it gathered speed on the runway. Corie sat with her hand gripped in Granger's strong fingers, watching his face grow more ashen by the second.

"Everyone does it nowadays," she said gently, leaning toward him to reassure him. "It's perfectly safe."

He gave her a quick glance. "I've heard that somewhere before."

"Once we've left the ground you'll hardly feel it." She almost laughed at his expression. "Don't worry, I've done this lots of times."

The plane lifted, and Granger closed his eyes. A few minutes later he opened them again and looked cautiously out of the window. "Amazing," he said, his voice hushed with awe. "I can't imagine what wonders you still have in store for me."

Corie grinned. "We've only just begun. Just wait until you see Disneyland."

He gave her a questioning look, and she shook her head. "You'll see."

"I've seen all I want to see. I have the woman I love by my side, and that's all I need."

"It's all I need, too." She looked into his eyes, her pulse quickening when she saw her love reflected in their depths. "I do love you, Granger."

"And I love you. More than you can possibly imagine." He lifted her hand and pressed his lips against her fingers.

"I need to find a job. I need to support myself somehow."

She hesitated, not sure how he would take her suggestion. "I have enough money to start a business. I'll need help with it, though. Would you consider taking on the job?"

"I would indeed, if you think I could handle it. What kind of business?"

She smiled. "We'll think of something."

For a long moment he didn't answer her, then he shook his head. "You are a very special lady, Corie Trenton. Tell me, do people still marry in the old-fashioned way?"

She had to catch her breath before answering him. "Well, they sometimes find odd places to do it, but yes, people still get married."

"This might not be the right place, but I don't want to wait any longer." He grasped both her hands in his. "Corie Trenton, I have nothing to offer you but my heart, and my undying love. But I need you, and I can't live without you. Will you do me the honor of becoming my wife?"

Breathlessly she looked up at him, her heart filled so full of love she thought it would burst. "I would love to be your wife, Granger. I need you, and I'll do my best to make you happy."

His finger traced down her cheek as he said softly, "We will make each other happy. This was meant to be."

"I believe that, too. Even the distance of time couldn't prevent us from being together." Her smile faded, and she gripped his hand as if afraid to let it go. "I almost didn't go to Arizona. Dr. Richards told me Specturne had veered from its orbit."

"What do you think happened?"

He lifted her fingers to his lips again, and she shivered as his mouth caressed them. "I don't know. But I suspect he told me that so that I would forget about what happened and wouldn't report him to the government for what he did."

"What made you go back, if you thought the star wouldn't return?"

She shook her head. "I don't know. I felt compelled to say goodbye one last time, by being in the same place at the same time, even if we were separated by a hundred and thirty years."

"I felt you there," Granger said softly. "I felt your presence and knew what to do. I didn't forget."

He put his arm around her and pulled her close. "How could I forget you, when I loved you more than life itself?"

She smiled up at him. "We have a lifetime of memories ahead of us now. And I think it's appropriate that you proposed and I accepted, high above the earth."

His smile spread across his face as he looked down at her. "I have you now, my sweet Corie. Thanks to a special star. Wherever it shines now, I hope it brings as much happiness to others, as it has to you and me."

"Thank you, Specturne," Corie echoed softly. "Wherever you are."

* * * * *

COMING NEXT MONTH

MILLION DOLLAR SWEEPSTAKES (III)

No purchase necessary. To enter, follow the directions published. Method of entry may vary. For eligibility, entries must be received no later than March 31, 1996. No liability is assumed for printing errors, lost, late or misdirected entries. Odds of winning are determined by the number of eligible entries distributed and received. Prizewinners will be determined no later than June 30, 1996.

Sweepstakes open to residents of the U.S. (except Puerto Rico), Canada, Europe and Taiwan who are 18 years of age or older. All applicable laws and regulations apply. Sweepstakes offer void wherever prohibited by law. Values of all prizes are in U.S. currency. This sweepstakes is presented by Torstar Corp., its subsidiaries and affiliates, in conjunction with book, merchandise and/or product offerings. For a copy of the Official Rules send a self-addressed, stamped envelope (WA residents need not affix return postage) to: MILLION DOLLAR SWEEPSTAKES (III) Rules, P.O. Box 4573, Blair, NE 68009, USA.

EXTRA BONUS PRIZE DRAWING

No purchase necessary. The Extra Bonus Prize will be awarded in a random drawing to be conducted no later than 5/30/96 from among all entries received. To qualify, entries must be received by 3/31/96 and comply with published directions. Drawing open to residents of the U.S. (except Puerto Rico), Canada, Europe and Taiwan who are 18 years of age or older. All applicable laws and regulations apply; offer void wherever prohibited by law. Odds of winning are dependent upon number of eligibile entries received. Prize is valued in U.S. currency. The offer is presented by Torstar Corp., its subsidiaries and affiliates in conjunction with book, merchandise and/or product offering. For a copy of the Official Rules governing this sweepstakes, send a self-addressed, stamped envelope (WA residents need not affix return postage) to: Extra Bonus Prize Drawing Rules, P.O. Box 4590, Blair, NE 68009, USA.

SWP-S795

He's Too Hot To Handle...but she can take a little heat.

SILHOUETTE
Summer Sizzlers

This summer don't be left in the cold, join Silhouette for the hottest Summer Sizzlers collection. The perfect summer read, on the beach or while vacationing, Summer Sizzlers features sexy heroes who are "Too Hot To Handle." This collection of three new stories is written by bestselling authors Mary Lynn Baxter, Ann Major and Laura Parker.

Available this July wherever Silhouette books are sold.

He's an everyman, but only one woman's lover. And we dare you not to lose yourself—and your heart—to these featured

In May: NIGHT OF THE JAGUAR, by Merline Lovelace. Jake MacKenzie was a seasoned operative used to calling the shots. But when feisty Sarah Chandler and her three young charges became his newest mission, he knew he'd lost all control—along with his heart.

In June: ANOTHER MAN'S WIFE, by Dallas Schulze. Gage Walker had only intended to get his best friend's widow back on her feet. His idea of help had *never* included marriage—or fatherhood. Then he learned that Kelsey had a baby on the way—*his!*

In July: WHO'S THE BOSS? by Linda Turner. Riley Whitaker *never* lost a good fight. So when single mom Becca Prescott threw down the gauntlet in the race for sheriff, Riley accepted her challenge—and offered a seductive one of his own....

Heartbreakers: The heroes you crave, from the authors you love. You can find them each month, only in—

▼INTIMATE MOMENTS®
™ *Silhouette*®

ROMANTIC
TRADITIONS

Romantic Traditions sizzles in July 1995 as Sharon Sala's
THE MIRACLE MAN, IM #650, explores the suspenseful—
and sensual—"Stranger on the Shore" plot line.

Washed ashore after a plane crash, U.S. Marshal
Lane Monday found himself on the receiving end of
a most indecent proposal. Antonette Hatfield had
saved his life and was now requesting his presence in
her *bed.* But what Lane didn't know was that Toni had
babies on her mind....

Lauded as "immensely talented" by *Romantic Times*
magazine, Sharon Sala is one author you won't want
to miss. So return to the classic plot lines you love
with THE MIRACLE MAN, and be sure to look for more
Romantic Traditions in future months from some of the
genre's best, only in—

INTIMATE MOMENTS®
Silhouette®

SIMRT8

As a Privileged Woman,
you'll be entitled to all these *Free Benefits.* And *Free Gifts,* too.

To thank you for buying our books, we've designed an exclusive FREE program called *PAGES & PRIVILEGES™*. You can enroll with just one Proof of Purchase, and get the kind of luxuries that, until now, you could only read about.

BIG HOTEL DISCOUNTS

A privileged woman stays in the finest hotels. And so can you—at up to 60% off! Imagine standing in a hotel check-in line and watching as the guest in front of you pays $150 for the same room that's only costing you $60. Your *Pages & Privileges* discounts are good at Sheraton, Marriott, Best Western, Hyatt and thousands of other fine hotels all over the U.S., Canada and Europe.

FREE DISCOUNT TRAVEL SERVICE

A privileged woman is always jetting to romantic places. When <u>you</u> fly, just make one phone call for the lowest published airfare at time of booking—<u>or double the difference back</u>! PLUS— you'll get a $25 voucher to use the first time you book a flight AND <u>5% cash back on every ticket you buy thereafter through the travel service</u>!

*F*REE GIFTS!

A privileged woman is always getting wonderful gifts. Luxuriate in rich fragrances that will stir your senses (and his). This gift-boxed assortment of fine perfumes includes three popular scents, each in a beautiful designer bottle. <u>Truly Lace</u>...This luxurious fragrance unveils your sensuous side. <u>L'Effleur</u>...discover the romance of the Victorian era with this soft floral. <u>Muguet des bois</u>...a single note floral of singular beauty.

YOURS FREE!

$50 **VALUE**

*F*REE INSIDER TIPS LETTER

A privileged woman is always informed. And you'll be, too, with our free letter full of fascinating information and sneak previews of upcoming books.

*M*ORE GREAT GIFTS & BENEFITS TO COME

A privileged woman always has a lot to look forward to. And so will you. You get all these wonderful FREE gifts and benefits now with only one purchase...and there are no additional purchases required. However, each additional retail purchase of Harlequin and Silhouette books brings you a step closer to even more great FREE benefits like half-price movie tickets... and even more FREE gifts.

L'Effleur...This basketful of romance lets you discover L'Effleur from head to toe, heart to home.

Truly Lace...
A basket spun with the sensuous luxuries of Truly Lace, including Dusting Powder in a reusable satin and lace covered box.

*C*omplete the *E*nrollment *F*orm
*in the front of this book and
mail it with this Proof of Purchase.*

PROOF OF PURCHASE
Offer expires October 31, 1996

SIM-PP3